HEIR OF DARKNESS

Heralds of the Culling

Book 1

M.J. Stewart

Also by M.J. Stewart

Heralds of the Culling (Vampire action/horror)
>   *Heir of Darkness*
>   *Blood of the Third*

Displacement (Time Travel Sci-Fi)
>   *Displacement: The Long Sleep*

Kingdom of Lorr Novels (Epic Fantasy)
>   *The Kingdom of Lorr: WorldGate Crossing*
>   *The Kingdom of Lorr: The Return*
>   *Demon of Lorr*
>   *Key Quest*

Previews and purchasing information at:

https://majorstewart.com/

Humans are our favored prey, but they outnumber us exponentially. Their superior numbers, in addition to our intolerance of the sun and talismans blessed by the faithful, allow humans to compensate for their physical weakness. We have thrived this long because most humans do not believe we exist.

– Manuel Del Sol, vampire, traveler, and scholar
19th century

Prologue

Camillia's Story

Mid 1970's

He was all she ever wanted. She knew it the moment they met. He was all she had ever dreamed about. It was in his eyes. There was something about his eyes that drew her to him, *into* him, that made her love him. Until the day she met him, Camillia Williams *thought* she was in love with another man named Richard Stewart, but what she thought was love for Richard was nothing compared to what she felt for this man.

This man named Andre. She met Andre a few months after Richard was murdered. He was found with his throat cut and his wallet stolen. Camillia was sure she would never love another man the way she loved Richard. And then Andre came along and swept her off her feet.

"Andre," she said as the two of them walked through the night, "I would usually be scared to death of walking through Jackson Park at night, no matter who was with me. But with you, I'm not afraid."

Andre smiled into her mahogany brown eyes. "That's because you feel safe with me. You know I'd never let anything happen to you."

Camillia believed him. She believed everything he told her from the moment they met.

"The park is beautiful at night," she said wistfully, "I just wish we were able to take one of these strolls in the daytime. There's so much more to see in the sunlight."

"I wish we could, too," Andre said sincerely, almost sadly. "But you know my job doesn't give me any free time during the day."

"That's alright, baby, we'll do it sometime."

"For sure," answered Andre. "Sometime."

Camillia did not know what his day job was and it did not really matter to her. She asked him once and his answer was so vague she barely remembered it. He was a manager at a brokerage firm or insurance firm or some other well-paying job that required a suit.

She did remember when she met him. It was a Tuesday night three months earlier at a movie theater or "the show" as Camillia and everyone she knew called it. After the death of her fiancé she often went to the movies alone. She would catch a cab to the theater and then her father would either borrow a friend's car or ride with a friend who owned a car to pick her up.

Her friends and parents did not understand why she would go to the movies alone. Camillia explained that going to the movies with Richard was one of their special things. After his death, going with anyone else would feel like a betrayal of his memory. To her, it was on the same level as marrying another man the day after her husband's death. That alone time was special to her. It was a chance for her to work through her grief. She would always find two empty seats at the end of a row so she could occupy one without having anyone next to her.

When she and Richard went to the movies together, she would reach over and touch his leg or shoulder when something made her laugh, or hug him when something scared her, or rest her head on his shoulder if something made her sad. Even after his death, she would still reflexively reach over to the chair next her, a habit which proved embarrassing the first time she went to the movies with one of her girlfriends.

Andre changed all of that. When they met he was standing behind her in line at the concession counter. He took a chance and touched her shoulder. Camillia did not turn all the way around to face him. Instead, she turned slightly and politely said:

"Yes?"

"Please forgive me for being forward," he began. "But are you here alone?"

Camillia's first instinct was to lie and say she was with someone, or to tell him that yes, she was alone and intended to stay that way. But there was something about his voice...there was compassion, sincerity and a kindness that made her turn all the way around and face him. When she did, she saw the same compassion, sincerity and kindness in his warm brown eyes.

"As a matter fact, I am here alone," she said graciously.

"So am I," the stranger returned. "My name is Andre, by the way. If you don't mind, would it be alright if I sat next to you?" He saw the reluctance in her eyes and quickly added, "I promise I won't talk through the movie. You won't even know I'm there."

"How do you know we're going see the same movie?" Camillia asked suspiciously.

Andre dropped his head sheepishly with a guilty half-smile. "I heard you at the ticket counter. But I promise I had already planned to see the same thing. I like comedies, too."

Camillia tilted her head slightly to the left, a sad smile on her pretty face. "I'm sorry, but I'd rather sit by myself."

"I understand," Andre assured. The sadness in his eyes was genuine. "I had planned to sit alone, too, until I saw you. But hey, maybe next time."

Camillia turned to place her order. After she received it and turned to make her way to the theater, Andre softly touched her shoulder again.

"I never got your name," he said.

"I know," Camillia replied.

To her surprise, Andre did not sit anywhere near her. In fact, he sat all the way at the front row, craning his head to watch the comedy and action of *Uptown Saturday Night*. Camillia found herself watching him almost as much as the movie.

She made it a point to wait for him outside the theater complex after the movie. As he walked by, she surprised him by coming up from behind and touching him softly on his shoulder. He turned quickly and smiled when he saw her.

"Yes?" he said, playfully – and rather skillfully – mimicking her voice.

"I didn't mean to be rude, Andre. My name is Camillia. I appreciate you respecting my wishes. A lot of guys would've sat next to me anyway, or very close."

"Don't mention it," Andre said with a dismissive wave. "Besides, I'm nothing like most guys. Hey, I don't know how often you go to the movies but if we run into each other again, maybe you'll be in the mood for a next-chair-neighbor."

"We'll see," Camillia told him.

Three nights later they saw each other at the same theater and she did indeed allow him to join her. At the end of that movie they exchanged numbers and became fast friends, much faster than she had ever befriended anyone in her adult life. And they soon became much more than friends.

Andre had what her parents would call an "old soul." He could not have been more than a few years older than her, which would have put him in his mid twenties, but he was mature beyond his years. He was settled both professionally and emotionally. He made her feel special about herself and never asked for anything more than she was willing to give.

Camillia never saw him until after sunset but they made the most of their nights. They would go to the movies, to live shows at the Chicago Theater or the Regal, out to eat, or for walks like this one. After they dated for a month, their nights ended with them making love at her apartment and then he would disappear into the night. She never intended to sleep with him so soon. She had even made Richard wait six months. But every time she looked into Andre's eyes, or at his smile, both her heart and her resistance melted.

While their relationship was mysterious to her from the start, the mystery only heightened their romance. In the three months they had been seeing each other she had never even been to his home. She asked him more than once about going to his apartment.

"Later, when the time is right," was always his answer.

She did not push the issue. The time she spent with him was so magical that she was afraid to change anything about it. Tonight, however, something *would* change. He was finally bringing her to his home.

"I can't wait," Camillia said. "I've been wanting to see your place for some time. But tell me, what's so special about tonight?"

He smiled. "Later."

All that did was increase the suspense. She loved it.

After their stroll through the park they caught a taxi and headed north on Lake Shore Drive. Camillia was a resident of a lower-middle class neighborhood on the south side. The only time she went to the north side was to shop. She liked most of the neighborhoods on the north side but there were a few areas she knew to steer clear of. She had enough of rough neighborhoods as a child when she lived with her family. She lived with her parents and younger sister until she finished junior college, got a job and was able to move to a better neighborhood.

As soon as she and Andre began to head north the thought crossed her mind that the reason he never brought her to his home was because he probably did live in one of those bad areas and was ashamed.

Even if he does live in a bad neighborhood, I don't care. I know I'll be safe with him.

To her relief, he lived in a nice area, on the top floor of a three-story apartment building. When they got to his apartment door he kissed her softly and let her in.

"Wow," was all she could say when she stepped through the door.

His lavish apartment was entirely black and gray. The couches in the living room were covered with jet-black leather. The carpet and walls were a soft gray. Even the cocktail table was made of polished black glass. The walls were decorated with some of the best African and African-American art she had ever seen. On the mantle over the imitation fireplace were authentic wooden carvings from the Motherland.

"I didn't know you were so into art," she said.

"I'm into beauty," he answered, "That's why I'm so into you. I want to make you my most prized possession." There was something in his dark eyes that made everything else in the room invisible to Camillia.

"I'd usually knock a man out if he talked about making me a possession," she said with mock anger, "But damn, you make it sound nice. I don't know what kind of spell you've got on me, sugar, but it's a good one."

"If you like this room, wait until you see where I sleep."

Camillia followed him into a huge bedroom with the same color scheme as the rest of the apartment. The gray walls and the soft plush gray carpeting were soothing to the eyes. The bed on the far side of the room was a king-size waterbed but the water mattress was replaced with a regular one.

The frame of the bed, like the chest-of-drawers, was made of ivory that was painted a metallic black. The only thing in the room made of wood was the door.

Soon they were both under black satin sheets. Marvin Gaye's "Distant Lover" played on the turntable as Andre kissed Camillia softly on her lips, down her neck to her collarbone, and then back up to her lips again.

"So tell me," Camillia started, almost whispering, "What's so special about tonight? Why do I now get to see this beautiful place of yours?"

"Tonight is the night I let you into my world," Andre replied with a strange look in his eyes. "I had to make sure you were the one."

"The one?" Camillia asked. "The one for what?"

"This is the night I make you my queen. This is the night I make you immortal."

Camillia pulled away and looked at him curiously. "What does that mean?"

He smiled, his mouth opening slowly, revealing long, pointed fangs. Camillia thought this was some sort of sick joke but something in the back of her mind and in the depths of her soul began to scream for her to run.

She tried to move but all she could do was look into those deep, dark brown eyes. Pinpoints of blood red light appeared in the middle of his pupils.

He's got me under a real *spell, but I can't fight him. He would never hurt me.* The words echoed in her mind yet they could not quite drown out the screaming deeper within her, the pleading for her to fight. But she could not fight. Andre's gaze would not let her.

He looked up an instant before bedroom door came crashing in. His face twisted into a terrible mask of bestial savagery and hunger. His mouth gaped impossibly wide and a frustrated roar tore through the room.

One of four men clicked on the light as they rushed into the bedroom. Two were dressed in police uniforms, their guns drawn. One was dressed in plain clothes with a long tan trench coat. He had a gun drawn as well. The fourth man was dressed in a black shirt and slacks and wore the straight white collar of a priest. A large crucifix hung from a thick chain around his neck and he a held small crossbow in his hands.

Once Andre looked up, the spell he had on Camillia was lifted. The scream that was trapped in her mind and soul suddenly exploded from her mouth.

She tried to move but her efforts were in vain because Andre was still on top of her. He was not, however, on top of her for long. He moved with incredible speed to the side of the bed opposite the intruders. Gunshots exploded as the police peppered Andre with bullets. The bullets caused him to twitch as they slammed into him but that was the only damage they did.

Andre lifted a shining black glass nightstand and hurled it across the room. The stand smashed into the wall directly of above the ducking priest and to the right of the other four men. The shower of glass caused the men to duck and shield their eyes. That was all the time Andre needed. He literally flew across the room and into the two uniformed officers who stood to the left of the priest and plainclothes officer. The three of them went down in a heap.

In little over a second, before the uniformed officers had a chance to scream, Andre was up again and coming toward the plainclothes cop and priest. Blood dripped from his clawed hands. A twisted grin cut across his face, which had morphed into an unholy permutation of man and beast. Death danced in his dark eyes.

The officer raised his gun and emptied his .45 caliber Smith and Wesson into Andre's chest. The shots did not really hurt Andre but they were powerful enough to send him stumbling into the corner of the room. He quickly regained his footing and started toward the two men again. The officer was trying desperately to reload as the priest stepped from behind him and leveled his crossbow.

Andre was close enough now to see what the crossbow held. It was loaded with a thin wooden stake a foot-and-a-half long. Andre had just enough time to widen his eyes in surprise as the priest triggered the weapon and sent the crossbow bolt into his chest.

Camillia's scream was a whisper compared to Andre's howl when the stake hit him. The force of the blow threw him back into the corner. The priest produced a small vial from his pocket and flung it at Andre as the vampire writhed in pain in the corner of the room.

The priest's aim was true. When the vial struck, it exploded and blanketed Andre in flames. Andre lunged across the room, clearing the bed and Camillia by at least two feet, and went crashing through the window.

All was silent. The priest rushed to the bed where Camillia lay. She had fallen silent but she was conscious. Her eyes stared blankly at the ceiling and the priest could see that she was suffering from shock. He lifted her gently to a sitting position and respectfully took care to keep the satin sheet wrapped around her torso, and inspected her neck. The plainclothes officer ran to the window.

"It's alright, ma'am," said the young clergyman. "He didn't bite you."

Camillia remained silent as a tear ran down her cheek.

"It's *not* alright," the plainclothes officer countered. "I don't see him outside...anywhere."

A few weeks after her ordeal, Camillia discovered she was pregnant. Her first instinct was to panic, but when the doctor told her how far along she was, she knew that she had become pregnant some time just before Richard's death, probably the last time they were together.

Richard always gave her wonderful gifts, but he left her the greatest gift of all before he died. She moved in with her parents, not wanting to live alone while she was with child.

Nine months later she was sitting in her parents' living room watching television. Her baby boy was sleeping quietly in his crib a few feet away. Her mother and father were sitting on the couch across the room. The setting sun cast the sky in a beautiful orange-purple hue.

"You look tired," Camillia's mother said, "Maybe you should lay down."

"I am," Camillia admitted. "But I think I'll wait until the baby goes to sleep."

"Don't worry about the little fella," her father assured, "He'll be alright with me and Ethel."

"No, really," Camillia answered, "I can stay up."

"Now Cammy," Ethel argued, "Jack and I can watch the baby for a few hours. You need some rest. You haven't been away from the child for a half hour since he was born."

"I'm O.K., momma," Camillia said, "Really. You two have to stop worrying about me."

"You're our daughter," Jack said, "our only baby. We can't help but worry about you. I know you love the boy but you need to breathe every now and then."

Ethel's eyes narrowed. "What's the matter? You don't trust us to take care of him?"

"Momma--"

"C'mon," Jack pressed, "You can't stay here with us forever. You gotta go back to work in a few weeks and you can't take him with you. You'll have to leave him with somebody. Look, just take a nap and when you get up call one of your girlfriends and go out or something."

"Yeah," Ethel agreed. "At the rate you're going, you'll never be able to leave the baby with anybody."

"Ok, ok," Camillia surrendered. "When the *Jeffersons* go off, I'll lay down."

A few minutes later the sky turned from the orange and purple of dusk to the black of night. The baby woke up and began to cry.

"That's a hungry cry, I'll take care of him," Ethel said.

"Don't get up, momma," Camillia said. "I'll do it, then I'll lay down."

Camillia went into the kitchen and to the refrigerator. She opened the refrigerator door and reached for one of the many bottles of formula. The bottles, however, were not filled with formula. Camillia snatched her hand away when she saw them. The bottles were filled with an opaque, dark, almost purplish liquid.

"Momma," she called, "What did you put in the baby's bottles?"

No answer came from the living room. The only thing Camillia heard was the crying baby.

"They must be going deaf," she muttered to herself. She took one of the bottles from the refrigerator and shook a drop of the dark liquid onto the back of her hand.

"This ain't tomato juice," she mumbled, "It's way too dark."

She tasted the small drop. It had a salty, familiar taste. It was the same flavor that she tasted if she accidentally bit her tongue too hard. It was the taste of blood.

She stifled a scream as she dropped the bottle to the floor. The nipple of the bottle popped off and the thick dark liquid began to ooze out onto the floor. She wiped the back of her hand against her shirt to remove the remainder of the blood and slammed the refrigerator door closed.

"Momma!" she yelled as she turned to run to the living room. She bumped into a man's chest and stumbled backwards into the refrigerator. She looked up into the man's face and saw a familiar pair of deep brown eyes.

"No..." she said quietly.

Andre grabbed Camillia by the throat and held her against the refrigerator.

"Our son's hungry," he began. "Warm up a bottle. We'll feed him together."

Camillia looked over Andre's shoulder and saw her mother walk into the kitchen. Ethel's dark-brown face was ashen and had a far-away expression.

"Hurry," Ethel said with a ghostly smile, "The baby's hungry."

Camillia broke away from Andre's grasp and ran toward the living room. She pushed past her entranced mother and sprinted out of the kitchen. When she reached the living room she saw her father still sitting on the couch. He was staring blankly at the television with dead eyes. His shirt was soaked with the blood pulsing from his slit throat. Camillia screamed.

The sound of her baby's cries broke her out of her momentary panic. She ran to the crib and picked up the infant. She looked at the baby and almost dropped him.

The child's face was horrible. The baby's big bright eyes had changed. The whites of his eyes were now as black as midnight and the irises were just as black. The baby's face was contorted into an evil snarl. His mouth was toothless earlier that evening but now a pair of short feral fangs protruded from black gums. The child-like cries became little high-pitched growls.

Camillia closed her eyes and screamed so loud she could feel her throat burning...

And then she opened her eyes. She was sitting on the couch in her parents' living room. The credits to the

Jeffersons were rolling. She looked for the baby's crib but there was no crib to be seen. Her parents were sitting on the couch facing Camillia. They both looked at her with frightened surprise.

"What's wrong, baby?" Ethel asked.

Camillia looked around with a frantic, puzzled look on her face. She then looked down at her swollen stomach. She touched it to make sure, felt the baby kick, and then breathed a deep sigh of relief.

"Another nightmare?" Jack asked.

"Yeah, daddy," Camillia answered, "This one was a doozie."

"I'm worried about you, Cammy," Ethel said.

"I know, momma," Camillia replied, "But the nightmares don't come like they used to. After a while I probably won't have them at all."

"You've been through a lot, baby," Ethel began, "You're a strong woman but I know finding out that the guy you're dating is a serial killer is a lot to handle."

Camillia thought it would be best to tell her parents that Andre was a serial killer instead of what he really was. She did not know whether they would believe the truth or if they would think she was having a nervous breakdown. The detective, the priest and Camillia were the only living people that knew what transpired that night.

"Thanks, momma. I just thank the Lord that I wasn't his next victim." At that moment, a strange look came across Camillia's face. Her eyes bulged with surprise and pain.

"Cammy..." her father began.

"It's the baby," Camillia answered as she clutched her stomach, "I think it's time."

"Push!" the doctor commanded.

Ethel leaned close to her daughter's left ear. "C'mon, baby."

"You can do it, Cammy!" her father cheered from the right.

Camillia pushed as hard as she could. The pain was unlike any she had ever felt. It was even worse than she imagined it would be. But instead of pausing to try to ease the pain, she used it as motivation to push even harder. She was sweating and crying profusely, the salty liquid dripping into her mouth and stinging her eyes before her mother wiped it away. All Camillia could see was blurred, pale white light from fluorescent bulbs. All she could hear was the sound of her own breathing. The room began to spin as the pain intensified.

"Here it comes," the doctor said calmly.

Seconds later Camillia heard the sounds of a baby crying. She wanted to smile but the pain was still there. She became even more light-headed than before.

"There's internal hemorrhaging," she heard the doctor say. "We've got to stop the bleeding."

"Oh, God," she heard her mother whisper.

"C'mon," the doctor yelled. "We're losing her!"

Camillia's vision started to waver. The baby's cries and the doctor's voice faded to white noise. She felt herself losing consciousness and then everything went black.

When Camillia came to she was lying in a hospital bed. She looked down to see her hand being held by a larger one. She looked up into her father's eyes and smiled.

"How you feelin', sweetheart?" Jack asked.

"I'm alright," Camillia answered weakly.

"The doctor said you lost a lot of blood. He says you should stay at the hospital a few extra days to get your strength back."

"How's the baby?" She asked. She thought about her last nightmare and became gravely concerned. "Where's the baby? Where is he?"

"Calm down, sweetheart," her father cajoled. "We'll see in a second."

The door opened and her mother walked into the room holding a small bundle. Ethel brought the bundle to her daughter as Camillia sat up in the bed.

"Let me see him," Camillia said nervously. Her heart began to race as she reached out impatiently for the bundle. Ethel placed the baby carefully into the new mother's arms. Camillia looked down into the most beautiful pair of brown eyes she had ever seen.

"A boy?" Camillia asked softly.

"A boy," her mother answered with a smile.

The baby looked up at his mother and smiled. Camillia kissed him gently on the forehead.

"My baby," Camillia said as a tear rolled down her cheek, "His eyes...just like Richard's.

Chapter 1

Late May; Early Nineties

He was all she could ask for. The moment she saw him she knew that she was blessed. He was her son and his name was Richard. She liked to call him "Li'l Richard." He hated it. Little Richard the entertainer was a bit too wild for him.

It was just Camillia and Richard now. Her parents passed away within two years of one another while Richard was in elementary school. If not for Li'l Richard, his comforting innocence and his infectious joy, Camillia did not believe she would have been able to keep her sanity through it all.

The Lord took away her fiancé but gave her a beautiful son in return. Camillia didn't think about the ordeal with *him* very much anymore, only in very rare nightmares. She was a totally different person than the twenty-year-old college girl that was quite literally entranced.

Camillia absently stroked the silver cross hanging an inch below her neck from a silver chain. She took to wearing the cross after her son was born. While she had always believed in God and rarely missed attending her Baptist Church on Sunday, she had never felt compelled to outward displays of her faith.

The combination of Richard's birth and the traumatic experience a few weeks earlier, however, was more than enough incentive for her to begin wearing the silver cross and hanging a Black Jesus crucifix in her living room, kitchen, and bedrooms.

Camillia suppressed the smile that tried to come to her lips, listening to her son plead his case as they sat adjacent to each other at the kitchen table, their unofficial conference area for years. She had to keep up the façade of stoicism so her son would know she was serious.

Li'l Richard was a lot like his father. He always excelled in schoolwork but was never considered a nerd by his peers. He was not a superstar in sports but he always made the team. He went out of his way to help people and was hurt if someone needed help and he could not give it. All in all he was a good kid, Camillia thought. He was a good, normal kid.

He was ending his first year of junior college and it was registration time for his second year. Richard received academic scholarships from a number of universities but he turned them all down.

"We had this talk a hundred times, momma," Richard argued, "The scholarships pay for my tuition and housing but you wouldn't be able to send me any kind of money for other expenses. I ain't gonna have you putting yourself under financial strain tryin' to. Besides, it's too late now. I turned everybody down already."

Camillia shook her head irritably. "I still get pissed every time I think of you turning down a chance to go to a four year university. That's just crazy."

"It's not crazy, momma. I don't wanna leave. I can stay here and work while I go to school. You need all the help you can get around the house. Besides, you may start having the nightmares again."

"So that's it? Scared to leave mommy by herself?"

"Stop trippin', woman. Look at it this way, as long as I'm gettin my education it don't matter where I get it."

"That's bull and you know it," she argued. "A bachelors degree carries a helluva lot more weight than an associate's. I should know."

Richard folded his arms stubbornly. "I transferred one of my scholarships to the junior college and I'm not leaving. I can always go to a four-year to finish up my bachelor's."

"So you say," Camillia shot back. "Why would you feel any different two years from now?"

"By then, I'll have found you a man to take care of you," Richard teased.

She swatted him on the back of the head in mock anger. "What did I tell you about that?" she demanded. "You know I don't *need* a man. And don't change the subject."

"Momma, I promise," Richard assured. "Honestly...I'm just not ready to leave. I guess I'm a momma's boy."

"Alright, you big baby," she said incredulously before kissing him on the cheek. As much as she knew she would hate to see him go, she hated the idea of him turning down prestigious universities because of her. But once her son made up his mind it could not be moved with a bulldozer. "You're as bull-headed as your daddy. So what's your plan?"

"Check this out," Richard's favorite phrase, "I just got this night job as an orderly at South City hospital. I'm gonna take three classes in the morning and work four hours a night."

"Are you sure you can handle work and school?"

"I did it all through high school."

"Yeah, but this is college, it's a lot tougher."

"If I can't handle it I'll give up the job, I promise," Richard haggled. "Deal, momma?"

"Deal," Camillia said. Richard kissed her on the cheek. "So what are you doin' this afternoon?"

"Shootin' ball with Tim and Major."

"Tell them I said hi. Hey, before you go, run to the store and get me a newspaper."

"You got it."

About twenty minutes later Richard was gone and Camillia had her paper. A headline on the front page caught her attention.

WOMAN FOUND SLAIN

Stories like that always caught her attention. Nineteen years earlier the newspapers ran a story like that almost every morning shortly before she met *him* and while they were dating. Back then the cause of death was always a slashed throat. The victim would have already died from loss of blood by the time she was found. The twist in those murders was that the throat was not just slashed. It was destroyed, ripped apart.

It was *his* way of hiding the evidence of what really happened.

Camillia began to read. She read that the woman was found in an alley the previous night. The story revealed that the victim had multiple stab wounds and other mutilations. Camillia said a silent prayer for the woman and breathed a small sigh of relief. She was relieved because for nineteen years she had been reading the papers to see if *his* method of murder would be repeated. There were similar instances like this one by psychopaths that were eventually found and brought to justice, but nothing to make her believe that *he* had returned.

"Give up the rock, punk!" Major called to Richard. "That wasn't a damn foul!"

Richard scoffed. "You must be sick in the head. You hacked the shit outta me."

Tim raised his hands in a placating gesture. "Fellas, fellas, just do a jump ball. I'll toss it up."

"Now both you boys know Richard can't out-jump me. I don't care if he *is* two inches taller than me. You might as well just gimme the ball, Tim."

Richard passed Tim the basketball. "Toss it up."

The ball was tossed and sure enough, Major won the tip. He hit the ball into the air and ran to retrieve it.

"Now, let's hoop. It's my rock, suckers. Check ball," he tossed the ball to Richard and Richard tossed it right back. "Now watch this..."

Major dribbled the ball inbounds, executed a quick spin move on Richard and pulled up to shoot the ball before Tim could reach him to block the shot. The net made a swishing sound as the ball passed neatly through the hoop. "Twenty points, fellas! When I hit this free-throw the game is over."

"Go ahead and shoot, choke-master," Richard dared. "If you miss, this game is mine."

Tim waved his hand. "Don't forget about the kid. I ain't too far behind Li'l Richard."

Richard grabbed his crotch. "I got your Li'l Richard right here, punk. Shoot the ball, general."

"The name is Major," Major corrected as he shot the free-throw. "And now the game is over."

The ball hit the front of the rim and bounced right into Richard's hands.

"You damn right it's over!" yelled Richard. "Mage, you just dropped to thirteen, Tim you got eighteen, and I got nineteen."

Richard dribbled back behind the free throw line as both Major and Tim defended him. Richard turned his back to the two defenders, faked left, faked right, and shot a turn-around jumper. It probably would have been a good shot if Tim, who was about three inches taller than Richard, hadn't blocked it. Tim quickly gathered the ball and took it to the hoop for a two-handed dunk.

"Hell yeah it's over," Tim teased. He went to the free throw line and, despite taunts and jeers from his friends, calmly sank the free throw. "You girls wanna run it back?"

"Maybe later fellas," came a voice from beyond the court. "Richard and I need to talk."

The three young men turned to see a late-middle aged man in a tan trench coat standing on the other side of the playground fence.

"Detective Weller," Richard greeted. "You wanna run with us?"

"No thanks," the detective answered. "I don't wanna embarrass anybody."

"I got no problem with that," Tim said to Major. "I don't care much for playing with cops anyway."

"Let's walk, Rich," said Weller, ignoring Tim's comment. Richard shook hands with Tim and Major and left with Weller.

"So what's up, man?" asked Richard as the two men walked along.

"You know you really should wear a sweatshirt or something," was Weller's response. "It's unseasonably cool out here for late spring, even in Chicago. The wind is pretty high, too."

"I'm straight, Weller. I can't hoop good with too many clothes on. What's up?"

"Rich, we've been tight since you were a toddler, right?"

"Right. You're about the only cool white guy I know."

Weller grinned. "We're not all bad. But anyway...you've got to be honest with me. Where were you last night?"

"I was at a club. Why? What happened?"

"Someone you go to school with was murdered."

"Who?" asked Richard, suddenly very serious.

"A young lady named Vanessa Strickland."

"Oh, shit..." Richard said softly, "What happened?"

"It's in the papers. She was found in an alley cut up real bad."

"That's foul," Richard looked at Weller, "But why are you asking where *I* was?"

"I don't think you did it or anything," Weller said quickly. "But maybe you know who did. Vanessa wasn't robbed or raped, just murdered. Did she have any enemies?"

"None that I can think of, but we weren't really that tight. We know a lot of the same people, though. I'll let you know if something comes up."

Camillia was sitting in the living room watching television when she heard the door open. She went to the door and saw Richard and detective Weller entering the house.

"What's up, old lady?" greeted Weller.

"I think you got the wrong house," Camillia answered, smiling. "There's only a young lady here."

Camillia got a beer for herself and Weller before the three of them took seats around the living room. Weller wasn't supposed to drink on the job but one beer wouldn't hurt. It never did. Richard had an iced tea.

"So what brings you over here, detective?" asked Camillia.

"Work," he answered, "I know you read the paper today."

"Yeah," Camillia replied, her tone darkening just a bit. "But what does that have to do with you coming here?"

"The paper withheld the victim's name, but she was a friend of Richard's. I was just asking him a few questions..."

"Like where I was last night," Richard interrupted. "I thought he was about to accuse *me*," he said with mock anger.

Camillia gave Weller a sharp look.

"Anyway," broke in Weller, "I was just doing it by the book. I've been to see five other people that knew her."

"Any leads yet?" asked Camillia with a colder tone.

"Not yet," answered Weller. "But we'll come up with something."

Once again Richard interrupted, "Hey folks, I hate to leave in the middle of such an interesting conversation but I gotta go take a shower. I'm going to Tim's crib to watch the Bulls game." He got up and left the room.

"You asked him where he was last night?" Camillia asked. "What the hell kind of question is that?"

"A standard cop question. Don't start with me."

"Standard cop question, hell. You make it sound like he was a damn suspect." If not for Camillia's dark brown skin, she would have been red with anger.

"Alright, Camillia, no more bullshit. Let me fill you in on some of the things that were kept out of the papers..."

"Bulls win!! Bulls win!!" Richard, Tim, and Major shouted in unison. High fives were going on all over the place.

"Damn! Look out," Major said to Tim, laughing. "You almost made me drop my beer."

"Damn your beer," Tim said. "There's more of that in the fridge. The Bulls won!!"

"I wish *I* could have another," said Richard. "But I gotta get home."

"Gotta go home to mommy?" Major teased, "Poor baby."

"Poor baby this," Richard said, grabbing his crotch, "I'm outta here." He finished off his beer and left for home.

Camillia didn't usually approve of Richard walking around outside after sunset. She didn't mind if he rode in a car but she had what Richard thought was an unreasonable fear of being out in the open at night. Tim lived only a few blocks away, and Richard was almost twenty years old, so she grudgingly made an exception. It was just after nine-thirty, though, so Richard knew that he had better walk fast. His mother always watched the Bulls and since the game was over she would be expecting him home soon.

As he walked he thought he heard soft footfalls behind him. The hairs on the back of his neck rose and he turned around casually to look. He saw nothing.

When he reached the corner he was startled by a large German shepherd standing to his right. Richard was terrified of stray dogs, especially big ones, but this one scared him even more than usual. The dog did not snarl or make any aggressive motions but something about it was decidedly not natural. It just stood there and looked at him. Richard thought he saw a glint of recognition in the unsettling gaze, and not a pleasant recognition. Richard did not how he knew, but he knew the dog was sizing him up, like a predator deciding whether or not the focus of its attention was worth the effort of attacking. Richard could feel his blood turning cold.

"Dogs can smell fear," he whispered to himself, "Don't be afraid, and whatever you do, don't run." Richard walked by the dog as if it was not there.

As he passed the dog, it let out a thundering bark. Richard stumbled and did all he could to keep from bolting.

"Please...don't run," he said to his quaking legs. "Please." Richard risked another look behind him to see where the now silent dog was. It was gone. "Thank you, God. Thank you thank you thank you."

When he got home his mother was in her usual place, standing just beyond the front door. She always heard him putting the key in the lock and went to make sure it was him. Richard did what he always did when his mother met him at the front door: he kissed her on the cheek.

"You see the game, momma?"

"You know I did," she answered with a smile, but Richard could see that something was bothering her.

"You ok?" he asked.

"Stomach's a little upset. I was waiting for you to get home so I could go to bed."

"Well you can go to bed now, momma. I think I'm about to crash, too. G'night."

They gave each other a hug and Richard headed for the stairway to go up to his bedroom. "Momma, guess what happened to me on the way home. I was almost attacked by a gigantic German shepherd!"

Camillia inhaled sharply at the word "attacked" but exhaled in relief when Richard finished the sentence.

"I'm glad you're alright. Goodnight, baby."

Richard realized later that night that he had left his wallet over Tim's house. He was walking back to his friend's place and berating himself for his forgetfulness.

"I *never* leave my wallet over someone's house," he fussed. "I'm glad it didn't have money in it."

He heard a growl over his shoulder.

"Uh oh..." he whispered. He turned his head slowly. The German shepherd was back, and this time it was snarling. "Don't run...don't run..." he pleaded to himself.

He looked over his shoulder once more and when he did the dog was growling and baring his teeth. Richard could feel the contents in his lower intense shifting.

The animal charged.

"Oh shit."

Richard finally gave in to his shuddering knees and exploded into a full run. He ran faster than he had ever run in his life. He felt his heart pounding violently in his chest as the sound of paws beating the pavement grew louder and louder. The hairs on his neck stood on end and tingled almost painfully.

It seemed as if he had been running forever. His breath grew ragged and burned his lungs. He looked over his shoulder again, praying the dog would disappear as he did earlier. The beast, however, was less than an arm's length behind him.

Run! was the only thought in his mind. The animal leapt and all Richard could see was those hideous fangs...

And then he woke up. Cold sweat ran down his face like water and hot tears streamed from his eyes. He must have cried out in his sleep because an instant later his mother burst into the room.

"Are you alright, baby?" she asked worriedly.

"Just a wild nightmare," he answered.

"About what?" his mother was deathly serious as she held his shoulders in a firm, almost painful grip.

"I don't remember exactly...but that dog..." he shook his head in an effort to remember more of the dream. "I can't remember now. You know how a dream of fades out."

"I can't believe you had me run up all those stairs for a nightmare about dogs," Camillia smiled nervously and sighed.

There were no more bad dreams that night. The next morning was a Saturday morning but Camillia woke up earlier than she did during work days. She peeked in on Richard and saw that he was still fast asleep. She quietly got dressed and drove to St. Anselm's Catholic Church. Her intention was to talk to Father Burns alone, but when she arrived she found that detective Weller was already there. Weller and Father Burns were seated in a pew at the back of the church having a serious conversation. Camillia went over and joined them.

"Talking about me, gentlemen?" she asked.

"As a matter of fact, we were," the priest answered.

"We were talking about you and vampires," broke in Weller.

"You still on that vampire-child trip, huh?" questioned Camillia.

"You sayin' it's impossible?" argued Weller.

"I have said it, I'm sayin' it now, and I'll always say it because it *is* impossible."

"Look," Weller began, "Nineteen years ago I thought the existence of vampires was impossible. I was investigating this Andre character under the assumption that he was just some rich psychopath, then I run into a priest," he said, pointing a finger at Father Burns, "Who just happens to be after the same guy.

"When the padre tells me this Andre is a vampire I just thought he was drinkin' too much communion wine or something, but I worked with him because he had some solid leads. Next thing I know we're bustin' into his apartment and he's about to make you his next victim.

"I still didn't believe he was a vampire...but when he flew across the room and I looked into those eyes...and those fangs..." Weller shuddered at the memory. "I'll put it like this, after what I saw I won't rule anything out."

"I've heard the story before, Weller," Camillia said in an irritated tone. "My son is *not* a vampire. "Do you have any idea how many times that thought has crossed my mind over the years? Of course you don't. You checked in maybe once or twice a month like it was some sort of damned chore..."

"Camillia –" Father Burns interrupted. He could see her anger growing and tried to cut her short. Camillia was having none of it.

"I *lived* with the boy," she continued. "Every day for more than the first fifteen years of his life I watched and prayed and looked for any sign that he might be...different. Believe me, if he was, I would know. Li'l Richard is Richard senior's son. Why won't you just believe that Andre is back?"

"I don't believe it because if we didn't kill him that night he would have made his presence known way before now," Weller argued. "We didn't find a body because he crawled off somewhere and disintegrated or something."

"My son is *not* a vampire."

The priest interceded. "We don't know if it is or isn't possible and it's pointless to go on arguing about it. What we have to do now is just concentrate on the facts, and the fact is that the killings have started again. Let us work under the assumption that Andre has returned. And if it isn't Andre, if it's some other vampire, perhaps we can use what we know about Andre to help us track it down."

"Whatever we do we'd better make it quick," the detective said. "I don't know how long I can keep this information out of the papers. If the press ever gets to one of the murder sites before we can wrap up the body they'll see that the corpse is almost completely drained of blood with almost no blood on the scene. That's the same way they were nineteen years ago.

"The papers called him the 'Vampire Killer' because they thought it was a catchy name, but the name stuck. People remember it. If they thought he was back or that there was a copycat out there, they'd put the whole city in a panic."

"I just wish someone would have informed me earlier," said Camillia. "I could have been able to help."

"You can still help, Camillia," Father Burns assured. "But you may have to recall some rather unpleasant memories."

"I can handle it," she promised. "I learned how to deal with it a long time ago."

"Good," Father Burns said. "Let us begin. Detective, do you have anything to add?"

"Yeah. Let's get to it."

The remainder of that Saturday morning and afternoon was spent trading information about Andre. Each person knew something about him that the other two did not. Father Burns was the authority on vampires in general. He studied the undead for years and learned how to recognize signs and warnings. He knew the ways to kill the creatures and prevent them from returning.

Detective Weller knew about Andre from an investigative perspective. Weller was familiar with Andre's patterns of behavior and the types of victims that he chose.

Camillia knew him personally.

She never understood why Andre didn't simply kill her when they first met the way he had killed the other women. Her assumption was that he was toying with her. Andre did, however, share a lot about himself with her.

She knew many of his likes and dislikes, the places he liked to go, the things he liked to do, etc. It would have been incredibly naïve of her to discount the probability that he had lied about all of it, of course, but she had a strange feeling he had been truthful for the most part.

It was a long afternoon.

Chapter 2

When Richard woke up, the sunlight shining through the open blinds was unusually painful to his eyes. He went quickly to the window to close them and then jumped back in bed. As soon as his head hit the pillow the phone beside his bed began to ring.

"Shit..." he swore as he picked up the receiver. "What?"

"That ain't no way to answer the phone, boy!" It was his mother.

"Oh, sorry momma, I just woke up."

"That's no excuse," she said. "It's one in the afternoon. Why are you still asleep?"

"I got up earlier..." he said, "to use the bathroom."

"Don't get smart. I just called to tell you that I'm going to be out for a while. I'm going to a friend's house. There are some leftovers in the icebox when you get hungry. I'll be home before dark."

"Ok, momma. Is it alright if I go to a party tonight with the fellas?"

"What kind of party?"

"A party, you know, music, dancing, women--"

"Alcohol, drugs, orgies..." Camillia interjected.

"No, no, no. The party's at a friend of Major's house. There may be a little beer, but I won't drink any. And you know I don't mess with drugs... and an orgy? I wish!"

"Just take your protection with you. And don't catch anything you can't throw back!"

"Momma..."

"You *will* be home when I get back won't you?" It was more an order than a question.

"I'll be here. The party don't start until nine o'clock."

"It *starts* at nine?" Camillia asked. "I know you're not catching the bus or el that time of night. Who's driving?"

"Tim."

"I guess that's ok. I don't want that damn Major driving you anywhere. I don't trust that boy."

"Don't worry, momma. That's my boy and all, but he's a fool. I wouldn't ride with him to the corner."

"Alright," Camillia relented. "I'll bring back some Chinese food or something. You need to put something in your stomach before you start drinking."

"Momma, I just said I wouldn't be drinking."

"And I wasn't born last night. Talk to you later."

Richard chuckled as he hung up the phone. He was too hungry to wait for his mother, so he made short work of some leftover chicken. The chicken didn't sate his hunger so he looked in the refrigerator for something else to eat. A short search uncovered a half-pound package of fresh ground beef.

"Burger time!"

About twenty minutes later, just as Richard was about to sink his teeth into a huge homemade hamburger, the doorbell rang. He put the snack down and went to the front door. He looked through the peephole and saw the distorted images of Tim and Major.

"Whatup fellas," Richard said as he opened the door.

"Whatup," they answered.

"Damn, what's cookin'?" asked Major between sniffs.

"Don't worry about it. You can't have none," Richard replied.

The three young men made their way to the kitchen. Tim turned on the small television and Major went straight for the burger. He reached for the food and a steak knife stabbed into the table between his hand and the burger.

"Alright, fool," Major said as he snatched his hand back. "You don't have to stab me."

"Yeah, I thought so," Richard sneered.

"Check it out, fellas," Tim said, pointing at the television set. "They're talking about Nessa."

The midday news was indeed talking about Vanessa Strickland. The newswoman was saying:

"Vanessa Strickland is the name of the woman found slain two nights ago in an alley on Chicago's south side. She attended a Community College downtown and is the fourth woman found slain in as many nights.

"When asked, the police stated that there was no evident connection in the four slayings. Each woman was found in a different part of town and each manner of killing was different. The women were also of various ages. Two of the women were Caucasian, one was Spanish, and the fourth, Vanessa Strickland, was African American. Detective Weller was asked his opinion on the slayings."

Weller's image appeared on the television screen.

"As of now, the killings are being treated as unrelated incidents," he said. "We haven't found anything to link the victims. This town is just like every other big city. It's full of sick individuals."

"So what'cha think, guys," Tim asked. "You think the killings are connected?"

"Shit," Major answered. "I hope not. The last thing we need in this city is another serial nutcase."

"I kind of think they are," Richard said. The other two turned to him.

"I thought you liked your burgers *cooked*," said Major, indicating a spot of blood-red juice on the bottom corner of Richard's mouth. Richard wiped it away.

"I do...usually," Richard wondered aloud. "Oh well, I'm still hungry. Think I'll have another."

"*Cook* this one," Major advised. "And while you're at it, fix me one, too."

"Go to hell," Richard scoffed.

"Anyway," said Tim, "Why would you think they're connected?"

"I don't know," Richard answered. "I just do."

Tim shook his head. "I'm just sorry somebody we knew had to go out like that."

"And somebody that sexy," Major added, shaking his head. "It was probably her boyfriend. You know she was kickin' it with some crazy white boy. The law probably got his ass jacked up somewhere already. But enough about all this sad shit. We still partying tonight or what?"

"You don't care about nothin' do you?" questioned Tim.

"We didn't know her *that* well," Major argued. "It ain't like she was givin' us the ass."

"Have some respect for the dead," Richard broke in, finishing his burger.

"Why don't *you* have some respect for that dead cow you just tore up," countered Major. "And wipe that blood off your chin."

Tim shook his head. "Major, you are sick."

That Night

"Eleven o'clock and all is jumpin'!" shouted Major over his shoulder to Tim above the blaring House Music. They were back to back, both dancing with a scantily clad young woman.

"I gotta admit," Tim confessed, "You're boy throws some slammin' basement parties. Where'd he find this DJ?"

"He spins at Mendel and the Country Club sometimes," Major explained between breaths.

"So your boy got ends, then," Tim noted. "Them studs don't come cheap."

"It's his cousin," Major explained. "He's gettin' that family discount. Mark my words, he's about to blow up like Ron Hardy or Frankie Knuckles!"

Tim nodded and danced for several more beats, and then looked around. "Hey, where'd Richard go?"

"Somewhere mackin', like always," Major guessed. "I got too much ass over here to worry about Richard, and so do you. Just dance, fool!"

Just as Major said, Richard was where he usually was when he went to a house party: in the corner talking to an attractive young woman. Her complexion was that of coffee with a touch of cream. She was very well endowed in the posterior and had thick, shapely legs. She wore black stretch pants and a white shear blouse that showed off her black halter-top and flat stomach. Her short hairstyle reminded Richard of a model from *Essence* magazine.

"I had to get over here and talk to you before one of these other brothers scooped you up," he began. "I was surprised to see you standing by yourself at all. I figured a woman as fine as you would have a line of men waiting to dance."

"I suppose *you* want to dance," she replied with a disinterested sigh.

Richard caught the tone of her voice but refused to give up. "That would be nice, but I was hoping we could talk for a little while first."

"I'll dance with you for *one song* if you want to dance. I didn't come here to talk."

Richard became frustrated. "You fine, baby, but you ain't all that. It's not like dancing with you would be some kind of privilege. Now I know why you're standing over here by yourself."

He turned walked away. As he walked around the edge of the dance floor he saw many other attractive women but none seemed to really strike him. He bumped into one of his friends from school. They greeted each other with a couple of "whatup's" and a handshake.

"I saw what happened with ol' girl," his friend said, pointing at the girl in black and white. "Your problem is you're too picky. You passed up a gang of fine broads just to get shot down by her, and you just passed up another bunch of honeys. What the hell are you looking for?"

"I don't know," Richard said, "A female just has to make somethin' in my head click. If she don't I can't swing it."

"You be lookin' for the finest honey at the party," the friend explained. "But the finest one is usually the biggest bitch. Lower your standards a little. You'll never get it wet the way you work."

"Yeah? I been gettin' it wet for years the way I work," Richard countered. "No need to change now."

"Well I wish you luck with that one," his friend said before he walked away.

Richard continued to walk around the perimeter of the dance floor. After a few strides he gave in and took his friend's advice. "Excuse me," he started, approaching another woman. "Would you like to dance?" He decided to leave out the extra comments this time and that decision proved to be a wise one.

"Sure," she answered with a smile.

They walked out to the dance floor and began to dance. Richard found her attractive but not like the first young lady. He couldn't keep his eyes from wandering over to where she was standing. The girl he was dancing with noticed his diverted attention and let him know.

"Look," she said, "If you wanna dance with her just go ask."

"I did," he answered, "But she wasn't with it."

"Well if you're gonna keep starin' over there I'm not with it either."

She walked away.

"Damn!" he said to himself.

A pale hand clutched his shoulder. He turned quickly to see the owner of the hand. What he saw startled him.

The hand belonged to a gaunt white man who looked to be at least thirty years old and stood about six feet-six inches tall. The stranger was dressed in an old beat up black leather jacket, a dirty white T-shirt, and a pair of faded blue jeans.

He was incredibly pale with dark maniacal eyes. Dark bags swelled beneath them, suggesting a severe lack of sleep. His head was shaved and he wore earrings constructed of metal loops, each with an old yellowish animal fang dangling from it. He was definitely out of place at this party.

Richard quickly pushed the hand away and took a step back. "Can I help you with somethin'?" he challenged.

An ugly smile spread slowly across the misfit's face. His yellow teeth and dark gums stood out even in the dim lighting. The red and blue strobe lights cutting through the darkness didn't do him any favors.

"Your friend didn't know what the hell he was talking about, homeboy," the stranger said in a confidential tone.

"Never...*never* lower your standards. If you see something you want, let nothing stop you from getting it. Nothing."

The man snapped his fingers and a beautiful young woman with chocolate brown skin stepped up to his side. She was by far the most attractive woman at the party. Had Richard saw her first he would have never wasted so much time with the girl in black and white.

The misfit's companion wore a soft gray cat suit that displayed all of the curves of her athletic body. She beamed a beautiful smile and large, dreamy light brown eyes. But Richard noticed that there was something about those eyes that was decidedly not right. She looked as if she were under hypnosis. Richard stared with his mouth open. Words escaped him. His new acquaintance, however, was far from speechless.

"Look at her," he said. "You wouldn't think a crazy-looking white boy like me could pull a beautiful sister like this. I have a philosophy, though: Nothing is out of your reach. Isn't that right, sweetheart?"

She nodded wordlessly with a faraway look in her eyes. The misfit then looked her in the eye and said, "How about a kiss for your man."

The woman nodded again and kissed him on his thin, almost purple, lips. Richard stared in disbelief. Then the stranger said, "If I can do it, I *know* you can."

"Thanks, man...I'll...I'll remember that," was all Richard could manage before the unlikely couple strode away and disappeared into the crowd.

"I done seen it all!" Richard said to himself.

An hour or so later he bumped into Major and Tim at the refreshment table. He couldn't wait to tell his friends what he saw earlier that night.

"Fellas," he started, "you wouldn't believe what I saw this evening..." He went on to tell them all about the girl in black and white, the friend from school, and the mismatched couple. "There's the girl in black and white," he said, pointing to her. She was dancing with a very happy looking young man.

"That freak is TIGHT!" Major exclaimed.

"She is that," agreed Tim.

"She ain't got nothin' on the broad that was with that white boy."

"I'd love to see *her*, then," Major said.

"I don't know where the odd couple is," Richard continued. "But if you saw them two together you'd freak the hell out!"

The three friends were heading home at about two o'clock in the morning in Tim's '95 Chevy Cavalier. They had been riding for a few minutes when they noticed flashing lights. When they reached the source of the lights they saw police cars and an ambulance gathered around a convertible forest green late model Mustang. Several television reporters and cameramen surrounded the area. Paramedics were loading a full body bag into the ambulance.

"I wonder what happened there," Richard said.

"The Mustang don't have a scratch," Tim added. "It don't look like an accident."

"Damn," Major said. "I wonder who gets the car."

The other two just looked at each other and sighed.

"Let's check it out," offered Richard.

Tim frowned. "Why?"

"I don't know..." Richard answered. "I just... C'mon man. Just pull over and wait for me. I'll be right back."

"Don't be all night," Tim warned. "I'll leave your ass."

Richard chuckled. "No you won't."

Tim parked about a half block away from the scene. There was an alley that separated the block right at the midpoint. As Richard jogged pass the alley he thought he heard a voice call his name. He stopped abruptly and looked back.

"Richard!" came the familiar voice that he could not quite place. He may have recognized it if the voice was more than just a loud whisper. He glanced into the alley in the direction of the sound. The shaved head of the misfit he had met earlier that night peeped around the corner of the building at the edge of the alley.

"C'mere, Rich!" He whispered.

"I don't think so," Richard answered, wondering how the hell this weirdo knew his name.

"Aw, c'mon. I got a little present for you. The boys at the ambulance forgot something!"

He brought his left arm from behind the building. In his outstretched hand was the severed head of the beautiful, dreamy-eyed girl the misfit was with earlier that night. Richard's eyes bulged to almost the size of eggs and he turned to run.

When he turned around he saw that Tim's car was gone. He ran anyway. He dared to look over his shoulder and was sorry he did. The misfit was standing in the middle of the street with the head in one hand and the other hand pointing at Richard. That huge German shepherd was now at the misfit's side. The beast snarled evilly and frothed at the mouth.

"Go fetch 'em, boy!" the misfit laughed, and the dog exploded into motion.

The animal moved with unnatural speed. Richard could have sworn the dog was nearly flying. Within seconds the German shepherd was on him.

Richard screamed and jumped up out of his sleep. He looked around to see that he was still in the passenger seat of Tim's car. His chest was heaving and his heart was beating to the point that he thought it might burst. Tim and Major looked at him as if he'd lost his mind.

"What's wrong?" exclaimed Tim. "You scared the shit outta me!"

Richard was still disoriented as he looked over his shoulder and down the street. "Y'all see that shit?"

"What shit? " Major asked. "I don't know what the hell you had in your punch but I'm glad it wasn't in mine!"

"Wait a minute," Richard said as he calmed himself, "What about the Mustang and the ambulance and cops?"

Major shrugged. "What about 'em?"

"You went to sleep right after we passed them," Tim added.

"Man," Richard went on. "That was a helluva dream."

"About what?" asked Tim.

"A man and... damn! I can't remember who he was... But that damned dog was in it, too! It had to be the biggest German shepherd I ever saw."

"Boy, I hate to tell you this, but you losin' what little mind you had," declared Major.

Later that morning, on the outskirts of the city, a beat up 1975 Camaro pulled to the curb in front of an older and even more beat up house. All of the windows were boarded and the grass in the front yard was waist-high. An individual with the sharpest eyesight would have had a hard time locating the walkway under the overgrown weeds. An instant later the Camaro's engine died and the headlights blinked out. The car sat idle in front of the house for a few minutes.

The house looked like it should have been torn down long ago. In fact, the house looked as if it would fall apart on its own at any moment. A tall figure stepped from the Camaro. The figure was skinny and had a pale, shaven head. He wore a dusty black leather jacket and torn faded blue jeans.

The misfit made his way to the cracked stairway that led to the front door, which was the only opening to the house that was not boarded. The misfit opened the door, walked through a foyer and went left into the living room. As he turned on the light a booming bark exploded from somewhere in the house. A monstrously huge German shepherd came charging into the living room.

The misfit dropped to one knee and spread his arms wide. The dog skidded to a stop just short of the open arms. It gave a small growl and a disinterested sniff before turning and trotting away. The misfit laughed and stood up straight.

"Stop acting like you don't love me, pooch!" He went to the couch and sat down. "I just can't get over this place." he said to no one in particular.

He did however, have a good reason for the comment. The interior of the house was a startling contrast to the exterior. The living room was decorated with plush, soft gray, wall-to-wall carpet. Every piece of furniture was covered with black leather. There was all manner of African and African-American art on the mantle and hanging on the walls.

The misfit reclined on the couch and picked up a remote control. He hit the power button and turned on the thirty-six inch television in the corner of living room.

The morning news was showing a newswoman talking about a young woman found beheaded on the south side. She was found in a green convertible Mustang parked on the street. After a short chuckle, the misfit flipped through the channels until he came to his favorite morning cartoon. He then reached into his jacket and pulled out a large machete filthy with dark dried blood.

"I get to do all the dirty work," he mumbled as he put the big knife on the cocktail table. "I *guess* I'll get it clean before he wakes up. He's such a damned neat-freak."

Camillia had also been watching the morning news. It appeared the one thing detective Weller feared most had come to pass. The press arrived at the scene of the murder before the police. News of the beheaded woman almost totally drained of blood was all over the newspapers and television. Camillia's telephone began to ring as soon as the newscast ended. She did not even have to look at the caller ID to know who it was.

"What is it, Weller?" she asked when she picked up the receiver.

"You must've been watching the news," he answered. "You know what I want. I wanna know where Rich was last night."

"He was at a party, dammit! And if you don't have anything else to talk about, don't call me."

"Camillia," he began, "I don't like this anymore than you do, but I haven't found any sign that would point to Andre's return."

"What about all these damned murders?" Camillia challenged.

Weller ignored the statement and continued. "Have you even talked to the kid about it?"

"About what? About his father? I've told him all about Richard senior."

"Have you told him about why you used to have those nightmares? Have you told him about Andre?"

"Why would I tell him that, Weller? That has nothing to do with him."

Weller sighed. "I give up, Camillia. I'm coming over to talk to him."

"Don't bother."

"Look, the woman was killed about three blocks away from a party, the same party Richard and his friends went to. I asked around and found out that she had been at the party earlier that night."

Camillia was silent.

Weller continued. "I'm going to ask him if he or his buddies saw her."

"I don't know," Camillia said with a slight shakiness in her voice. "Maybe Andre *is* back and he's trying to get at me through Richard..."

"I don't know either, Camillia. I'm sorry, but I have to talk to Richard. He may have seen something... anything."

"Alright," she conceded. "You can come over."

The time was three forty-five in the afternoon and Richard was still asleep. Camillia had not tried to wake him up because she knew he had been out late and had a hard time sleeping the night before. Weller was sitting in the kitchen with her and nursing a can of beer.

"You need to start bringing your own beer with you so you stop can drinking up mine," Camillia joked, her attempt at levity failing to mask the worry in her eyes.

"You don't drink much," Weller countered, "One six pack would last you over a week. I'm just tryin' to help you get rid of it. So when is the kid gonna get up, anyway?"

"Yeah, it's about time to wake his butt up." She turned toward the stairs but stopped when Weller called to her.

"Camillia, thank you," Weller said with uncharacteristic tenderness. "You've gotta be the strongest woman I've ever met. I can't imagine how hard this must be for you."

Camillia went up the stairs and into his bedroom to find Richard lying peacefully in his bed. The room was relatively dark because the blinds were shut. Camillia gave her son a nudge but he didn't move. She shook him vigorously and Richard did not so much as budge.

It was almost as if he was dead, but the steady rise and fall of his chest put that fear to rest. She grew impatient and began to shake him violently. He grumbled a bit but still didn't move.

"Alright sleepy-head," she said as she made her way to his window. She snapped opened his blinds and flooded the room with sunlight.

Richard jumped straight out of his sleep and shielded his eyes.

"SHIT!" he yelled.

"What?" Camillia asked.

"Oh...sorry, momma. I didn't know you were in here."

"I guess not. Get your lazy butt out of bed. You've got company downstairs."

Weller was just finishing his beer when Camillia and Richard came into the kitchen. Richard was wearing a T-shirt and boxer shorts and he looked like he had not had any sleep for days. He got a glass from the sink then went to the water cooler to fill it.

"You look like hell, kid." Weller stated.

"I just woke up, Weller," Richard grumbled. "What's your excuse?"

"Smart ass," Weller said. "Hey, I heard you went to a party last night. How was it?"

"It was pretty live. I saw some weird stuff, too."

"Like what?" Weller asked, suddenly very interested.

"Like a scary-lookin' white boy with one of the finest sisters I've ever seen. And then, on the way home I saw a body being pulled out of a nice Mustang."

Camillia and Weller looked at each other. Richard noticed the eye contact and was concerned.

"What?" Richard asked. "What's wrong?"

"Describe the girl with the white guy, Weller ordered.

"Well, she was dark-skinned, long curly hair. She had a very, *very* nice figure and was wearing a gray cat suit."

"A body was found last night," Weller told him. "The body was that of an athletic woman in a gray cat suit. We don't know what her face looked like because...well...the body was headless."

Richard almost choked on the water he was drinking. The dream he had in Tim's car came vividly back to him.

"Richard?" his mother asked.

"I had a dream...a nightmare in Tim's car on the way home last night. I dreamt that the crazy-looking guy she was with had cut her head off, then he sicced that big dog on me."

A look of realization came to his face.

"Vanessa used to mess around with a white guy, too!" Richard continued. "I never saw him but I heard he was weird. Major saw him once, I think. I have to ask him about it. This guy may be the killer!"

"Tell me about him," Weller demanded. "I need to know how he looked, how he acted, everything!"

"He was tall, real tall. His head was shaved and he was white, I mean *really* white! He was the palest *living* man I've ever seen."

"Get Major on the phone," Weller said excitedly. "Ask him about Vanessa's boyfriend. If his description matches yours we may have our man."

Richard ran to the phone and dialed Major's number. A few seconds later his friend answered.

"What's up big Mage? Remember that odd couple I told you about last night?"

"Yeah, I remember," Major answered.

"That girl was the one being pulled from that Mustang last night."

"You bullshittin'."

"No bullshit... Oops...umm, sorry momma." Camillia waved it off. Richard continued. "And check this out, her head was cut off."

"Damn...that's freaky as hell. It had to be that dude you told us about."

"That's what me and Weller think. Tell me somethin', you remember that white guy that Vanessa used to kick it with?"

"You think it was the same guy?" Major asked.

"Probably. Do you remember how he looked?"

"Vanessa's man? Never saw him. I just heard about them going together and that he looked weird. I can ask around, though."

"Cool," Richard said. "If you find out anything, let me know and I'll tell Weller. I gotta go. Later."

"Yeah, I'll holler atcha."

Richard hung up the phone. He turned to his mother and the detective. "Major never personally saw the guy Vanessa went with. He said he'd ask around."

"Now you have something to go on, Weller," Camillia said triumphantly.

"Yeah, and I'm damn glad of it!" Weller returned. "I'll go back to the station and let 'em know I've got a lead."

"Let me walk you out," Camillia offered.

As they went to the front door Camillia began to speak in a hushed tone. "Are you satisfied, detective? You've got an actual suspect."

"I won't be satisfied until I've nailed the son of a bitch," Weller answered. "But like I said before, I'm not ruling anything out."

Chapter 3

Richard's Story

Monday - The first day of summer classes

Tim drove himself, Richard and Major to their community college campus just a few blocks south of downtown Chicago. Tim and Major joked and laughed. Richard sat quiet and contemplative in the back seat.

The three of them had been friends for years. Camillia and Richard moved into the neighborhood when all three were entering the fourth grade. They were drawn to each other on the playground during recess and had been best friends ever since. Even then the three youngsters seemed to share an uncanny bond that none of them could quite put into words. Each could tell when something was wrong with one of the other two, no matter how much they tried to hide it, so Major knew Richard had something troubling on his mind.

Major turned to his friend. "So what are you supposed to be, Rich? A psychic or something?"

"I don't know. But my dream had to be more than a coincidence."

"Who knows?" Tim asked. "You might be able to help the law catch this sick bastard. Them sorry-ass cops need all the help they can get."

Major chuckled. "This fool couldn't catch herpes from a hype!"

"Damn right I couldn't! I wouldn't mess with one. But you probably *have* been burnt by one."

Tim shook his head "Anyway, did Weller get back with you about that crazy white boy from the party?"

"Not yet," Richard said. "But I should hear somethin' from him tonight. He told me to let him know if I have any more of those crazy dreams."

"This is wild," Major said. "You think this is a fluke or do you really think you have some kind of powers?"

"I don't know, man. I don't really think I have powers or nothing but this is crazy."

"Boy, if I had powers like that," Major began. "I'd do all kinds of shit! I'd hit the Lotto for weeks! Fuck work! Y'all think I'm tripping but I'm serious. I'd hypnotize the finest freaks in the city of Chicago...hell, the world! Y'all just don't know –"

"Alright, Major, calm your ass down," Tim chuckled. "You gotta admit, though, a brother would be tempted to do some stuff with powers like that. I think I'd do real subtle things. I'd just make sure I got whatever job I wanted. You know, stuff like that."

"Listen to y'all," Richard interrupted. "My dreams ain't nothin' compared to the fantasies you two fools are having!"

"Tell the truth," Major demanded. "You tryin' to say that if you find out you got psychic powers you wouldn't use 'em to get whatever you wanted?"

"I'd use them to get something I really needed," Richard answered. "But only if I couldn't work for it. You don't appreciate things that come too easy. I would definitely help my mother get outta debt."

"Oh, you're such a nice boy," teased Tim.

"Yeah," Major agreed. "Nice and full of shit."

A few minutes later they pulled into the campus parking lot. Tim saw a parking space next to a dirty, dented old black Camaro and decided to pass it up for another place to park.

"So," Major began, "the Cavalier's too good to be seen next to an old Camaro, huh?"

"Cars like that don't have insurance," Tim answered. "I don't want that piece of shit to scratch my ride."

"That car would be smooth if it had a little bodywork." Richard said.

"Ain't that much bodywork in the world," Major scoffed.

Later that day Richard was reluctantly walking to his eleven o'clock History class. History was not one of his favorite subjects and he was not looking forward to going to class. He took his time even though it was already five minutes after eleven. It was the first day of class so he thought he would get pass for being a few minutes late.

Hell, this is college, he thought. *The instructors here are supposed to give the students some leeway.*

He arrived at the classroom and checked his schedule to make sure he had the right place. The door was closed so he tried to open it. It was locked. Richard tentatively knocked on the door and waited. Seconds later the door was snatched opened by a short, dark-skinned balding, chubby, cranky-looking middle-aged man wearing glasses and holding a roll book in his hand.

The instructor looked up at him and said in an irritated voice: "Young man, you're late."

"I know," Richard responded. "I had a little trouble finding the class."

"If you had trouble finding a class on this tiny campus you're going to have a helluva hard time finding your way *out* of my class with a passing grade. I will *not* tolerate tardiness. What is your name?"

"Richard Williams."

"Richard Williams..." the instructor echoed, looking through his roll book,"...yes you're on the roll, and you have one tardy against you already. Two more and you will have earned yourself an automatic F. Three absences will earn an F as well."

Richard made his way to the back of the classroom. He already hated History and this teacher was not going to make it any better. He was thoroughly embarrassed and wanted nothing to do with anyone.

A few seconds later, another knock sounded from the classroom door. The instructor opened the door and a young lady entered. Richard was surprised when he saw that it was the young lady with the bad attitude from the party Saturday night. He almost felt sorry for her. He was sure she was about to be thoroughly embarrassed, so he was both shocked and disgusted by the instructor's reaction.

The instructor looked at the young lady and a perverted smile spread across his face. "Young lady," he said, "What is your name?"

"Paula," she answered with a shy smile, "I'm late because I had a little trouble finding the class."

"Oh, that's quite alright," he said, still smiling. "But please, don't make this a habit. You may take a seat."

"Well I'll be damned!" Richard mumbled to himself.

The only available seat was right next to Richard. She went to the back of the classroom and sat beside him. Richard wondered if she remembered him and doubted that she did. He figured their little conversation was replayed several times by different men at every party she attended. Richard made it a point not to look at her until she sat down. When she did he turned to her and nodded a greeting. She gave him a quick and obviously phony smile and opened her notebook.

What a bitch, he thought.

Camillia loved working as an administrative assistant in the Sears Tower. The building was such a majestic sight as it stood sentry over the beautiful downtown Chicago skyline. It always gave her a sense of pride to work in the tallest building in the world. She had read that a pair of taller buildings was being built somewhere in Malaysia, but for the time being the Sears Tower held the title.

Camillia was enjoying her lunch break in a sandwich shop on the ground floor of the super structure when Father Burns and detective Weller met up with her. Every time she saw them together she couldn't help but smile.

The two men were almost exact opposites. They made an odd-looking pair as they entered a room together. Father Burns stood well over six feet tall while detective Weller barely reached five feet seven inches. The priest had a full head of distinguished gray hair. The detective's thinning hair was hidden under the fedora he always wore to protect his ever-expanding bald spot from the elements. Burns' black priest's garb always gave him a formal appearance. Weller's full-length tan trench coat made him resemble a comical imitation of detective Columbo.

Burns walked tall and straight with confident strides. Weller walked with a quick stride and a bit of a bounce, looking over his shoulder every few steps. He did not appear to be nervous, just very cautious. It was as if he was always watching for someone watching him.

Camillia greeted the two men, finished the last bite of her sandwich and dropped her money on the table. She stood and then all three of them left. They walked outside the Tower and got into Weller's '95 Cutlass Ciera. Father Burns was the first to speak.

"Camillia, the detective told me about Richard's dream. I have to know if it was the first of that nature that he's had."

Camillia thought a moment. "He had a dream about a huge German shepherd the night before that. It was the same dog that was in his second dream."

"You really think he *dreamed* about the beheaded girl?" asked Weller. Camillia gave him a stern look. Weller continued. "I talked to Major and Tim. Tim didn't have much to say. He apparently has somethin' against cops; especially white ones. Major told me the three of them weren't together all evening. He said that Tim was with him the whole night but Richard broke away for a while."

"I don't like where this is going, Weller," Camillia warned. "Maybe Richard went off somewhere with a friend."

"Yeah, a *lady* friend," Weller said.

"Look you sonofabitch," Camillia said in surprisingly calm tone. "I'm not gonna sit here and let you insinuate this nonsense about my son."

"Camillia, please," Father Burns pleaded. "And let us not jump to conclusions, detective. The dreams may quite possibly be a gift. Richard may be getting psychic warnings of Andre's return because his mother may be in danger."

"Let's deal with *facts*," Weller began. "First off, the fact is that the killings have started again. Second, we don't know for a fact that Andre's back. And third, Richard's dreams...if they *are* dreams...have to be more than just a couple of mere coincidences. Father, have you found anything concrete that would suggest Andre's return?"

"Honestly...no."

"Okay," Weller continued, "I know we can't rule out the possibility that he's back but by the same token we can't rule out the possibility that Richard may be –"

"Enough!" Camillia exploded. "I'm outta here!" She got out of the car and slammed the door behind her.

"I'm sorry she feels that way, padre," Weller admitted. "I really am, but we've got to face facts."

"True," Weller conceded. "But can you blame her for feeling the way she does?"

"Not at all. Still, she's got to be realistic."

"One could say the same for you."

"Hell, I hope I'm wrong. I hope Andre is back. I pray every night that Richard isn't...you know. I watched him grow up and I love him like a son. We both know he's a good kid and nobody wants something like this to happen, but like I said before –"

"We can't rule anything out," finished Burns. "I'm not an expert on vampire biology. I only know about the legends and histories. I've read some accounts of male and female vampires spawning vampire children, and according to the literature, even that is extremely rare.

"I've never read anything suggesting that a vampire could sire a son with a human, though I dare not say it's impossible. Though even if it was, I know for a fact that Camillia has had Richard's blood tested on at least two occasions. She did a blood type test shortly after he was born and it matched Richard's type."

"I know," Weller said. "I also know that she had a DNA test done a few years ago when that technology went public. It was supposedly to see if Richard would be a suitable organ donor for his paternal grandparents down south. It turned out he was, for his dad's father. All the science stuff checks out, but what we're dealing with...this goes beyond science, padre."

"Indeed," Weller agreed. "I suppose we can't rule out the possibility that perhaps Camillia was pregnant with the elder Richard's child and Andre's seed infected the fetus."

Weller shivered. "That's a scary thought."

"But perhaps," Weller continued, "there is one more possibility that we've overlooked. What if we're all right?"

"What do you mean, padre?

"What if what you think about Richard is true...*and* Andre *has* returned?"

"Then we'd be in a helluva jam, old buddy."

Richard was sleeping on the couch when his mother got home from work. Camillia stormed into the house and slammed the door behind her. She then went into her bedroom and slammed yet another door. Richard was immediately concerned. He went to her bedroom door and knocked softly.

"Momma," he called. "What's wrong?"

"Rough day at work."

"You wanna talk about it?"

"Maybe later."

"You dressed, ma?"

"Yeah, why?"

"Because," Richard said as he barged into the room, "We need to talk about it now."

"Rich, please –"

"Please nothing. I've never seen you come home so upset." The grave look in her son's eyes unsettled her. "I swear, momma, if someone's done something to you I'll kill 'em. Just tell me."

Richard's concern brought a smile to her face. "Really, baby I'm alright. One of my girl friends got fired today."

"You two must've been real tight," Richard said. "Have I ever met her?"

"No. You don't know her, but we are good friends. Enough about that depressing subject. How was your first day at school?"

"It was cool 'till I got to History class. I got a real butt-hole for a teacher."

"You've got to expect to have one or two bad teachers every semester. Hell, you're gonna run into some of your worst teachers in college. If you let them get to you, though, you won't pass the class."

"I'm gonna pass, believe that."

"Richard," Camillia asked, suddenly very serious.

"Yes, momma?"

"Tell me about the nightmares."

"I told you about them."

"Did you have one last night?"

"I don't remember having one," Richard said. "What do you think? You think I have psychic powers?"

"I hope so." She then quickly changed the subject. "Don't you start working at the hospital tonight?"

Richard nodded. "I hope it's not too gross. I'm gonna be cleaning up after sick people and stuff."

"You'll get used to it."

"I don't know. You know how I get at the sight of blood."

"Your father couldn't stand the sight of blood either," she laughed. "He'd damn near faint if he cut his finger."

Richard chuckled. "I don't think I'm quite that bad."

The floor of the hospital lobby was covered with blood and Richard did indeed come very close to fainting. He took a few deep breaths as he approached the mess with his mop at the ready. A few seconds earlier, a man had run into the lobby holding his side. He had been robbed and assaulted. Richard could not figure out why the man didn't go into the emergency room entrance.

As he mopped up the blood, Richard started to feel light-headed once again. An older orderly walked by Richard and saw the look of discomfort on his face.

"What's the matter?" He asked with amusement. "Can't stand the sight of blood?"

"Somethin' like that," Richard answered.

"Then you got the wrong job, boy!" He laughed as he gave Richard a couple of firm pats on the back. The pats were so firm that Richard stumbled forward.

Richard looked up at the older man for the first time. He was a couple of inches taller than Richard and almost twice as wide. He looked to be in his mid to late thirties. He had a muscular build and tattoos covering his forearms. The man was dark-skinned and wore a moist curl under his hair net.

"I *would* like to finish, if you don't mind," Richard said in an irritated tone.

"Be my guest, li'l fella. If you need some help, don't ask me." The man laughed and walked away.

Richard continued to clean. As he mopped he felt a strange pain in his stomach. The pain was not the queasiness that he had expected. It was a sharp burning sensation. He clutched at his stomach for a few seconds until the pain passed.

His break came at seven thirty and lasted until seven forty-five. He was ravenously hungry so he bought a hot dog and hamburger from the cafeteria vending machine. When he opened the microwave door to put in his food a big dark hand came out of nowhere and inserted a full Tupperware bowl.

Richard looked up, "What the hell –"

It was the big orderly from earlier that evening. "Sorry boy, but it's first-come first-served around here."

"I *was* first!" Richard said angrily.

"Then why is my food in the microwave?" He asked with an annoying grin. He closed the microwave, set the timer and turned on the machine.

"Just hurry up so I can eat," Richard snapped.

"Slow up, youngster," the orderly began in a confidential tone. "Let me fill you in on some things. The name's Slab. I'm the head orderly on this shift. I got seniority, pull, muscle and all kinds of other shit around here. It would be best for you to..." he looked for a way to say what he wanted to say, "...Let me put this in a way you'll understand. I think it would be best for you to cooperate and stay the hell out of my way."

"You don't know me, man," Richard countered. An unusual anger built up inside of him. "It's just a microwave so it ain't no big thing, but for future reference, don't play with me."

"You and me gonna have fun, boy," Slab assured.

A familiar, maniacal voice came from the side of the two men:

"Not half as much fun as me and you are about to have, Slab!"

Richard and Slab turned to the misfit, wearing the same ratty leather jacket and seeming even paler and gaunter in the severe hospital lighting, coming toward them. He hid one hand behind his back. Richard took a couple of steps away but Slab stood his ground. He folded his big arms defiantly across his chest and smirked at the other's ragged appearance. The misfit stepped up to the big orderly and pulled a machete from behind his back.

Slab cried out as the machete whistled through the air. Richard threw up both hands to shield his face from the flying blood.

When he brought his hands down he saw Slab backing away from the misfit. Both of the big man's hands were covering his throat while blood spurted from between his fingers. Richard looked around at the other people in the cafeteria. They all continued to eat and socialize as if nothing was happening.

The misfit looked at Richard and laughed that insane laugh. "Looks like home boy can't stand the sight of blood either! At least not his own!"

Slab fell to his knees gagging and then fell on his face. Blood gushed from below his face and neck and spread slowly out across the cafeteria floor.

The pain Richard felt when he cleaned the blood in the lobby exploded in his belly. He grabbed his stomach, staggered backward and then doubled over in agony. He tried to call out for help but the pain stole his breath. He looked to the others in the cafeteria for assistance. They all acted as if they saw nothing.

"You feel that?" asked the misfit. "That's the hunger, kid, the *hunger*. Don't fight it, stand up straight and give in to it. Get up –"

"Get up, li'l fella," Slab said as he shook Richard awake. "How the hell you gonna rush me to heat up my food and then fall asleep?"

Richard lifted his head from the table with a wild look in his eyes and panting like he'd run a marathon.

"What the hell's wrong with you, boy?" Slab asked when he saw the younger man's face.

"Nothing..." Richard calmed himself. "...nothing."

"I should'a let yo' ass sleep," the big man said. "But the boss gets pissed when people are late clockin' in from break. I don't want you to get fired on your first night. I still have to torture you some more."

"Thanks," Richard said sarcastically. "I owe you one."

"Damn right you owe me one. And I don't forget shit."

Major and Tim were on a double date at the movies that night. They were waiting in line for popcorn while their dates waited in the theater seats.

Major put a hand on Tim's shoulder. "So what do you think about your boy Rich?"

Tim shook his head. "I don't know what to think."

"Those dreams are a trip, Tim. That type of shit can drive a man crazy."

"Richard is pretty strong, though," Tim said. "If this is some kind of phase, I'm sure he can handle it."

Major was quiet for a moment, hesitant to continue, then he spoke. "Weller came by the house the other night asking questions about ol' girl at the party."

Tim nodded. "I'm not surprised. He called me. You know I didn't talk to him, though. I hate pigs, especially white ones."

"He asked if the three of us were together all night," Major continued.

Tim looked at him. "You told him we were, right?"

"I told him the truth, Tim. Rich broke off to holler at some freaks like he always does. So what?"

"Damn, Mage. Weller's tryin' to pin this on Rich."

"That's crazy," Major denied. "He damn-near helped Ms. Williams raise Rich. Why would he want to bust him?"

"I don't ask questions about law-boys. They're dirty, man. I don't trust 'em."

A strange voice floated up from behind them. "I don't blame you, brother."

Tim and Major looked over their shoulders. The voice came from a tall, thin, ghastly pale white man. He wore a Chicago White Sox baseball cap and had long kinky dark hair hanging from under it.

Tim gave him a blank stare. "I ain't your brother."

"Get you some business, boy," Major advised.

The two young men turned away from the disguised misfit to place their respective orders.

"I've *got* business," the misfit assured them. "My business is one you wouldn't believe. I'm a detective, so to speak, but not the kind you hate so much, Tim."

This got Tim's attention. "How'd you know my name?"

Before the misfit could answer, the woman working behind the counter came back with Major and Tim's food. They turned to take it and when they turned back the stranger was gone. They looked at each other.

Major shrugged. "Don't ask me."

Later that night, after Tim and Major took their dates home, Tim drove up to the front of Major's house. Major got out of the car and closed the door, but instead of going right to the house, he bent down and poked his head through the open passenger window.

"I'm tellin' you," he began. "Two more nights and those freaks will be comin' out the panties."

They laughed, shook hands, and Major made his way up the walkway. When he reached the porch he went into his pocket and found his keys. He opened the door then waved to Tim. Tim waved back and drove away after Major stepped into the house. He always waited for Major and Richard to get safely into the house before he left. They lived in Chicago, after all. They all had known of or read tragic reports of people being assaulted just outside of their front doors.

Major closed the door behind him and put his keys back in his pocket. While his hands were in there he felt a crumpled slip of paper. He thought it was a receipt, but when he pulled it from his pocket he noticed that it was not. The paper was yellowed and wrinkled.

"Where the hell did this come from?" he asked himself. He opened it and began to read:

Major, I gave this letter to you instead of Tim because I knew Tim would just throw it in the trash. If you're wondering how I know you guy's names, I'll tell you.

Like I said earlier at the movies, I'm a detective. I'm not a police detective, either. I detect and destroy things that most people don't believe exist. I live in a world of darkness and violence. I am a vampire hunter.

At this Major had to laugh. He kept reading.

I know that sounds hard to believe but it's true. The recent killings are related. Your schoolmate Vanessa Strickland as well as Susan White were killed by the same man. Susan, if you don't already know, is the young lady that was at the party that you, Tim and Richard went to, the young lady that was found dead later that night.

All of the amusement left Major's face. He read on.

I believe Richard may know something more about the murders than he's led everyone to believe. I know he's been having nightmares lately. My colleagues and I are afraid that they may have been more than simple nightmares.

Any help you could give us would be greatly appreciated. Please don't dismiss this as the raving of a madman. A lot of lives are in danger.

Major balled the paper up and threw it into the trash as soon as he reached the kitchen. He told himself that this letter certainly *was* the raving of a madman.

He did not get much sleep.

Camillia went to the kitchen for a glass of cold water. The door to the back bedroom was open. That bedroom served as the guest room and was adjacent to the kitchen. From certain parts of the kitchen, a person could look through the bedroom window and see the back yard and the detached garage. The neighbors' barking dogs drew Camillia's attention that window. When she stepped into the kitchen and looked more closely she noticed the window was open.

The security-conscious mother chided herself for forgetting to close the window before dark. She had been so preoccupied that she had forgotten about it while checking the rest of the windows in the house. The cool breeze blowing through the screen was refreshing, but not enough to leave an easy, quiet means of ingress for an opportunistic home invader.

She pulled a glass out of the cupboard and filled it from the tap before going over to the freezer, where she scooped out three ice cubes and dropped them into the water. After a quick shake to cool the water faster and a refreshing gulp, Camillia made her way around the kitchen-slash-conference table to the bedroom to close the window.

When she stepped into the room she saw a figure, draped in shadow, seemingly crouched on the roof of her garage. She did not see any eyes, but she *felt* something looking into her home, looking at her.

Camillia choked back a scream and squeezed the glass so forcefully that it shattered in her hand. She gasped and took a step backward in fear as well as shock and pain from the frigid ice water and broken glass striking her bare feet.

She glanced down at the mess on the floor and quickly looked up and out the window again.

The figure was gone.

She looked down again, at the blood dripping from her cut fingers and oozing from a cut on the top of her right foot.

Blood.

"Oh no…" she breathed.

Without another second of hesitation, Camillia pulled the silver cross out from beneath her nightshirt to let it hang in full view. She dashed to the kitchen drawer and pulled out her decorative silver carving knife.

The barking suddenly stopped and an ominous silence fell over the house. Camillia felt the fine hairs on her arms and on the back of her neck stand on end.

Inhaling deeply, slowly, and as silently as possible, she crept back to the open bedroom door. She clutched at the cross with her left hand and brandished the knife out in front of her with the right. She said a silent prayer to herself and padded slowly into the bedroom.

The light was off but the light from the kitchen lent enough illumination for her to see that room was empty. With another silent prayer, she stepped to the window.

You can't come in if you're not invited, she thought, still too afraid to speak aloud. *I know you can't.*

An icy breeze buffeted her as she quickly closed and locked the window, never releasing the knife, and then shut the blinds.

Camillia peeked through the blinds at the garage roof and saw nothing but shadows. She searched as much of the night-shrouded back yard as she could through her narrow vantage point and saw nothing but grass and the concrete patio.

She finally exhaled.

When Richard got home his mother was up watching television. She met him at the front door like she always did. Richard noticed the bandages on her fingers and foot.

"What happened, momma?"

"Just clumsy, baby. I'm fine."

"You sure? You look a little frazzled."

"Positive," she lied with a forced smile. "So how was your first night at work?"

"It was cool 'till I met the head orderly. He was a real butt-hole, just like my History teacher."

"Welcome to the real world, Li'l Richard," Camillia teased. "There'll be assholes everywhere, as far as the eye can see."

Richard grunted. "That's good to know."

"I guess I can go to bed," Camillia said. She paused and regarded her son for along moment. "Richard?"

"Yeah?" he responded, a little unsettled by his mother's concerned gaze.

"If you have a nightmare, tonight tell me. Please."

"Ok, momma. I will. I promise."

Richard didn't have the heart to tell her that he had already had one that night. He was tired of seeing her so worried. Even now he could tell she was uneasy. He was not about to make her feel any worse.

Besides, he didn't think the dream was a premonition. And hell, even if it *was*, he would not miss Slab one bit.

Father Burns was restless that night. It was two-thirty a.m. and he was wide-awake. His body was deathly tired but his mind refused to let him rest. His nightmares had returned. The nightmares began that terrible night he and Detective Weller faced Andre. They visited him almost nightly for several years before finally going away. He thought the nightmares had stopped for good almost fifteen years earlier. He prayed that they had. That reprieve had apparently ended.

The recent reoccurrence of grizzly serial murders brought all of the bad dreams back with the dizzying force of a tornado. They seemed to be even more vivid than they were when he had them so long ago. Burns could not seem to escape the image of the monstrous Andre flying at him across that bedroom, face distorted into a sickening amalgam of bat, wolf and human, monstrous fangs and claws glinting in the moonlight.

Burns thought of Psalms 23:

Though I walk through the valley of the shadow of death, I will fear no evil...

At this he smiled ironically. He wished that were true. He wished he did not fear the evil that was Andre. For years the priest would tell himself that the fear was natural, that courage comes from facing and overcoming fear. As true as all that may have been, he nevertheless wondered if he had the strength to face that fear again.

Nineteen years ago he was young, strong and ignorant. Nineteen years ago, even once he had all the evidence he could ever need, deep down he still doubted that vampires actually existed. When he finally met the beast face to face the fear hit him like a sledgehammer.

He did not fight Andre out of courage that terrible night. He fought Andre out of his fear of dying. Adrenaline and reflexes took over and made him do what had to be done. If the young priest had known exactly what he was getting himself into, he doubted he would have gone to Andre's apartment.

I will fear no evil, for you are with me; Thy rod and Thy staff, they comfort me.

He did have the rod. The rod was made of solid oak and sharpened at the tip. He had the staff, a staff of pure silver and six feet long. On the upper tip of the staff was a shining silver crucifix surrounded by a gilded wreath.

Yes, he had the rod and the staff yet he felt no comfort. The priest was not as young as he used to be. The mere thought of facing the beast once again ripped his breath away and made him feel much older than his actual fifty-one years.

As he looked out of his window at the starlit night sky he began to question himself. Would he be quick enough to strike in time? Would he be strong enough to strike at all? Would he have the courage to even get close enough to strike?

The most disturbing question, however, was who he would actually be facing. Had Andre returned? Or would he have to do battle with the son of one of his oldest and dearest friends? The thought of killing Richard saddened him as much as the prospect of fighting a vampire frightened him. Would he be able to harden his heart enough to strike Richard down?

Every one of these questions invaded his mind constantly. He wished he could avoid the answers; that someone else could be burdened with this task. Unfortunately, he knew these wishes had no chance of being granted. For some reason that he could not explain, he knew he was fated to meet the beast once again, whoever that beast might be.

The first meeting with the vampire was not the true test. Father Burns knew this all too well. The second meeting *would* be the true test, now that he knew what awaited him. It would be a test of his faith, of his courage, of his resolve. It was a test he dreaded with all his heart.

"Well, since I'm up," he said to himself. "I may as well do something productive."

He reached under his bed and retrieved a small stack of newspapers. He read through various stories about the recent murders. It had been nine days since the killings started. Five bodies had been found in those nine days. The priest knew that there had been at least four more killings because the beast fed every night.

Just because the murders had not been discovered did not mean they had not been committed. There was no telling how many times Andre may have killed before the first body was even found. The priest jotted down the locations of each murder and got dressed.

Rod in one hand and staff in the other, he made his way to his car. The halls of the rectory seemed smaller that night, the shadows darker. He could hear every creak of wood in the large old house. The whispering wind mocked him. He was thoroughly spooked by the time he got into his car.

Father Burns lived on the city's north side. The first body was found on the north side. The location was about ten minutes from his home. He drove those ten minutes before pulling his car to a curb getting out. The chill nighttime breeze made him zip his jacket up to his chin. He made his way to the alley where the body was found.

He made a mental note that all of the bodies were found in or near an alley. That was not an unusual place for a victim to be found but he did not want to miss a thing. Burns had no idea what he was looking for so he searched the area for any clue he could find. On one end of the alley was a small liquor store. When he walked to the other end of the alley he found a church. The whole time he was scribbling on a little note pad.

The priest looked at his watch and saw that it was fifteen minutes to four a.m. The neighborhood was quiet and still with the exception of a few pre-dawn drivers on their way to work. He stood at the edge of an alley on the city's south side. From where he was standing he could see a church in the middle of the block and a liquor store on the end of the block. This was where the fifth body was found. A liquor store and a church were either on the same block or one block away in each case. There had to be a connection.

A strong hand gripped his shoulder. The priest reacted very un-priest-like as he turned quickly, knocked the hand away and drew back a fist. He came very close to smashing detective Weller in the nose.

"Wait a minute, padre!" Weller yelled as he shielded his face. "What kind of priest goes around knocking people out?"

The priest dropped his fist and let out a loud sigh. "You shouldn't sneak up on people, detective," Father Burns admonished, "especially at night."

"Night?" Weller asked. "Hell, it's almost daybreak. What are you doing out this time of morning?"

"A little detective work of my own. I decided to check on some things. I see you're putting in a bit of over-time."

"Yeah," Weller said. "I couldn't sleep, either."

"Weller, I think I've found something you might like."

"What is it?" the detective asked.

"Every victim was found in an alley of a street that was very near both a liquor store and a church."

"Hell, there's a liquor store and church on just about every other street in certain parts of the city," Weller reminded.

"There are many streets like that in certain parts of the city, it's true," Burns agreed, "but not so many in others. Remember, the killings almost never take place in the same location where the bodies are found. It seems the killer intentionally placed the bodies in these locations."

"So what do you think, Padre? Is this creep is trying to make a point or something? Is this some kind of social commentary?"

Father Burns thought about it for a few seconds. "I think the killer is certainly trying to make a point, but not about social ills. I think the killer knows us, and is mocking us."

"You mean you and me specifically, don't you?" Weller asked.

"The bodies may be placed near churches to mock me, a priest, and the liquor stores to mock you."

Weller frowned. "Why do *I* have to be related to a liquor store?"

"Your drinking prowess is no secret, detective," Burns assured. "You are a good policeman but when you're off duty... It's just a guess. It may not be that personal. It may be a commentary about the urban plight or simply a statement about the duality and hypocrisy of man."

"Yeah, yeah, yeah," Weller interrupted. "You're calling me a lush. But anyway, I've been doing some homework and I think I've found something you may be interested in. Come back to the station with me."

Back at the police station, there was a large map of the city on the wall of Weller's office. The map had five colored tacks stuck into it.

"So padre," Weller began, "What does that look like to you?"

"The colored tacks form a small arc," Burns answered.

Weller nodded. "That's right, an arc. Each tack represents where a body was found. If this pattern keeps up, the tacks will form a full circle. I don't know exactly what that means but I do know I don't like it."

"A circle can represent infinity," the priest offered. "No beginning and no ending. Perhaps he's trying to say that he himself is infinite."

"Not if we find his ass," Weller promised.

"If this is a circular pattern," Burns said, "then perhaps you can pinpoint the general area of the next murder."

"Not necessarily," Weller differed. "The geographical pattern is circular but the chronological order in which the bodies have been found is completely random so far.

And like you said earlier, the murders haven't been committed where the bodies have been found."

"I see what you mean," Burns said. "Besides, the arc only covers roughly sixty degrees. There are three-hundred degrees of possible locations left."

"Right," Weller grunted. "By the position of the tacks the circle would be damn near as large as the city itself."

"So what do you suggest?" asked the priest.

"Assuming the circle pattern is on the money, what do all points of a circle have in common?" Weller asked.

"The center point, of course," Burns said as a look of realization rushed to his face. "You think we should see what's at the center of this circle."

Weller marked down the coordinates of the center point and the two men hurried to Weller's unmarked car. It was daylight by the time they reached their destination. Their trek took them into downtown Chicago. They drove around the area that Weller had marked for them.

"If you see something fishy, padre," Weller instructed as he drove slowly down the street, "just holler."

They drove around in silence for quite some time. The serenity of predawn soon gave way to the sounds of morning rush hour. It started as just the sound of a few car motors. Within a short time it grew into the thunderous sounds of car and truck motors and honking horns as rush hour came on in full force.

Despite the noise outside of the Cutlass Ciera, the inside of the car was deathly silent.

"Padre," Weller started in a tired voice, "I don't think we're gonna find –"

Both men saw it at the same time. The building stood out from the surrounding buildings. It didn't stand out in size, but in shape. It was a concrete, circular building standing three stories high. Weller checked the address of the building against the coordinates he had written down in his office.

"This building's in the exact center point of the arc," Weller confirmed.

The building was a church.

"He's mocking us," concluded Father Burns. "He's mocking *me*."

Camillia tried to shake Richard awake but he didn't budge. She noticed he was sleeping much harder than he used to sleep. She attributed his heavy sleeping to the fact that he had probably worked very hard the night before. There was one thing that always seemed to work though, so she did it. She walked over to the window and opened the blinds. Once again Richard sat bolt upright as the sunlight poured in. Once again he shielded his eyes for a few seconds. The alarm clock next to his bed was beeping. He reached over and turned it off.

"Do you have to do that every morning, ma?"

"Apparently," she answered. "I'll stop when you start waking up when the alarm goes off."

"I didn't know I was that tired," he said while he stretched.

"Did you sleep well?" Camillia asked.

"I slept like a baby," Richard answered.

"If this job takes too much out of you, you're going to have to give it up. You know school comes first."

"I'll be alright, momma. I have to get used to getting up early again. I got lazy over the summer."

The downstairs phone began to ring. Camillia rushed to answer it. The phone rang three times before she got to the kitchen to pick up the receiver.

"Hello?" she greeted.

"Camillia, don't hang up," Weller's implored. "I have some news for you."

"What?" Camillia asked with ice in her voice.

"You asked me and the padre to keep you informed, you got it, but I don't want to talk about this over the phone. When can I meet with you face to face?"

"Come by this evening about five. I'll be home and Richard should be on his way to work by then." Camillia cautioned Weller: "Look, detective, if plan on spouting more nonsense about –"

"I promise," Weller interrupted. "No talk about vampire children. Before I go, do churches and liquor stores mean anything to you?"

"What?"

"Never mind, I'll tell you about it later."

"I'll see you at five."

I do not *need this*, Major thought as he lay awake in his bed that Tuesday morning. He had too many problems already. The last thing he needed was to find out that one of his best friends was some kind of psycho killer. The thought of Richard being a vampire was the height of insanity, though it was possible that he might know something about the murders.

Major did not want to think about something like that but he could not help it. Coincidences never meant that much to him. He was one of those people that believed everything happened for a reason. The fact that the tall freaky white guy knew who he and Tim were made Major wonder what the hell was going on.

How did he know about Richard's nightmares? Richard made him and Tim swear not to tell anyone. Could the man have been a cop? Major doubted that. He considered sharing all of this with Tim but then he thought it would be better not to. Tim would categorically disagree with everything the misfit guy had to say on general principle.

Vampires. It almost made Major laugh out loud. The misfit guy was obviously implying that he thought Richard was some kind of unholy bloodsucker. How could a sane person believe that? If the guy had not mentioned anything about the living dead Major would have been able to take him more seriously. He could not deny, however, that Richard's nightmares made him nervous. He did not believe in vampires but he never believed people had psychic powers, either. He did not believe it, that is, until he found out about Richard's dreams.

"I'll give this some time," Major said to himself. "If anymore crazy shit goes down, I'll fill Tim in."

He turned over and tried in vain to go back to sleep.

There was one thing Camillia could not deny about detective Weller, and that was his promptness. As soon as her grandfather clock struck five Weller was ringing her doorbell. Minutes later they were in a deep conversation about what the priest and the detective learned that morning. Camillia listened intently to everything Weller had to say.

"So far," Weller concluded, "that's the closest thing to a pattern that we have."

"Interesting," Camillia said. "He was regimented. Whenever we went out it was the same routine: One night we'd go to dinner, a movie, then home; the next night we'd go to dinner, a play, then home; the next night we'd go to dinner, a walk in the park, then home; the next night we'd start over again with the movies and the pattern began again."

"That's something to go on," Weller said. "If you had to guess, where would you think he'd strike next?"

"I think the body would be somewhere in that circle, but like you said earlier, that's a lot of ground to cover."

"Too much," Weller agreed. "We don't have the manpower to cover that much territory."

"You should do some random checks around the circle," Camillia suggested. "Use the liquor store and church pattern on the circle path. There may be a body in that area that hasn't been found."

"My captain's got some men on that. It's still a large area to cover, though. There has to be some way to narrow it down."

"But that's not enough," Camillia added. "Finding the bodies is not finding him. I think he's killing them a very long way from where the bodies are being dumped."

"What makes you think that?" Weller asked.

"He's real...classy, if that's what you wanna call it. He's very neat and ordered. I think he'd consider killing on the street or in an alley beneath him."

"And he's not killing them at their homes," Weller observed. "At least, if he is, he isn't leaving any evidence of it. Maybe he's killing them at his place."

"Possible," Camillia allowed. "But I doubt it."

"Why?" Weller questioned.

Camillia took a deep breath and forced herself to recall the time she had spent with Andre all those years ago. The heartbreak, fear, and anger she experienced threatened to overwhelm her, but she composed herself and pushed through.

"Well, we dated for weeks before he brought me to his apartment. Before that we went to some very public places. Dozens of people saw us together and he didn't care. That hasn't been the case with his other victims, then or now, has it?"

"No," Weller concurred. "We couldn't find anyone that said they ever saw any of the victims with a man matching his description."

"He had something special in mind for me," Camillia admitted.

This is the night I make you my queen. She shuddered at the memory.

"Otherwise, he could've killed me at any time before then. So no, I don't think he's taking any of them to his place, not to kill them. I don't think he'd defile his home with his...his prey."

A thought suddenly occurred to the detective. "Maybe he isn't working alone."

"You think so?" Camillia wondered.

"If what you say is true, if he wouldn't sully his home with his victims, how would he transport them?"

Camillia's eyes widened. "The weird guy Major and Richard mentioned, you think he could be working with Andre?"

Weller shrugged. "Could be. But even if he is, how the hell do we find *him*?"

"You're right," Camillia said, crestfallen. "The only way to stop Andre is to find out where he sleeps."

"Yeah, the padre said something like that, too. But the 'scary-lookin' white boy' would stand out. People would remember someone like that. I'll ask around about him. Hell, he might even be the killer."

Something like hope brightened Camillia's expression. She was terrified at the possibility that Andre had returned and even more afraid of the chance that her son might somehow be involved. The very notion that it could be anyone else...

"You really think maybe Andre hasn't returned?"

"I've said it before. I'm not ruling anything out. Besides, if it really was Andre..." the detective trailed off.

"What?" Camillia asked, eyes narrowed.

"If it was Andre," he continued, "Why hasn't he come after you by now?"

The memory of the shadowy form on her garage roof flashed in her mind. She was not sure if it was really there. Either something was watching her or she was losing her mind. She could not decide which was worse.

There was no moon out. There were no stars. Richard stood staring out of the hospital window with a strange longing while absently holding a mop.

He always did like the night more than the day. There was something mysterious and exciting about the night sky. When he was a kid he hated to have to come in before the sun went down. His mother never left him much choice, though. Two options were given to him: either come in when the streetlights came on or come in after sundown and get his ass beat.

Times were different now. Now he could stay out as long as he wanted. Now he could enjoy the night, and he did. As long as he let his mother know where he was going, who he would be with, and when he would be coming home, she did not give him any problems. Her main concern was that he was safely indoors and not out on the dangerous streets.

Just looking at the night sky mesmerized him. He looked into the infinity of space, the eternity of darkness between the twinkling stars. Sometimes he felt as if he could float away into that endless ocean of night. This was one of those times. All he was aware of was the beautiful blackness. The cold darkness caressed him.

"Wake up, boy!" a huge hand slammed into Richard's back and woke him violently from his trance.

An unnatural anger surged through Richard as he struggled to keep from swinging his mop around to strike at the owner of the voice. Instead of lashing out he turned around slowly.

It was Slab, the big orderly. This man became more and more annoying every time Richard saw him.

"Look, man," Richard warned, "all I'm asking is for a little respect, and I think it'd be wise if you gave it to me." Richard looked at him with smoldering eyes and calmly said: "You don't know me."

Something in the young man's eyes seemed to unnerve Slab. Maybe he was surprised that a kid so much smaller than him showed absolutely no fear of him. Slab, however, would not be outdone.

"No, I don't know you, you little fucker, but you don't know me either...so you better hope it don't never come down to me an' you 'cause I'll break your little ass in half."

For some reason that not even he understood, Richard began to chuckle. He could see the uncertainty in Slab's face and he could also see the anger. He knew full well that the most dangerous man in the world is a man who is afraid, but Richard chuckled as if the thought of Slab hurting him was amusing.

"Now, Slab," Richard began. "You and I both know that's not happening." Richard smiled an evil smile.

Slab did know it. He would never admit it but somehow, on a primal level, he knew the smaller man was right. Slab could see it in his eyes. For just a split second Richard had the eyes of a madman.

Slab's bullheadedness, however, as well as his pride, got the best of him. The bigger man had to save face.

"Oh, I get it," Slab said, a nervous smile spreading across his face. "You're joking. You gotta be. You got nuts, li'l fella. I like that. I think we'll get along pretty good after all!" The big orderly walked away, laughing all the while.

Richard heard a small quiver in that laugh.

Chapter 4

About a mile away from the hospital where Richard worked, someone else was admiring the beautiful blackness of the night sky. This someone else was walking down the street holding the hand of a lovely young Asian woman with almond-brown eyes and flowing, silky black hair.

"The night is beautiful, don't you think, Yi?" he asked.

"Very," answered the woman.

Yi did not normally date African American men, Caucasians, either, for that matter. She'd always made it a point not to date anyone that was not of her ethnicity. There was something about this man, though. This particular man was markedly different than any other she had ever met.

He was about five feet ten inches tall. His hair was cut short and neat. He had smooth medium brown skin with no facial hair. While not very large or muscular, strength radiated from him. There was an aura about him that she found somewhat threatening yet exceedingly enthralling.

Other than his handsome face, at a glance the man did not appear overly impressive physically. His eyes, however, held the promise of mystery and excitement. His eyes held the promise of an unforgettable experience. Yi simply could not keep her eyes off of his.

The two turned into the entrance of an upscale downtown hotel. They were nearly invisible among the throngs of people dressed in suits or business casual attire milling in and just outside the lobby. The nametags and lanyards worn by the majority of the people evidenced some sort of conference. Yi could not tear her attention away from her companion long enough to tell what kind of conference it was. She could only think about the man at her side.

"I don't usually do this," she said timidly. "I don't want you to think that I'm some sort of depraved woman."

"I know you're not," the man assured. "You know that you'll be safe with me."

"Yes...I'll be safe with you," she said. Her heart beat fiercely in her chest. Was it...fear?

No, not fear, assured a soothing whisper deep in her subconscious. *It's excitement. You're about to have a night you will never forget.*

The beat-up black Camaro came to a stop on the sand of a deserted lakefront beach on the city's north side just before dawn. The misfit jumped out of the car and looked around to make sure no one else was there. He went to the trunk, popped it open and looked down on the pale, pretty face of an Asian woman with long black hair.

Her almond-brown eyes were open wide and staring blankly into eternity. Just below her chin was a mess of dried blood and gore that trailed from her neck to her navel. She was naked from the waist up and her neck and torso had been ripped open.

"I don't know why that sonofabitch won't just drain 'em and be done with it," he complained as he struggled with the limp, dead weight.

"'We don't want people catching on,'" the misfit said, mimicking the voice of his master. "'We don't need too many people looking for us just yet' he says. Fuck people! What the hell can they do to him? He's *already* dead! These damned bodies are messy!"

He finally lifted the body out of the trunk. "They're heavy, too! She's *so* pretty, though." He kissed the dead lips before tossing the body into a small rowboat.

Weller was going to hate this. Up until now he was able to able to steer clear of the police Lieutenant. Standard operational procedure called for him to converse with Lieutenant Stone from time to time as it was, and even that was too much for Weller to stand. Any extra contact with the ultra-conservative, straight-laced, stubborn superior officer was dreaded. If there was any other way to do this Weller would have gladly tried, but unfortunately there was no other way. Weller took a deep breath and entered the lieutenant's office.

Lt. Stone looked at Weller and nodded his head in acknowledgement. Weller nodded in return. No attempt was made by either to hide his dislike for the other. Stone continued to page through the various papers stacked neatly on his desk. The lieutenant made a conscious effort to not look at the older detective when he spoke.

"Is there something I can help you with, detective?" The tone of Stone's voice made it clear that he hoped there was nothing he could do for Weller.

"As a matter of fact, yes," answered Weller. "You know about the serial killer we have on our hands..."

"You know how I feel about that," Stone replied in a condescending tone. "I don't think there's enough evidence to connect these murders and call them the acts of a serial killer."

Here we go again, Weller thought with a sigh. "Listen, captain, this isn't a reporter you're talking to."

"All of the mutilations are different," Stone argued. "The backgrounds of the victims are different. Their physical descriptions vary. What have you got to suggest one killer?"

Weller was getting frustrated. "You *know* what we have. They were all killed somewhere else and dumped in a location where they'd be found fairly easily. Did it ever occur to you that the killer might be purposely mutilating these women in different ways to throw smart cops like yourself off the scent?"

"So you think we've got a crazed vampire running around?" Stone asked with a grin.

The detective bit back an angry retort. The lieutenant was younger than him but old enough to remember the "Vampire Killer" headlines from two decades earlier. Weller had never used the word "vampire" to describe the serial killer, but as an up-and-coming detective taking the lead in an investigation for the first time, the label was quickly associated with him.

He had been quickly climbing the ladder of success within the CPD. All of the accolades he received earlier in his blossoming career promptly became scathing criticism after coming so close to catching the killer and then allowing him to escape. His career stalled after that. And here this little bastard was, using that disgrace to try to get a rise out of the hot-tempered older detective.

Weller refused to take the bait. "Yeah, well, anyway," he snarled. "I think I've discovered a pattern."

"What kind of pattern?" Stone became mildly interested.

"A circular pattern," Weller said. I've marked each place where the bodies were found on my wall map of the city. So far, the marks construct a huge arc."

"Each mark is equidistant from a common point?"

"I know what an arc is. The locations form one."

"Let me check it out."

The police lieutenant picked up a few papers from his desk and rose to follow Weller to his office. When they reached the desk Stone looked at each mark on the map and looked at one of the papers in his hand.

He turned to Weller. "I've checked each mark against the locations of the bodies in the reports. Everything checks out."

"You didn't think I'd mark the wrong spots did you?" Weller challenged.

Stone ignored the question and gave him a look that confirmed that he thought exactly that. "Have you checked to find out what's in the center of this arc?"

"Of course," Weller snapped. "The big, concrete, circular church downtown is in the exact center of the arc. We've checked the church and the surrounding area thoroughly but we came up with zilch."

"The killer is mocking you," the lieutenant noted. "So what do you plan to do?"

"Well," Weller began, "It occurs to me that there may be bodies that we may not have found yet. I suggest we do detailed searches in random areas on points of the curve."

"That arc suggests a very large circle. Do you know how much time and manpower that would take?" Stone was again using that condescending tone.

"A whole helluva lot, but I think it's worth it."

"If this circular theory is right, detective..." Stone began as he studied the map. He sounded as if he were about to shoot the theory full of holes, "A few of those points run right out into the lake." He indicated points on the circle that did indeed extend out into Lake Michigan. He looked at Weller with a patronizing smile. "Would you have us drag a Great Lake?"

"Yes. As a matter of fact, I'd suggest that we check the lake *first*. If we do find a body or two out there on the circle my theory would be solidified."

Stone's smile disappeared. "Are you insane? That's *Lake Michigan*. Do you think we'll get approval for that kind of search based on what you've found?"

"Yes," Weller repeated. "We know what area to search. Sure, it's a large area, but if the killer is mocking us the way we suspect –"

"Mocking *you*," Stone corrected.

"My guess is he weighted the body, or bodies, down to minimize the effect of the tides, and there will be at least one body close to the shore. The key is that he *wants* his victims to be found. He'll place them somewhere where we can find them relatively easily."

Lt. Stone thought for a moment. "I'll see what I can do. This is going to be a lot of trouble, Weller. You better hope like hell we find something."

"To be honest with you," Weller replied, "this is one time I really hope I'm wrong."

Tim and Major were in the Chevy Cavalier on their way to pick up Richard. Major sat in the back seat with his winter jacket unzipped. He stared distractedly out the window.

"What's wrong, Mage?" Tim asked.

"Huh? Oh, nothing. I'm straight."

"Straight, hell. You ain't this quiet in your sleep. What's on your mind?"

"Alright," Major said. He made up his mind to fill Tim in. "Remember that tall freaky sumbitch behind us at the concession stand the other night?"

"Yeah. What about him?"

"To make a long story short, he slipped a note into my pocket and –"

"Uh oh!" Tim laughed. "A love letter?"

"Fuck you, man. I'm serious."

Tim could see that for the first time in a long time Major actually *was* serious. Tim became concerned. "What was it?"

"The letter proved he knew a lot of shit. He knew a lot about you, me, and Rich. He even knew about Rich's nightmares."

"A cop," Tim said. "I bet he was a cop!"

"I don't know what the hell he was. I just know he knew things he shouldn't have. The letter said that he thinks Rich knows more about those murders than he's letting on."

"He's a cop, man," Tim insisted. "Don't you get it? Weller told him about the nightmares Rich was having. Weller told him to screw with us about it. They're using us to try to get to him, to find out what we know."

"I don't think even Weller knew some of the things in that letter," Major argued.

"The law thinks Rich is killing those people," Tim countered.

Major shrugged his shoulders and looked out of the window. Tim's eyes narrowed as he glanced at his friend.

"You think so too, don't you?" Tim accused.

Major said nothing, he kept staring out of the window.

"You do!" Tim pulled the car to the curb. "Don't tell me you sellin' out on Rich, man. If you are you can get the hell outta my ride right now."

"I don't know what to think, Tim." The confusion was evident in Major's face and voice. "I just know some strange shit is going down. I don't think Rich is a –" he caught himself, knowing that if he mentioned vampires he would definitely be walking to school, "– a killer or nothing, but there's somethin' to this that we don't know."

"Don't sell out your boy like that, Mage. And *please* don't sell out to some cracker-ass law dogs. We grew up with the brother. If Rich knew something more about this he wouldn't hold it back from us." Tim pulled back out into traffic.

"The weird guy knew you wouldn't buy it," Major said. That's why he slipped me the note. How would he know that?"

"Weller!" Tim replied, flabbergasted. "Don't you get it? Weller knows I don't like him. He knows I don't like cops. You can't trust any of them."

"I don't think that guy was a cop." Major insisted. "I can spot a cop when I see one. I saw his piercings up close. They're real, and so are the tats. Dude looks like he's starving and smells like he don't know what soap is. Cops don't look like that. Cops don't *smell* like that."

A look of realization came over Tim's face. "I'll be damned," he said as Major looked over at him. Tim continued. "Maybe he wasn't a cop. Remember that white guy Rich told us about at the party? Remember when he asked you about the white guy that Vanessa used to kick it with? It could've been the same dude! Rich said he was tall, pale, and ugly as hell."

"He also said the guy was bald and had a big fang for an earring," Major reminded. "This fool had hair down to his shoulders."

"You can take an earring off," Tim replied. "And I know you've heard of wigs."

Major nodded. "Me and Rich thought that guy may have been the killer," he said.

"He probably is," Tim said. "He could be a cop, too, just deep undercover. That would explain how he knows so much. He could be trying to throw everybody off the trail by making them think Rich is the killer."

"Damn..." Major said. "You could be right."

"I know I am." Tim pulled in front of Richard's house and honked the horn.

"Who's gonna fill in Rich?" Major asked. "Me or you?"

"Both of us," Tim answered. He glanced at his friend and noticed something he had not noticed earlier. "What's that around your neck?"

Major looked at Tim out of the corner of his eye. "What's it look like? It's a crucifix."

Tim scoffed. "It's nice, man. Looks like real gold. When did you get religion?"

"Always had it," Major said with the shrug of one shoulder. "Catholic school, remember?"

"Yeah, Major...but, uh...what about all of the weed and the drinking and the cussing and the many, many failed attempts to get laid?"

"I ain't no angel. So what?" Major said defensively. "I still believe in God and Jesus Christ. This crucifix and chain, which *are* real gold, were consecrated and everything. My pops gave it to me. I usually don't wear it. You know how cats snatch gold around here."

"Why wear it now?"

Major shrugged one shoulder again. "I just feel like wearing it."

Tim gave Major a suspicious side-eye as Richard approached the car and ducked into the front seat. He wore a pair of dark sunglasses and wrinkled clothes.

"Sorry you had to wait so long, fellas," Richard began. "I got up pretty late. I couldn't go to sleep for nothin' last night. I finally dozed off at about four."

"Say Rich," Major piped up from the back seat. "What do you think of this chain?"

Richard turned to look at Major and his jewelry and his head snapped back. A pall of dread washed over Major's face.

Richard chuckled. "When did your foul-mouthed, alcoholic, herb-smokin', wanna-be player ass start wearing a cross?"

Tim laughed out loud.

The fear on Major's face twisted into embarrassment. "Both of y'all can kiss my yellow ass."

"You have another nightmare?" Tim asked when his laughing fit subsided.

"Naw. I was just sitting up. I guess I was charged up from what happened last night."

"What happened?" Major asked.

"I punked Slab at work," Richard said with a satisfied smile. "He stepped to me and I called his bluff. He backed down real quick like."

"Well, me and Tim are pretty charged up too, dog. Listen up..." Tim and Major went on to share their theory about the tall misfit.

By the time they finished they were pulling into the campus parking lot. Once again, one of the few parking spots available was next to the dusty old Camaro. Once again Tim passed that spot up for another one.

Tim spoke as the trio got out of the car and headed for their respective classes. "So what'cha think, Rich?"

"I think that was some good info," Richard answered. "When I get back to the crib I'm gonna let Weller know."

"I don't know about that," Tim warned. "If that white freak *is* a pig, the only way he would know about us is if Weller told him. If Weller can't keep this to himself telling him definitely ain't the move."

"I know you don't like him," Richard said, "but he practically helped momma raise me. He wouldn't put me in danger like that. If this freak is a cop Weller should know. I'm damn sure not about to trust any other cops with this info."

"It's your call, dog," Tim conceded with a shrug. "But don't say I didn't warn you.

Richard entered his History class at three minutes before eleven o'clock that morning. Most of the class was already there and the instructor was sitting behind his desk. The grouchy little man looked up at Richard.

"You've made it to class on time two days in a row, young man," the instructor said. "Keep it up."

"What about Paula?" Richard asked. "She was late Monday, Tuesday, and I bet she'll be late today. You haven't chewed her out at all."

The shorter man stood up from his desk. "Listen, young man," the instructor said as he pointed a bony finger at Richard. "How I conduct my class is no concern of yours. Just make sure *you* don't slip. And never wear sunglasses in my classroom again. That's the same penalty as being tardy. Strike two." The instructor made another small mark next to Richard's name.

White-hot rage warmed Richard from his head to his feet. In the next instant his hands were wrapped around the instructor's throat and lifting him easily from the floor. The students behind gasped or yelped, but no one moved. All of them were frozen in shock and fear.

With a swift jerk and twist, Richard heard the man's neck snap. The vibration of the snapping vertebrae was soothing to his hands and wrists. He could hear man's fading heartbeat and he could smell the fear.

The sudden rush of sensations blurred his vision and caused him to shake his head to clear it. When his vision cleared, the instructor was once again standing in front of him. His haughty glare, however, had changed into something markedly less pompous.

The flash of anger in the student's eyes was enough to unsettle the smaller man. The instructor sat back at his desk a little quicker than usual.

"You may be seated, Mr. Williams."

Richard exhaled with something resembling relief. He knew his rush of anger and violent fantasy was an unreasonable reaction to the instructor's disrespect, yet it took all of his self-control to keep his hands at his sides and away from the other's neck. Would he be able to stop himself the next time?

Later that evening, Weller and Father Burns stood out in the unusually cool weather next to Weller's Cutlass Ciera. They were on a south side beach experiencing firsthand why Chicago is called the Windy City. Their coat collars were closed tight against the chill while their coat tails flapped loudly in the gale blowing off the lake. There were over a dozen marked and unmarked police vehicles parked on either side of the Ciera. A score of police officers stood at the water's edge. Everyone's attention was riveted to the police boats out on lake.

"I don't know why you're still out here, padre," Weller said as he pulled his collar up. "The only reason I'm here is because Stone made sure I'd have to oversee this operation."

"You don't have to be concerned about my comfort, detective," Burns assured. "This jacket is warm, and besides, if this pans out I want to be here to see it."

"I gotta tell ya," Weller confided, "a part of me hopes it doesn't. The last thing I wanna do is tangle with Andre or anything like him again."

"Neither do I, detective." Burns paused for a few heartbeats. "I hate to seem pessimistic but I think we'll have to do just that."

"Yeah, me too," Weller agreed. "I've been having nightmares about Andre lately. I've had a couple about the kid, too."

"Richard? Yes, I think he's going to play a part in this as well, if for no other reason than to give his mother strength. I haven't had any nightmares about him, but like you, I've had more than my fair share of bad dreams about Andre."

"It's hard not to," Weller said.

The detective looked toward the lake and saw that some of the men on one of the boats were very busy pulling something out of the water. A uniformed officer on the edge of the water lifted his radio and a few seconds later he sprinted to Weller.

The detective looked at the priest with worry etched on his face and the priest turned a grave look to him. The young officer made it to the two men breathing heavily.

"Well, detective," the young officer began. "You can tell Lt. Stone you were right. We found one."

Camillia sat in her living room reading. She loved mystery novels and she was completely engrossed in this one. It was well after sundown and Richard was due home from work in a few minutes. She loved her son's company but sometimes she enjoyed the peace and quiet of solitude.

When the sun rose that morning, Camillia convinced herself that what she saw, or what she thought she saw, on the roof or her garage was merely a product of a worried mind. Still, though, all of the windows were shut and locked and all of the blinds were closed. In this silence and safety she wanted to get as much reading done as she could, so of course, the doorbell rang the moment she began reading an exciting part.

"Shit," she muttered as she went to answer the door. A look through the peephole revealed Father Burns and detective Weller. She opened the door and greeted them.

"So what've you got?" she asked as the priest and police officer entered her house.

"Too much," answered Weller.

"We have concrete evidence that the pattern theory is solid," Burns added. "A body was found in Lake Michigan. The spot where it was weighted down was consistent with the circle."

Camillia frowned, thinking again of the figure on her garage roof, hoping against hope that it had been her imagination.

"We still don't know that it's Andre," she pointed out. "What about that weird guy Richard talked about, the one he saw at the party?"

The trio went into the living room and sat down. "We don't know that it's Andre," Weller agreed. "It still seems like he would have come after you by now if it was. But there's no doubt in my mind that the killer is a vampire, so just in case, the padre and I have decided you shouldn't be home alone at night."

"And since Richard works nights, we thought it would be best that either detective Weller or I should be here in the evenings," Burns concluded.

"Gentlemen," Camillia said with a sigh, "I couldn't agree more. Especially since, I think, I may have had a visitor the other night."

Weller's eyes widened. "What?"

"I thought I saw something... some*one*... on the roof of my garage, looking into my house."

Weller tensed. "Why the hell didn't you call me?"

"Because I'm not sure if I really saw it," Camillia admitted. "I looked away for a second and when I looked back it was gone. It might have been my imagination."

"That's it, then," Father Burns said with finality. "We won't leave you alone at night until this is settled."

"There's something else, Camillia," Weller started. "Rich is gonna wonder why you need bodyguards all of a sudden. Maybe it's time to talk to him."

"I understand what you're saying, detective," Camillia replied. "But I can't get Richard involved in this. We'll tell him I testified against a convict before he was born or something. We'll tell him that the guy just escaped from prison..."

"C'mon Camillia –" Weller began.

"I'm serious," Camillia interrupted. "I testified against a criminal and now he's out. Period. We doubt he'll come for me but you two want to stay here for a few nights until he's caught. That's all Richard needs to know."

"Perhaps it would be best to keep this to ourselves as long as possible," the priest agreed. "Richard is very protective of his mother. If he finds out that a creature like Andre is after her he may take it upon himself to find him. He could quite possibly endanger his own life."

Weller nodded. "If Andre is back, though, what makes you guys think he won't come after the kid? He may try to get to Camillia through Rich."

"That is a definite possibility," admitted Father Burns.

"So how do we do this?" Camillia asked.

"Maybe you can have an officer trail him," Camillia offered.

"No good," Weller said. "I might be able to get my boss to authorize a tail on the kid with the story that the serial killer is back and might target the two of you. But if Andre made a move on Rich, what the hell would a cop do? Shoot it?"

"We'll have to keep Richard at home," Burns decided. "We'll tell him that it's too dangerous for him to leave the house without one of us with him."

Just then they heard the front door opening. As usual, Camellia went to greet her son as he entered the house.

"We were just talking about you, baby," Camillia said after Richard closed and locked the door.

"Who is 'we'?" Richard asked as he kissed his mother's cheek. His mother answered him by leading him into the living room. Richard looked at the priest and the detective and chuckled. "I never thought I'd see you two in the same place. You fellas don't seem like you'd hang out together. I'm glad to see you, though. I'm especially glad to see you, Weller. I have some information about those killings."

"Shoot," Weller said.

"Well," Richard started. "Tim and Major think they met the same guy I saw with that girl at the party, the same guy that we think may have killed Vanessa Strickland."

Everyone in the room grew acutely attentive.

"They told me a tall, skinny, freaky-looking white guy slipped Major a letter saying that he thinks I have something to do with the murders," Richard continued. "We figure he may be doing that to throw suspicion off of himself."

"What's your theory of how the murderer would know about you all?" asked Burns.

"Well, we think he may be a cop," Richard said as he looked over at Weller. "No offense," he quickly added. "But maybe you mentioned my dreams to somebody at the station and it got back to him."

"You three have been doing a lot of thinking," Weller noted. "You may be half right. Years ago, there was a serial killer on the loose. He tried to get to your mom but we got to him first. He just recently escaped from prison. We have reason to believe that this guy may be back.

"I think prison and age may have taken too much out of him to make him a direct threat. The problem is we have reason to believe he had a son somewhere. We don't think he's a cop but he may be real smart and real interested in the woman responsible for sending his old man to jail."

Camillia and the priest looked at each other with surprise and then realization. Father Burns quickly picked up where Weller was headed and added: "He may come after you and your mother. We think it would be best if Weller, you and I stuck around here in the evenings, just in case."

"I'd have to quit my job," Richard said. "I'll do it tomorrow. Anything else I can do to help catch this guy?"

"You can come down to the station with me," Weller began. He continued quickly when he saw Camillia's suspicious glare. "Give us a description of the 'weird white guy' you three saw. Look at some mug shots. Maybe we'll get lucky."

"Ok," Richard agreed. "But what if we don't get lucky?"

"Then we'll need you to keep dreaming kid," Weller said seriously.

Chapter 5

SERIAL KILLER ON THE LOOSE!

The morning headline hit detective Weller like a fist. It was all he could do not to throw his mug of coffee against the diner wall. He went on to read about the police finding a body in Lake Michigan. Further reading revealed that his circle theory was included in the article. He became enraged when he read the section that mentioned the similarity between the killings of nineteen years ago and the recent killings.

Weller left his breakfast and a tip on the table and rushed to his car. He resisted the urge to turn on his flashers and sirens so he could run lights and clear traffic on the way to work. As soon as he made it to the police station he made a straight line for Stone's office. He barged into his boss's office and slammed the door.

Stone looked up from his paperwork. "What is it now, Weller?" he asked in an irritated tone.

"This," Weller tossed the newspaper on Stone's desk.

"Oh, that," Stone replied in bored tone. "Apparently someone leaked this story to press."

"*You* leaked this story," Weller accused. "No one else in the department knew about my circle theory."

"I may have mentioned it," Stone admitted absently. "The press came on pretty strong after that body was found in the lake."

"Whoever interviewed you remembered the 'vampire killings' from nineteen years ago. I was trying to keep this city from going into a panic but this article makes me look like either a moron or a liar."

Stone smirked in silence for a beat before replying. "This is Chicago, Weller; the 'City of Big Shoulders.' We're tough. You can handle it."

"That's exactly why you told the press," Weller realized. "You want them to think I'm trying to deceive the public by holding back information about the killings or I'm too damn stupid to make the connection. You want to make look bad so much that you'd jeopardize this whole damned case?"

"You ever stop to think that it may be best that the city knows? Maybe if people know what's going on they'll be more careful. Maybe the killer might high-tail it out of here because he knows we're on to him."

"And maybe he'll just lay low for a while and start all over again in a year or so; or just go set up shop in another city!"

Stone shrugged. "At least he won't be in Chicago."

"That's a load of bullshit, Stone. You're not concerned about the people. You just want to make me look bad."

"You've done a more than adequate of job of that yourself, detective. If you want to make yourself look better, go find this killer. And watch how you talk to me, old man. I *am* your superior, you know."

Weller scoffed. *In rank, only*, he thought. "I'll find him," he said aloud. "And when I solve this case I'm gonna have one more mystery to solve."

"What mystery is that?" Stone asked impatiently.

"The mystery of how the hell you got to be lieutenant." Weller turned to walk out the door.

"I strongly suggest that you don't slam the door on the way out, detective," Stone warned.

Weller walked out of the office and simply left the door open. Stone let out an irritated sigh and got up to close it.

When Weller went back to his desk he saw a man with a familiar face sitting in an adjacent chair. The face turned to him and smiled. The face was that of a late-middle-aged man with graying sideburns and crow's feet at the corner of both eyes. He had deep frown lines in his face from years of worrying. It had been a while since the two men had seen each other but they had no problem recognizing one another.

"Looks like your morning isn't starting off so great," the man said.

"Milton," Weller said with a smile. "The great beat reporter Keith Milton. I don't freakin' believe it."

The two acquaintances shook hands.

"My morning *has* started off crappy," Weller continued. "But only slightly more crappy than usual. What are you doing here? I thought you retired."

"I did," Milton said. "But when I read the paper I had to come see you."

"For what?" Weller asked as he sat behind his desk. "To give your condolences for my obituary in this morning's paper?"

"Yeah," Milton answered. "Every article I've read makes you look like a liar or a simp. I haven't seen you ripped up this bad in the papers since I used to do it."

"You were the best at it, my friend. But, honestly, I can't blame anybody but me. I was holding stuff back hoping I could keep this out of the news until I found the killer. Looks like I was wrong."

"I made a career out of following you and the vampire-killer stories," Milton told him. "It makes me kind of jealous to see others doing what I used to do so well. That's why I wanna help. Maybe we can steal some of their thunder."

"Help how?"

"I still have all the articles I wrote back then. There may be something in one of them that would spark a memory of a detail you may have forgotten."

"I'm not even sure we're dealing with the same guy," Weller admitted.

"It's either the same guy or a damn good copycat," Milton said. "The only difference is the pattern. Back then the killer used a cross-pattern, like a crucifix, and the place where you guys caught him was at the point where the two lines intersected. If it's not the same guy, someone's copying him so well that he may make some of the same mistakes."

"Already checked the center point," Weller informed. "He's *definitely* not there. I guess he was teasing us."

"Still," Milton offered, "You may want to come by my home office and check out some of those old clippings."

"Of course I will," Weller accepted gratefully. "I'll try anything to save face. You gotta work hard to regain respect from this city."

"Don't I know it," Milton concurred.

"But Milton, I know you," Weller began with narrowed eyes. "You want something out of this. You've never done anything out of the kindness of your heart, so just spill it."

"You know me too well, detective," Milton conceded. "I want *my* thunder back. It'd be nice to re-live a bit of my former glory. I want you to give me all the intimate details of the investigation. I promise I'll keep them under wraps until the case is closed. After that, I'll sell this story to the highest bidder. Who knows? I might write a book and make some real money. And of course, detective, I'll cut you in on the profits."

"Fame and money," Weller mused. "Two of the best motives a man can have. Let's go."

Weller, his spirits lifted slightly, left the station with Keith Milton laughing and talking about old times.

Their reminiscing went from happy to morbid in short order once they got to Milton's home office and began to research the killings from almost two decades earlier. The old clippings were well preserved and numerous, and brought back a flood of memories Weller wished could have remained buried in the back of his mind. The recent murders had been enough of a reminder.

Seeing Milton's old photographs, however, lent a staggering clarity to the horrors Andre left in his wake when Weller was a young detective. With each picture, Weller grew more determined to stop the new killings. The recent victims were brutalized more savagely than the ones back then, but in a strange way that made it easier for Weller to process. He could almost convince himself that a *human* psychopath had killed the recent victims. When Weller looked at the photographs of those poor women who were killed nineteen years ago...

Their ashen skin, bulging eyes staring at nothing, mouths gaping open in silent, frozen screams, with no blood left in their veins and no marks on their bodies save the puncture wounds on their necks... All of those things left no doubt that their murderer was anything but human. Their murderer was a predator of the highest order, a beast that not even a hail of bullets could bring down. And now he was back.

"Weller? Are you alright?"

The detective slowly shook his head from left to right. "No, Milton. I won't be alright until this is over."

"A lot of people criticized me for the 'vampire' talk back then," Milton said as he thumbed through photographs and articles. "I don't think I was too far off the mark."

Weller made himself scoff. "C'mon, Milton. You really thought the perp was a vampire?"

"No," Milton admitted. "But maybe the *perp* thought he was a vampire. He followed the mythology to the letter, and I'm not talking about the movie stereotypes. I did some research. I even worked with Father Burns. I helped him uncover some of the clues that he used to help you finally corner that murderous bastard."

"And I appreciated the assist," Weller said sincerely. "I hope you can help out just as much now."

Milton looked at Weller. "Tell me something. Do you think it's the same guy? I guess could be. It's been almost twenty years, but if he was young, and stayed in shape, he may have recovered from the bullet you put in him."

Bullet, Weller thought, stopping himself from laughing derisively. *Try dozens of bullets.*

"I don't see how he could've survived," Weller lied.

"Let's assume he did," Milton proposed. "Or we can assume it's a copycat who studied the original killer closely, possible even knew him. The woman who got away, you told me she said he was regimented, right?"

Weller nodded. "Right."

"So if today's killer is just as regimented, maybe he's doing the opposite, or near opposite, of what was done in the past? Consider this: He left the bodies in the pattern of a cross, and he actually lived at intersection point, the common point between the two lines."

"This time the pattern is a circle," Weller added. "He's *not* at the center, either."

Milton smiled. "Exactly. And his apartment was in the city, on the north side."

"Northwest, to be exact," Weller said. "So, by your logic, he'd be living outside the circle, in a house on the southeast side of the city."

Milton nodded and pointed at the detective. "Bingo!"

Weller's growing excitement was tempered by reality. "That's still a lot of area to cover, Milton. The CPD is already expending a shitload of manpower searching the circle perimeter for bodies. I don't think I can get the ok for a search of the entire southeast suburbs."

"Probably not," Milton acknowledged. "But it can't hurt to ask, can it?"

Weller shrugged. "Where's your phone?"

It was short phone call, and the only thing that ended up hurt was Weller's pride when Lieutenant Stone chuckled and hung up on the detective.

"This is some scary shit," Major said as he, Tim, and Richard stood on the outside of Tim's car. "A real psycho killer's after your mom. If there's somethin' I can do to help, man..."

"I'll damn sure let you know, dog," Richard assured.

"It's about that time, fellas," Tim reminded them. "It's almost eleven. You know you can't be late for class."

"Yeah, me either," Richard agreed. "I don't know how much more I can take from that teacher."

"Well," Major added, "at least you got that fine-ass freak from the party sitting next to you every day."

"That ain't shit," Richard scoffed. "She only speaks to me when she absolutely has to. She's a bonafide bitch."

"She's still nice to look at," Major pointed out.

The three friends went their separate ways. Richard made it to class early and went to his seat, making sure to take off his sunglasses. He and the instructor said nothing to each other, but unpleasant glances were exchanged.

At eleven o'clock sharp, the instructor stood up and asked for an assignment that was assigned the day before. The students formed a line to go to the instructor and hand in the work. Richard swore to himself because he did not have the assignment. With everything going on at home the homework slipped his mind. Richard went to the end of the line. When he reached the instructor, he tried to explain.

"Sir," he began, "I've been having a lot of problems at home and –"

"You don't have the work," the instructor interrupted. "I don't take excuses and I don't take late assignments."

"But if you let me explain--"

"You may be seated."

Once again the anger flared up, but instead of giving in to it, Richard walked slowly back to his seat. The instructor sat down, placed all of the assignments in his brief case, and then looked up at the students.

"Now," the teacher began, addressing the entire class. "Everyone in this class has turned in their assignments with the exception of two people..."

All Richard could do was sigh and hang his head. The instructor continued.

"One of them has not made it to class yet, and the other one tried to give me a lame excuse."

Richard could hear his own heart beating as anger grew within him and made him shiver.

The instructor continued, "I do not take late work, so late work is just like no work to me. The penalty for not turning in assigned work on the assigned date is a strike, and that gives a certain student his third strike. I made it clear on the first day of class that three strikes is an automatic F."

All eyes turned to Richard. The expression on the students' faces ranged from shock to pity to amusement.

Richard could take no more. He rose from his desk and made for the front of the classroom. The rage in his face was unnerving to anyone who dared to look at him.

The look in his eyes caused the instructor to stand up quickly and take hurried backward steps until he bumped into the wall and could back up no further.

"You...you may as well leave *now*, young man," the order sounded more like a plea. His brown skin took on a sickly pallor. "Don't do something you'll be sorry for...please."

The instructor's desk was soon the only thing between Richard and the frightened little man. With one hand Richard sent the teacher's desk flying sideways towards the wall. The resounding crash as the desk struck the wall drowned out the yelps of surprise and fear from the students. In two long strides Richard was face to face with the trembling, bespectacled man. He looked down at the instructor as tears welled up in the smaller man's eyes.

Richard's stomach twisted into a hungry, painful knot, which only served to stoke his anger. He could feel his jaws twitching and knew the other could see it. His hands trembled as he fought to keep them at his sides and away from the instructor's scrawny neck. It could only be his imagination, he knew, but in that moment he thought he could smell the man's fear.

"Go to hell," Richard finally said in an icy whisper.

With a mighty effort, he turned his back to the man and strode to the exit. Paula came in just as he reached the door. They bumped into each other and Paula came stumbling into the classroom. Richard slammed the door behind him so hard that the entire hallway shook. There was an awkward silence after he left.

"I don't know where he could be," Camillia told Father Burns as the two of them, Tim and Major sat in her living room drinking coffee. Richard was unusually late. In a few minutes the sun would be setting. "Richard's never come home this late from school without calling to let me know why."

"Wherever he is," added Major, "he's either on foot or on the bus. The last we heard he had gotten into it with his History teacher and stormed out of class."

"Maybe he's somewhere with Weller," offered Father Burns.

"Yeah," Tim said. "Like jail."

The doorbell rang and Camillia nearly sprinted to the door. When she opened it, Weller was standing there alone.

"What's wrong?" Weller asked, seeing the worry on Camillia's face.

"Richard's missing," she answered. "No one's seen him since this morning."

"Damn," Weller swore. He stepped into the house and went into the living room with the others.

"I just told Ms. Williams that Rich got into it with one of his professors this morning," Major informed Weller. "That was the last anybody has seen of him, at least that we know of."

"I'll get on the phone and tell all units to look out for him. He may be in danger."

"You mean he may be dangerous," Tim corrected. "I don't care what anybody says. I know you think he has something to do with the murders, don't you?"

Weller turned to the young man. "There are things going on here that you wouldn't understand, kid. The last thing any of us need is to start bickering with each other."

"Yeah," Tim replied. "I notice you didn't answer my question."

"No I didn't. You know why? Because I don't have to answer to a disrespectful, loudmouthed kid."

"Listen –" Tim began.

"No," Camillia interrupted. "*You* listen, Tim. We have to keep our cool. We don't need this right now."

Tim folded his arms and looked away stubbornly.

At sundown, Richard was fast asleep on a bus stop bench on a deserted south side street. Three teenagers eyed him from a coupe on opposite side of the street. One was female and the other two were male.

"Well," one of the boys began, "what'chu guys think?"

"I don't think we should," the other boy answered.

"Look, you cowards," the girl broke in. "The nigga is sleep. I say we go jack his ass before he wakes up. Look at those Jordans." She pointed to his basketball sneakers. "I'll bet he got mad loot...or at least a credit card."

The girl was apparently the leader because the two boys did as she said.

The trio exited the car, crossed the street and approached Richard. When they reached him, they heard an ear-jolting bark as two huge German shepherds bounded around the corner and charged them.

All three kids screamed and ran back to the coupe. They piled in through the driver-side car door and closed it an instant before the dogs slammed into it, scratching and biting at the window. The dogs continued to attack the car as the trio struggled clumsily to disentangle their limbs and settle themselves in their respective seats. The window was cracked and the crack was growing by the time the girl managed to get the key into the ignition.

The engine roared just as the driver-side window shattered. The girl's painful and frightful scream was drowned out by the screech of the rear tires when the coupe tore off down the street. The dogs immediately turned around and trotted back around the corner from whence they came. Richard woke up after the dogs were out of sight. He looked at his surroundings and tried to remember how he got there.

"After my run-in with that punk-ass teacher..." he recounted groggily to himself. "I left school and just started walking. I was waiting on the bus when I fell asleep. I was on my way to the...to the job. That's right!"

The fog in his mind cleared and he continued to talk aloud to himself. "I was going to tell them that I have to quit." He looked around at the gathering shadows.

The bus pulled up a few minutes later. Richard climbed aboard and found a seat.

Damn, I never fell asleep at the bus stop before. He thought. *I'm lucky I didn't get jacked.*

A couple of hours later Richard was walking into his home. As soon as he walked through the door his mother was on him, embracing him tightly. After a few moments of severe hugging, she pushed him roughly away and held him at arm's length.

"Where the hell were you?!" she demanded angrily.

"I went to the hospital to quit the job, momma," he answered. "But I...uh...I kinda fell asleep at the bus stop."

"How the hell did you fall asleep at the bus stop?" she asked as they made their way into the living room, where father Burns was seated on the couch.

"I don't know. I was tired, I guess. I've been crazy tired for the last few days. I didn't get much sleep last night. I was up worrying about you and all this stuff going on."

"Why didn't you call? How many pay phones did you walk past?"

"I...uh...I kinda forgot."

"You shouldn't forget things like that, especially at a time like this," Father Burns admonished. "Detective Weller is out looking for you now."

"Well you can tell him I'm alright when you talk to him again," Richard said. "I'm sorry, really."

"Are you alright?" asked Camillia. "I heard about your little incident in History class today."

"Oh, that," Richard said. "I blew up pretty bad. That's not like me but that little sonofa...sorry. Believe me, though, he had it comin'!"

"You'll probably get tossed out of school for that, Richard," his mother warned him.

"I know. I'm sorry."

"You've been having some serious temper tantrums lately, haven't you?" Camillia asked. "The way you tell it, you seemed to get into with Slab every night at work. You're right. That's not like you at all. You never used to go off like this."

"I never had people ride me like Slab and that teacher rode me," Richard explained. "I didn't know my temper was this bad until just recently. Maybe it's because of the lack of sleep."

Camillia stared at him for a few seconds, appraising him deeply. She took in every detail, from his weary eyes to his tired posture, looking for anything out of the ordinary. When no alarm bells went off in her mind, she finally relaxed.

"What, momma?"

"Nothing, baby. Call Tim and Major to let them know you're home. They're worrying about you, too."

"Since everything is alright," broke in Father Burns, "I'll turn in for the night."

"Alright, Father," Camillia replied. "The guest room is set up for you. You know where it is. I'll see you in the morning."

Later that night, Tim was lying in his bed watching sports news when his telephone rang.

"Hello?" he asked.

"Whatup Tim," Major greeted. "Did Rich call you?"

"Yeah. He said he'd already talked to you."

"You read the papers today?" Major asked.

Tim could hear the concern in his friend's voice. "No, not today," Tim answered. "Why?"

"The papers are calling this psycho the vampire-killer," Major told him. "One article mentioned how these killings are almost exactly like some killings that took place almost twenty years ago."

Tim grunted. "You don't believe that vampire crap?"

"Look," Major began. "There's something about that letter from the freak that I didn't tell you."

"What?" Tim asked.

"The guy said he hunted vampires," Major confessed.

"And you believed him?" Tim almost laughed.

"Hell no," Major said. "I just think this is weird. I think there's more to this that we don't know, just like Weller said."

"To hell with Weller," Tim swore. "There's *always* more going on than the cops tell you, but vampires? C'mon, man." Tim was silent for a moment before an idea struck him. "This could have something to do with the occult, though."

"You think so?"

"Hell, it's more realistic than Count Dracula! Cults are good for crazy shit like this. You know, human sacrifice, cannibalism...all that stuff."

"Yeah," Major agreed. "That dude looked like he'd be into somethin' sick like that."

Chapter 6

The hotels on Chicago's "Gold Coast" were outrageously expensive to say the least, so when the beat up old black Camaro with the tinted windows pulled up to the front, the valets were understandably perplexed. The old car came to a stop and the most odd, filthy-looking character stepped from the automobile. The tall, pale, bald man that stepped from the vehicle looked around expectantly but none of the valets made a move toward the dent-and-scratch-riddled Camaro.

"One of you jerks come get my damn car!" the misfit swore. "That's what you're paid for, ain't it?"

None of the young men moved.

"Don't worry," the stranger grinned. "She won't bite."

"Excuse me, sir," one of the valets said. "Are you sure you have the right hotel?"

"Positive." The misfit tossed the young man the keys. "And if there's one scratch on this baby when I get back, I'll have your fucking job!" The misfit burst into laughter and strode into the lobby.

Moments later he was on the thirteenth floor knocking on the door of room thirteen-thirteen. The door opened slowly and the misfit stepped in.

He looked behind the door to see who had opened it, but there was no one there. An African American man, appearing to be in his early to mid-thirties, was sitting on the bed watching television on the other side of the room.

There was nothing unusual about the way the man looked. Nothing, that is, except his dark, deep set brown eyes. When the misfit walked in the man did not even turn to look. He just kept watching television. The door closed on its own.

"How the hell do you do that?" the misfit asked.

"You're late, Eric."

"I had some car trouble, Andre," Eric the misfit answered.

"I won't hold you long. I want to discuss some things."

"Shoot."

"Have you read the papers today?" Andre asked.

"No. I've been following the three musketeers around all day. By the way, Richard quit his job this evening. Was there something about *me* in the papers?"

Andre ignored the question. "Things are progressing faster than I would've liked. They've already linked me to my past exploits."

"So now what do we do?" Eric asked.

"We proceed as planned, but at an accelerated pace. The authorities will begin an all-out search for me now that they believe I've returned. We must act with haste."

"Sure," Eric agreed. "It won't take me long to get to Major and Tim. All they need is a demonstration or two."

"Good."

"I was wondering...I put the finishing touches on the women to throw the law off the trail because you don't like the mess. Now, though, since your existence isn't a secret, do I have to keep butchering these broads when you're finished with them?"

Andre lifted an eyebrow. "I thought you enjoyed your work."

"Oh, I do," Eric admitted. "It just gets redundant after a while. I'm running out of new ways to mutilate. It's kind of like writer's block."

"As you know, Eric, I'm a creature of habit. I don't like to change things unless I absolutely have to. I see no reason to change our methods now. Besides, we have a deal."

"Right, I hack the women up and you make me like you...eventually. I won't gripe about it anymore."

"Good."

"There's one more thing," Eric said before he left.

"What?"

Andre was becoming annoyed. Eric could hear it in the clipped tone of his voice. He talked fast.

"If things don't work out with Rich's mom, can I do her? She's beautiful, you know. I could get real creative with her."

"If things don't go as planned, she's yours. You can have Tim and Major as well, but the priest and the detective belong to me."

"What about Rich?"

"Richard is the only part of this that I *know* will go along as planned. He can't deny who and what he is. Ultimately, he's the only one that really matters."

"But there's always a possibility..."

"No!" Andre snapped. "He *will* be my successor or he will die. Leave now, Eric. Come back in a few hours to pick up the young lady."

Just then a strikingly beautiful young woman stepped out of the bathroom. She had long, straight, black hair and wore a transparent negligee that silhouetted the perfect form underneath. She walked slowly to the bed and sat next to Andre, her eyes never leaving his. She said something in Italian and Andre answered her in kind.

Eric could only look and sigh. "Damn!" he muttered to himself after he left the room. He did not bother to close the door because he knew it would close on its own. "I can't wait till I can do that!"

A week went by. Weller, Father Burns and Keith Milton worked feverishly every day. They read through all of the old newspaper clippings in an unsuccessful attempt to find some kind of clue to the killer's whereabouts. Every night either Weller, Burns or both of the men stayed with Richard and Camillia. Burns kept his gold-wreathed crucifix staff by his side at all times.

The police continued to search the areas consistent with the circle pattern. Within that week only one new body was found, but they all knew that only meant the others were better hidden.

Richard had grown restless. All he did during that week was go to school and return home. He was not expelled as he expected because his classmates had come to his defense. They banned together to protest the crude and unfair methods of the instructor. Richard only received a written warning and the instructor a written reprimand.

All of "the old folks", as Richard started to refer to his mother, the priest, and the detective, kept telling him it was too dangerous for him to go out at night. He knew they were right but that did not keep him from being incredibly bored. Every night he found himself staring out the window at the night sky, wishing he could leave the house just for a couple of hours. His mother kept telling him that the confinement would not last long, that it was only a matter of time before the killer was caught.

Richard, however, did not care about the future. He was bored right then. Sometimes he felt as if he would explode.

Thursday evening, a few hours before sunset, Richard stood in his room gazing out the window yet again. He knew he could not bear sitting in the house another night. He had to get out of there or he would go crazy.

His mother came into his room. "Richard?"

"Yeah, mom?" he answered.

"Come downstairs. Dinner's ready."

"Momma," Richard began. "I've been fiending for some Chinese food. Can I go around the corner and get some?"

"I didn't cook all this food for you to go out and eat."

"Weller will help you eat it when he gets here. Besides, I know we both know I'll get hungry later on tonight. I can eat what you cooked for my evening snack."

"You know how I feel about you going out at night," Camillia reminded him.

"You said I could go out in the day, momma. It won't be dark for a couple of hours yet."

Camillia hesitated. He was right, of course. It would take less than forty-five minutes for him to order, get his food, and get back home. "Alright," she relented. "But make it quick."

Detective Weller and Father Burns strode down the busy street, drawing amused glanced from passerby for the diametrically contrasting duo they made. Keith Milton, leaning easily against a wall just beside the entryway to a near-downtown Irish pub, grinned at the sight of the approaching men.

"Good evening, gentlemen," he said jovially when they reached him. "Glad you could make it."

"Our pleasure," Father Burns said drily. "I relish every opportunity to visit Chicago's taverns."

"Ah, a priest with a sense of humor," Milton observed.

"That was sarcasm, Milton, not a joke," Weller corrected.

Father Burns cleared his throat. "Not to be rude, Mr. Milton, but we're in a hurry. I have an evening service to conduct. The detective has to get Ms. Williams'."

"Of course," Milton said. He walked into the bar and beckoned the two men to follow. The trio spotted an empty corner booth and made their way to it. Milton chuckled as they slid into their seats.

"What's so funny?" Weller asked.

"Us," Milton answered. "A cop a reporter and a priest enter a bar..." He frowned and fell silent when he noticed the blank stares of his companions.

"Alright, already," Milton surrendered. "I guess we get right down to business." He paused when a waitress came to their table. "Scotch rocks, darling," he ordered.

"Water for me," Father Burns instructed.

"Of course," the waitress said with a friendly smile. "And for the police officer?"

"Detective," Weller corrected. "And how'd you know I'm a cop? Is it that obvious?"

"It is, sweetie," she answered.

Weller sighed. "Oh well. I'm on duty, so get me a bottle of Highlife." The waitress nodded, chuckled, and left the table. Weller turned back to the reporter. "So what did you find?"

"I don't know how helpful this will be," Milton began, "Weller, you said that in your investigation nineteen years ago you couldn't find any evidence that the killer didn't spend as much time romancing his other victims as he did Camillia."

"That's right," Weller confirmed. "When we didn't find a body we started backtracking in an attempt to find him. A number of witnesses saw him with Camillia at different places. We couldn't find anyone who'd seen him with any of the others.

"I was thinking about why that is," Milton said. "After doing some more research and talking to some enthusiasts, I may have found some possibilities."

Father Burns raised an eyebrow. "Enthusiasts?"

"Vampire enthusiasts," Milton clarified. "There are quite a few of them out there, too; individuals and low-profile organizations. I'm not talking about movie buffs and dime store novel fans. I'm talking hardcore believers with access to obscure folktales and literature."

Weller feigned a scoff. "As if there really *were* such things vampires."

Milton nodded. "Exactly. But if this killer really thinks he's a vampire, or at the very least is sticking to the lore, there may be several explanations for why he treated Camillia differently than the others."

"Such as?" Father Burns asked.

"Plain old companionship, for starters," Milton began. "I suppose immortality could get kind of lonesome after a few hundred years."

Both Weller and Burns frowned skeptically.

"Yeah, I felt the same way about that one," Milton admitted. "Just thought I'd throw it out there, though. You know, Weller, not ruling anything out."

Weller shrugged. "What else you got?"

Milton paused as the waitress returned with their libations. Once the drinks had been distributed, all three men took a sip or swallow.

After a second swallow, Milton leaned forward conspiratorially. "Ok, gentlemen, here's where it gets really interesting: Maybe this guy believed he could sire a dhampir and thought Camillia would be the ideal mother for it."

"Dhampir?" Weller asked.

"A dhampir is a hybrid offspring of a human and a vampire," Burns elucidated. "It's supposed to have all of the powers of a vampire but none of the weaknesses. In legends, they often hunt vampires."

Milton was impressed. "I see you know your bloodsucker folklore, Father. Isn't that rather unusual reading material for Catholic priest?"

Father Burns shrugged. "Yes, suppose it is. But don't forget that we both assisted Weller all those years ago. I've done a bit of research myself."

"Question," Weller said. "What would be the point of making a dhampir when he could just, or *thought* he could just make and control other vampires?"

"Good question," Milton noted. "According to the legends, vampires are very territorial creatures, very competitive. He could use his dhampir to seek and destroy his rivals. Dhampirs aren't harmed by sunlight. That's a decided advantage."

"But he could also very easily turn on his master," Weller pointed out.

"True," Milton agreed. "But seeing as how we're talking about a kook who thought he was a vamp, I doubt he employed that much logic in his decision making."

"You've got a point," Weller allowed.

He and Father Burns shared a knowing glance. The look they shared acknowledged that neither of them believed that would be Andre's motivation. They didn't know him well, but it simply did not seem likely that he would purposely create a being with all of his considerable powers and none of his vulnerabilities. The potential for successful betrayal was too great.

"Interesting theory," Father Burns observed. "Do you have any others?"

Milton nodded. "One more," he said. "This is the scariest one. It's something I read and it's something that some of the more fanatical enthusiasts told me. There's this prophecy called 'the culling' that's been floating around for, if you believe the stories, almost two thousand years."

"Hmm," Father Burns murmured. "I'm not familiar with that prophecy."

"And I damn sure don't like the sound of it," Weller added.

"Nothing about it is likable," Milton concurred. "The culling is an apocalypse scenario. I couldn't get all of the details, but I got the gist of it. According to the prophecy, a vampire birthed from a human womb – not a dhamphir, mind you, but a full-blood vampire that is somehow born of a human woman – would have the potential to end the human race as we know it."

The observant reporter did not miss the flicker of change in his companions' postures. They quickly composed themselves, but the priest and detective stiffened for a moment. A shadow of something akin to dread flashed across their faces.

Milton laughed. "Calm down, guys," he teased. "You act as if this crap is actually possible."

Father Burns smiled uneasily. "Any mention of an apocalypse makes me slightly uneasy, Mr. Milton, no matter how far-fetched."

Weller took several large swallows of his beer before speaking. "It's not about him actually being able to do it, Milton. If the guy we're after now – whether it's the same killer from nineteen years ago or not – is thinking about apocalyptic scenarios, there's no telling how far he'll escalate. We *have* to take him down and fast."

"I agree," Milton said. "And whether he's lonely or wants a half-breed kid or an apocalypse, he's going to go after the one that got away. He was fixated on her back then so why wouldn't he be now?"

Weller and Father Burns finished their drinks with deep and fast gulps.

"That's my cue to get over there," Weller announced.

"And I have to get back to church," Father Burns said. "Mr. Milton, is it safe to assume the water was free?"

Weller pointed to his empty bottle and looked at Milton. "You'll take care of this right?"

"What?" Milton asked. "I give you all of this good dirt and you guys can't even buy me a drink?"

"I'll owe you!" Weller said as he and the priest rushed out of the tavern.

When they hit the sidewalk and started speed walking back the way they came, Weller said to Father Burns:

"I don't know if he told us anything that'll help us find Andre, but he definitely managed to scare me even more than I already was."

"He also underscored the need to stay as close as possible to Camillia and Richard. I'll catch a cab back to St. Anselm's. You should get over to Camillia's as quickly as you can."

"I will," Weller promised. "Say a prayer for us padre. Something tells me we're all gonna need it."

Major sat in the living room watching music videos while his father took a nap in the bedroom. His mother was working the evening shift at the post office. The phone rang and Major ran to answer it.

"Hello?"

"Whatup?" came Richard's voice.

"Whatup, dog?" Major greeted. He heard the drone of street traffic in the background. "You callin' from a pay phone?"

"I know you and Tim got somethin' planned for tonight, so spill it," Richard demanded.

"What on earth makes you think that?" Major teased.

"Don't bullshit me! We always kick it Thursday night."

"We? What do you mean 'we'? You're on lockdown for a while, remember?"

"I'm relieving myself tonight. So what's up?"

"We're just going to the show," Major admitted.

"With females?" Richard asked.

"We ain't *goin'* with females, but we do plan to leave with some!"

"I'm in, then."

"You don't even know what flick we're goin' to see."

Richard scoffed. "And I don't give damn. I'm in."

"Wait a minute," Major advised, "You sure you can kick it this evening? Your mom didn't sound like she wanted you to do too many nights until this whack-job gets busted."

"Like I said," Richard responded. "I'm relieving *myself*. Come get me from Wong's. I'm outside waitin'."

Richard did not have to wait long before his friends pulled up in Tim's car. Richard jumped into the back seat.

"You sure you wanna do this?" Tim asked. "Your mom's gonna be pissed."

"It's either this or stay at home and go fuckin' nuts." Richard snarled.

"I don't want your mom getting off in my ass about this," Tim complained.

"Don't worry," Richard assured. "I'll take the blame."

"Did you get anywhere with the artist's sketch?" Camillia asked, looking distractedly at the wall clock.

Weller finished chewing and swallowing a forkful of mashed potatoes before answering. "I got as far as I did with the photo lineups. Neither Rich nor his buddies saw the 'weird white guy' in the photos. Their descriptions are very similar except for the hair, but the lieutenant won't let us post it."

"Why the hell not?" Camillia demanded.

"Too general," Weller grunted. "The bald one looks like the average punk-rock or skinhead thug. The longhaired one looks like the average heavy-metal rocker or goth. Besides, the descriptions aren't identical. The hair, the piercings, they're just different enough to discourage the lieutenant from making them public."

Camillia looked at the clock again. "That's bullshit."

"What can I say, Camillia? The man doesn't like me. He's cutting me off at the knees every chance he gets."

"While a killer runs free?" Camillia asked, turning her gaze from the clock to Weller. "How irresponsible is that? Maybe Tim and Major were right. Maybe there *is* a connection between the police and the killer."

"I don't think so, Camillia. He's just an asshole. He thinks I'm so off base that picking at my case won't make a difference. Still, we can't rule anything out. The problem is I'd have a hard time investigating my own people without getting thrown off the case...or worse."

Camillia sighed and shook her head before looking at the clock again. "I don't know what's taking that boy so long," she complained.

"Maybe they've got a crowd tonight," Weller said around a mouthful of pork chop.

"The take-out place is right around the corner and they never take more than fifteen minutes on an order. It's been over an hour. Even if there was a long line, he should have been home by now." Camillia sat quietly for a moment and then spoke again. "I've been thinking."

"About what?"

"Richard. He seems to be changing. He's been restless and tense recently."

"He's going through a lot, Camillia," Weller said. "He's young. You have to expect this kind of reaction."

Camillia shook her head. "No. I mean even before we told him about this killer business. Right when the nightmares started, in fact, he started getting real short tempered. Not with me, though. He knows I won't have it, but with everyone else. At school, at work, I don't know..."

"What are you trying to say?" Weller asked.

"Maybe...maybe he's...I don't know...." She paused and took a deep breath. Weller saw the concern in her eyes as she measured her words. "He's been sleeping almost all day, staying up almost all night. This was even before he started having the nightmares. I mean...if he was...you know, he wouldn't be up at all during the day, right?"

"According to the padre," Weller admitted reluctantly, "a very select few of them can move around by day if necessary. The sun would exhaust and weaken them considerably, though."

"I *know* he's not like Andre!" Camillia continued. Her voice softened to almost a whisper. "But there *is* something different."

"You want me to go look for him?" Weller offered.

"No," Camillia answered, "*We'll* go look for him."

The three young men sat a few rows from the front of the movie theater. They were trying their best to enjoy the horror movie but there was too much of a racket behind them. Richard turned around to see where the noise was coming from.

There were five males in their late teens or early twenties six or seven rows behind them. They were passing a "blunt," a cigar filled marijuana and possibly some other substance, and talking at a higher volume than the movie. The theater was a popular hangout for teenagers so they were used to this type of disturbance. No one was complaining.

No one, that is, except Richard.

"Why don't them motherfuckers shut up?" Richard growled at his partners.

"As much as we come here?" Tim replied. "You should be used to this."

"You never complained before, Rich," Major observed. "Hell, we do that shit ourselves every now and then."

"I'm complainin' *now*," Richard returned.

The noise from behind them grew even louder.

"This is getting on my goddamn nerves!" Richard turned toward the boys behind him. "Say, fellas, why don't y'all hold that down?"

"Why don't you hold this down?" answered one the teens as he stood and grabbed his crotch. The five of them laughed riotously.

Richard had to check his anger before he said something he may have regretted. He turned quickly back to the movie.

"Look," Major said. "If you start somethin' tonight you're on your own. I'm ain't throwin' over no dumb shit!"

"I ain't gonna just let you get your ass kicked," Tim added. "But they outnumber us three to five. I'd hate to get my ass kicked over somethin' unnecessary."

"Y'all won't have to throw if it comes to that," Richard promised. "I'll take all five of 'em."

"Since when did you get so tough?" Major inquired. He injected an overly-proper tone to his voice as he teased: "You used to be such a mellow and peaceful young man."

"Major's right," Tim broke in. "Stupid, but right. I mean, I was listenin' to you talk about how you punked Slab and your History teacher. You never used to do stuff like that."

"Yeah," Major agreed. "We know you ain't never been no punk, but even if somebody charged you up you were always the one who walked away if you could. What's up with you lately?"

"I guess I'm changin' in my old age," Richard returned.

Just then an empty box of chocolate covered raisins flew over Richard's left shoulder and into his lap.

"I gotta go take a leak," Richard snapped.

"I'm serious, Rich," Major warned. "I came here to *get* some ass, not kick some ass."

Richard chuckled as he stood up and walked up the aisle. He kept his drink in his hand as he walked slowly toward the exit. When he reached the row where the noisy young men sat, he hurled his half-full cup of soda at them. All five of the men were thoroughly drenched. Richard ran to the exit. The people around the soda-covered group laughed loudly as the five young men jumped out of their seats.

"Aw *shit!*" one of them yelled.

"It's on, goddamit!" another of them exclaimed.

The five men gave chase. A countless number of teenagers ran behind them to see the on-coming fight. Tim and Major left their seats as well, but they were quickly caught up in the rushing crowd and loss sight of the five young men and Richard.

The five enraged teens made it to the sidewalk outside the theater and saw Richard about a half block away. He was no longer running. Instead, he stood on the sidewalk beckoning the young men to come to him.

They obliged with haste and the crowd inside the movie theater came pouring out behind them. Everyone in the lobby and the concession stands saw the chase and decided to join the flood of rushing youngsters. This made Tim and Major have to struggle even more to keep their footing as the crowd pressed them from the all sides.

"C'mon, pussies!" Richard taunted.

Within moments the first one reached him. He threw a punch and struck Richard in the nose. Richard laughed. The next two to reach him grabbed him by the arms and began trying unsuccessfully to wrestle him to the ground. When the last two reached him, three of them tried to bring him to the ground while the other two punched.

Richard laughed maniacally.

Tim and Major were still trying to push their way through the crowd to get to their friend. There were too many bodies in the way for them to see what was happening. All they could do was listen to the "ooohs" and "ahhhs" of the people from the front of the crowd.

The more Richard laughed, the harder he was hit. The harder he was hit, the more he laughed. His face was covered with bruises and blood but he laughed on and on. The five men still could not wrestle him to the ground. One of the men who bothered to look at Richard's face was frightened by the crazed look in his eyes. Richard saw him staring and looked right into the other's eyes as he was being pummeled.

"You havin' fun?" he growled.

The young thug shook off his fear and struck Richard in the jaw as hard as he could.

"ALRIGHT, BITCHES!" Richard yelled, "IT'S *MY* TURN!!!!"

The man holding Richard's left arm went flying into a parked car. His head struck the driver's side window and shattered it, his back struck the door and he bounced off of the automobile. When he rebounded off the car the crowd saw a deep dent in the door.

Richard caught the fist of another one as the man attempted to hit him again. Everyone nearby heard the sharp, wet crunch of something snapping as Richard crushed the man's hand. The thug fell to his knees and let out an ear-piercing scream.

"What's goin' on up there?" Major asked as he and Tim continued to push through the crowd.

The remaining three men backed away from Richard and their hands went into their jackets. The quickness with which Richard reacted was astounding as he rushed two of them. Before they could get their weapons out of their jackets, Richard was on them. He slammed their heads together as if they were in a scene from "The Three Stooges." His attack, however, was very real. There was a sickening thud and the two men crumpled, bleeding and unconscious, to the ground.

By that time the remaining man was aiming his gun right between Richard's eyes.

"NO!" Tim yelled as he and Major finally broke into the front of the crowd. The others backed away wildly when the gun came into view.

The young man made the mistake of looking over to see who yelled. By the time he looked back, Richard had grabbed his wrist. Two shots went harmlessly off to the side as the young man's wrist made a nasty popping sound and the gun clattered to the ground.

The scream the would-be shooter tried to scream was cut short when Richard grabbed him by the throat and the belt. Richard effortlessly lifted the man and held him horizontally over his head. Tim and Major could only look on in disbelief.

"I guess he *could* take 'em by himself," Major said.

Tim shook his head in denial. "Somethin' ain't right."

"Huh," Major scoffed. "No shit."

As Richard held his assailant high above the ground, he saw out of the corner of his eye the young man's reflection in the dark window of a store, but that was all he was able to see. His own reflection was not there.

Richard blinked a couple of times to clear his vision. The crowd was yelling, "SLAM HIM! SLAM HIM! SLAM HIM!" but all Richard was aware of was the reflection of the other man floating above the pavement with nothing below him.

Instead of slamming him, Richard set him softly to the ground, all the while watching the empty space in the window where his reflection *should have* been. The would-be attacker gave Richard a fearful look before he folded to his knees and massaged his broken wrist.

Richard released his attacker. His anger faded and he saw his reflection resolve slowly into existence and clarity. No one else had bothered to look at the store window while the real action was going on right there in three dimensions. The crowd began to boo as Richard sprinted into the night.

"Why the hell is he running?" Major asked with a smile. "He should be takin' bows! That was some pro wrestling shit he put on those bitches!"

"I don't know," Tim answered. "He didn't look proud to me. Somethin's really wrong, man. Let's go after him."

The two friends ran after Richard. When they rounded the corner a few seconds after him, he was nowhere to be seen. They paused and looked at each other. The block was long with no intersecting alleyways and very few parked vehicles to hide behind, and in any event, both men were sure Richard was not cowering behind a car.

"He's around here somewhere," Major said. "He can't run like the Flash."

Tim sighed. "After what we saw tonight, ain't no tellin' what that boy can do! C'mon."

Richard ran down a dark alley, his head pounding as if his heart was where his brain should have been. The only reason he knew his heart was not in his head was because his heaving chest felt as if it would explode.

How did he do the things he had just done? Adrenaline was the logical answer but he knew that was not the correct one. As far as he knew, adrenaline did not cause hallucinations, and his missing reflection *had* to be a hallucination. He had never heard of adrenaline sharpening someone's senses to a razor's edge. During the fight, the darkness seemed to light up like the day. He could smell his attackers' fear. He could taste the onlookers' excitement on the air. The din of dozens of heartbeats thundered in his ears. That was much more than just adrenaline but he had no idea what it was.

Tears ran down his face. His burning lungs struggled to support his erratic breathing. All Richard was aware of was the pain in his chest and head, and the dread as well as...something else he could not name...churning wildly in his stomach.

Richard could not even feel his legs but he knew he was running. He had to be. He could see the night rushing by around him and the ground rushing beneath him in a mad blur. Soon, however, he could not even see that through the streaming tears that blinded him as he ran. When he was finally able to feel his legs, he stumbled and crashed noisily into a row of metal trash cans.

He covered his face to shield it from the fall, held his breath and waited for the impact with the ground.

And waited...and waited....

When he finally opened his eyes he thought he was dreaming. He hoped he would open his eyes to discover that he had fallen asleep in the theater, praying that this was yet another waking nightmare. Unfortunately, he was still in the alley. The reason he had not yet hit the ground was because he was *floating above* it.

Richard's heart resumed its frantic dance as he stared dumbfounded at the ground below. He grinned insanely to keep from crying out in panic. He looked around to see if anyone else was there to watch the spectacle No one was. The alley was silent.

Tim and Major had been riding around for hours looking for their friend. They drove through every alley and down every street in the area. The only thing they noticed out of the ordinary was a mess of knocked-over trash cans with garbage strewn all over the alley.

"Where the hell is he?" Tim asked.

"Maybe he went home," Major offered, "where *we* should be."

Tim shook his head. "We can't just leave him."

"Hell, he left us!" Major countered.

"Something's wrong, man," Tim said.

"I told you that a long time ago."

"What're you talkin' about?" Tim demanded. "You on that psycho killer trip again?"

"I don't believe he's killin' people," Major began. "But you said it yourself, the boy's startin' to change on us."

"It's the stress he's been goin' through," Tim reasoned.

"He just damn-near killed five niggas with guns. He lifted that fool in the air like Hulk Hogan. You weren't lyin' when you said something's wrong with 'em!"

Tim was about to argue when he saw someone standing on the sidewalk about a half-block from the front the car. He pulled closer and saw that it was Richard. Richard spotted them and began to wave. The Cavalier pulled to a stop at the curb beside him.

"Rich," Tim began. "Where the hell you been?"

"Runnin'," Richard responded. "I was runnin' and learnin' things about myself."

"Learnin' what?" Major asked as Richard ducked into the back seat.

"That all this pressure is gettin' to me," Richard confessed. "My temper's gotten shorter than ever. I've never went off like I did tonight."

"No shit!" Major swore. "When'd you get so damn strong, man?"

"Must've been the adrenaline," Richard lied.

"You seem pretty calm for what you just went through Rich," Tim observed.

Richard stared absently through the window.

"Why'd you run off like that?" Major questioned.

Richard shrugged. "I figured the law was gonna pull up pretty soon."

"You know how the law is," Major said. "They never show up 'till everything's over. They pulled up right as me and Tim were leavin' to look for you."

"You ready to go home?" Tim asked.

"Fuck no!" Richard said, suddenly excited.

"Where to, then?" Tim asked. "We haven't been to the Hummingbird in a while."

Major scoffed. "That's 'cause we like to get out of the hood to party since we've been in college. I hear Silk Hurley's spinning at the Country Club."

"No good," Tim declined. "My cousin, the one who's folks and lives in the Manor, he said they're movin' on some four corner hustlers outside the Country Club tonight. I ain't trying to catch a stray bullet."

"What the hell?" Major asked with forced mirth. "If anybody steps to us, Super-Rich can handle it!"

"The baddest sisters are at the Warehouse," Richard suggested. "Or maybe we can hit LA Mirage. They have broads of all colors. I might be able to pull a nice Asian or white girl, or a fine Latina."

Major and Tim looked at one another and said in unison: "LA Mirage!"

Camillia sat in her living room wringing her hands. She was more worried than she had ever been. Weller sat next to her talking to someone on the telephone. He finished his conversation and turned to Camillia.

"Someone fitting Richard's description was reported as having just been in a fight at the movies."

Camillia stood abruptly. "Did he get arrested?"

"No. Everyone involved got away. I think we should go check the scene out. We might find something."

The five men that were in the fight with Richard drove around the area in a convertible BMW. The top was up in order to contain their smoke cloud of various illegal substances. A bass-heavy NWA rap song blasted from their speakers. Each one had a sawed-off shotgun in his lap or gripped a nine-millimeter handgun.

"That motherfucker's gotta be around here some-damn-where!" one of them declared between puffs.

"He took off on foot," another added, "but he could've caught a bus or something."

"What about those punks he was sittin' with," another asked. "Did anybody see where they went?"

"Not me, man," a fourth one admitted. He held a nine millimeter in one hand and folded handkerchief against the back of head with the other. "I ain't see shit after I hit that car." He brandished his nine. "I want that nigga."

"Look up there!" the driver said.

They thought they saw Richard dart into an alley down the street. Wheels screeched and smoked as the driver put the pedal to the floor.

The car raced down the street, skid-turned into an empty alley and then came to a stop. The driver turned off the ignition but left the lights on as the five men rushed out of the car with their weapons at the ready.

"Are you gentlemen looking for the young man that kicked your asses earlier tonight?"

All five of them turned around to see where the voice came from. All they could see was the shadowy form of an average sized man step from behind a dumpster at the rear of their car. The red glow from the taillights cast the figure in an ominous light. In the shadows, the figure looked to be about the same size and build as the young man they fought earlier.

That was all they needed to see. Their weapons exploded with light and sound as they fired. The figure spun back behind the dumpster.

"Did we get him?" one of them asked.

"Shit, man, we had to!" another answered.

One of the bolder young men stepped slowly to the dumpster as three of the others followed. One of them remained at the front of the car with his weapon raised and waiting. The first one to reach the dumpster peeked around its corner and saw nothing.

"AAAHHHHH!!!!!" The scream came from the front of the car. The shooter at the dumpster turned to see his friend dying. The young man had a gaping bloody hole in his chest where his heart should have been.

The other four men watched, dumbfounded, as their partner fell gasping to his knees, and then fell to his face.

Once again the night came alive with the thunder and lightning of gunfire. None of them knew exactly what they were shooting at, but they were all shooting in the general direction of where the dead man had been standing.

When the gunfire ceased again, another sound was heard. The three men standing by the rear of the car heard a gurgling, choking sound and turned to find the source. They saw the man who had peeked behind the dumpster slumped against it, holding his throat and gagging while blood spurted from beneath his hands. He slid to a sitting position on the ground and went still.

"OH SHIT!"

One of the remaining three ran off screaming down the alley in a panic. The other two hopped hastily into the car and took off in the other direction. As the vehicle roared down the alley, a figure stepped into the car's path. The car's headlights lit the figure from head to toe.

He was an African American man wearing a black full-length leather trench coat that was buttoned up to the chin. The coat reached almost to the ground, and a pair of shining black Stacy Adam shoes adorned his feet. The most noticeable things about him, however, were his eyes. Those eyes seemed to grow larger and more sinister as the car rushed toward him.

"Run 'em down!" the man in the passenger seat screamed. "Run that motherfucker *DOWN!*"

The driver pressed the pedal to floor once again as he attempted to hit the stranger. Just before the car reached him, he leapt into the air and out of sight.

Both of the men looked up and around in a frantic attempt to see where the other had gone but he was nowhere to be seen. The car turned out of the alley and onto the street.

"What the *fuck* is goin' on?" the driver demanded. He pounded the steering wheel in an unsuccessful attempt to calm himself.

"I don't know, man..." the passenger answered. He tried to sound composed but failed miserably. "I don't know...I don't know..."

"What about D?" the driver asked.

"Hell with D! That fool shouldn't have ran down the alley! He shoulda got his ass in the fucking car with us. He's dead by now, he's got –"

Whatever he was saying was cut short by a clawed hand exploding from his stomach. The driver screamed insanely as he looked over at his dying friend. The African American man in the black trench coat sat up in the back seat and grinned with terrible fanged teeth. He brought his other hand from behind the driver's seat and covered the driver's mouth with clawed fingers.

The beautiful BMW convertible swerved off the street and onto the sidewalk. The car came to an abrupt and violent stop as it smashed into the side of a building.

Derrick, or D, as his friend called him, did not know how long he had been running. All he knew was that he had to put as much distance between himself and that alley as possible. He had stumbled more than once as he made his mad dash down the sidewalk.

First they were beat up by one man and now another man was murdering them. He wondered if the two were related. And then he wondered if Wes and T-Dog were alright. He was beginning to wish he had gotten into the car with them. If he did, he thought, he would be moving a helluva lot faster than he was moving now. When he heard a loud screech of car tires and a violent crash from a few blocks away, however, he decided that he made the right decision and ran even faster.

As he reached the corner, a hand darted out from behind a building and grabbed his collar. He was snatched so roughly around the corner of the building that he lost a shoe. He was slammed against the wall hard enough to rattle his teeth and blast the wind from his lungs.

D found himself looking into the most sinister pair of eyes he had ever seen. The whites of the eyes were not white at all. They were blood red with irises as black as midnight and as deep as infinity. Set within those black irises were pupils that gleamed in the same shade of crimson as the sclera. The eyes belonged to the man in the long black leather coat.

When the frightened younger man finally gathered his breath and tried to speak, the stranger covered his mouth with a vice-like grip. Andre looked over the younger man like a wolf appraising a lamb.

"You ran away alone while the others took off in a car. You're a loner, at least instinctively. I like that."

The younger man's eyes were wide with fear as he tried in vain to look away from those hellish eyes.

Andre continued. "Loners make good servants. How would you like to be my...helper?" Andre moved his hand away so his prisoner could speak.

"I'll do anything you want, man! Just don't kill me!"

Andre appraised him further, breathing deeply through his nose to bask in the youngster's fear.

"Oh, Jesus," the youngster murmured.

"Oh, *Jesus*?" Andre's appraising stare became an icy glare of hatred. "That was the worst possible thing you could have said."

The man's pained, dying screams echoed through the night...for all of about two seconds.

Police lights were everywhere. Ambulances and police cars cluttered the street. Paramedics were busy loading their vans with full body bags while Camillia stood by Weller's car watching the activity. Weller was just out of earshot talking to another officer. After the uniformed officer finished talking to Weller, the detective walked back over to Camillia.

"Bad news, Camillia," Weller said, stating the obvious.

"What is it?"

"Five males in their late teens to early twenties were found dead in this vicinity. Two were found in a car about a quarter mile away, two were in the alley right there, and another on a corner just a few blocks away. The car matches the description of the car belonging to the five thugs at the movie theater. According to eyewitness descriptions, they're the same five who got into the brawl with the kid matching Richard's description."

"No..." Camillia exhaled. "Richard couldn't have done this. He couldn't have." Tears began to run down her cheeks.

"I don't want to believe it, either," Weller said sincerely. "But we've got to find him."

"Wait," Camillia said. "Maybe he's with Tim or Major. Can we call their homes from your car phone?"

"Do you have their numbers on you?" Weller asked.

"Here," Camillia answered, pulling an address book out of her purse.

Weller called Tim's home but got no answer. He disconnected and dialed again. "No answer at Tim's," he said. "I'm trying Major now."

Camillia waited, agitated but calm, until Weller finally spoke. "Major, this is Detective Weller," he began.

Camillia sighed with relief and half-smiled.

"We're looking for Richard," he continued. "Call me as soon as you get this message."

Camillia's smile faltered. "Wait," she bade. She took the address book back and turned a page. "Here are their parents' numbers."

She looked worriedly at her friend as Weller made two more phone calls He talked to Major's mother and Tim's father and the result was two separate but identical conversations.

"They're parents said they went to the show," Weller explained. "But that was a while ago, and neither has come home yet. They'll call me as soon as they see or hear from them."

"Andre was responsible for this," Camillia insisted. "I don't care if Richard did fight these boys earlier tonight. He's not capable of anything like this."

"Let's go, Camillia," Weller said tiredly.

Flashing lights and strobe lights turned the people on the dance floor to crazy animated characters. Blaring music shook the walls of the dance club. Dancers were caught in the spell of House music. They were completely lost in the driving bass and treble, mesmerized by the harsh, frenzied rhythm exploding from five-foot tall speakers. Some of the speakers were mounted high on the walls while others were bolted to floor. The floor speakers had people dancing on top of them and even right in front of them, oblivious to pounding beat.

The smell of sweat and musk was strong but no one cared. Men and women moved in and out of time with the music. Some were pressed tightly against each other, grinding erotically. Others danced a few feet apart matching one another enthusiastically move for move. And still others danced alone, spinning like tops, arms and legs flailing.

Major stepped away from the dance floor sweating profusely and walked over to Tim, who was sitting at a table drinking a soda.

"It's hot as hell on that dance floor, man," Major told Tim. "I should've worn my workout gear. Why aren't you on the floor?"

"I'm worried about Rich," Tim replied. "He's been actin' so different."

"I know," Major said as he sat down. He suddenly became very serious.

"Tonight, man," Tim continued. "He started that. An empty box of Raisinets ain't shit. It was nothing to start a brawl over. I've never seen him trip like that."

"I know he's trippin' off what went down earlier tonight," Major continued. "But he's been actin' funny for weeks now. And you gotta admit that he started actin' strange even before the nightmares started." Major looked around. "Where is he now?"

"Damn if I know," Tim admitted. "But I'm pretty sure what he's doin'."

Major nodded. "Tryin' to get his freak on like always."

Richard was, in fact, making his way around the club. He had already walked around the perimeter of the dance floor and checked out the few tables lining the walls. He was full of confidence that he had never felt before. The confidence, however, was laced with a hint of fear of the unknown. The nightmares and his explosive temper began to make sense. His recent inability to sleep at night and his exhaustion during the day came into perspective.

From the moment he failed to see his reflection in the store window, everything became clear. And then, when he saw himself floating above the filthy ground and trashcans in the alley, he was almost certain.

But he had to be absolutely sure.

A familiar song began to play. At the midpoint of the song, Richard knew, the tempo would change from feverishly fast to slow and sexual, with passionate pants and moans, before speeding up again. Its eroticism made it wildly popular and Richard was determined to dance to it with someone.

He was looking for a woman, that special woman that he always felt was beyond him. He was searching for a woman that fit all of the physical attributes for his opinion of the perfect body. There were certain facial features that he felt a woman should have to make her beautiful. He had seen many women that came close, but he had yet to find the real thing until he met Paula.

Paula was Richard's opinion of the perfect physical female specimen. When he first met her, her attitude was unpleasant, but he could not deny that it intrigued him. She became somewhat of a challenge. The fact that he never pursued her was not because of her bad attitude, but because he felt she was beyond his reach. He used her attitude as the reason for never making a move on her, but deep down he knew it was because he did not think she would have him.

Things were different now.

If Richard was what he thought he had become, he was confident he could have any woman he wanted. He probably always could. If he had known what he really was a long time ago his life would have been much different. The time had come to find out for sure.

He was searching for a woman like Paula. He had once overheard her talking to her friends about LA Mirage. It was one of her favorite clubs. That was the real reason he suggested it to Tim and Major. His only wish was that she was there that night.

His wish was granted. There she was. Paula sat with two female friends sipping ginger ale. All of the women at the table were attractive, but to Richard, none of them held a candle to Paula. As he approached he saw a few men come to the table to ask them to dance. He saw each man walk away alone and disappointed. After each man walked away, the women laughed more.

It was Richard's turn. Paula looked up, saw him coming and said nothing. She ignored him, turning her attention back to her friends. When Richard reached the table he put his hand on her shoulder.

"You sit next to me in History class," he said.

Instead of looking up at him, she looked at the hand on her shoulder and spoke in an irritated tone. "And?"

"Let's dance," he said. It sounded more like a command than a request.

"Is that the best way you know how to ask?"

"I'm not asking."

"*Excuse* me?" she began, still not looking at him She looked at her friends in disbelief. "I would appreciate it if you moved your hand."

"Let's dance, Paula."

"Why don't you step off?" asked one of Paula's friends.

"Yeah," added the other friend. "Maybe you should just dance your ass on away from here."

"Shut up," Richard said, quietly but firmly.

His voice managed to carry over the deafening music despite its low volume, as if he had spoken into their minds as much as their ears. The two women looked up at him with expressions of severe indignation, ready to unload withering verbal assaults.

When their eyes found his, however, they both quickly decided that it would be in their best interest to do exactly as he commanded. They looked down at their drinks in order to look at anything other than his frightening glare.

"Look, damn it..." Paula began as she knocked the hand away. She stood up quickly and turned to face Richard, "...you're a bold son of a bitch, but you better get away from –" she stopped short when her eyes finally met his.

"Let's dance, Paula."

"Let's dance," Paula echoed.

Richard smiled as he led her to the dance floor.

"I can't believe I couldn't find one broad to dance with me to 'French Kiss'," Major said with exasperation as he returned to the table with Tim.

"Did you see Rich while you were out there sweatin' and beggin'?" Tim asked.

"As a matter of fact, yeah," Major answered. "He was over there tryin' to get that fine freak from his History class to dance. That boy never quits."

Tim's eyes widened as he looked out at the dance floor. He turned to Major. "And it's a good thing, too. Check it out."

Tim pointed to the dance floor. Major looked where his friend pointed and his jaw dropped.

The music was slowing down, causing the dancers to slow their rhythm as well. Couples were bound in sensual embraces, their groins pressed together while their hips rotated in time with the ever-slowing tempo. Richard and Paula were locked together in the middle of the floor.

The dancers immediately surrounding them watched even as they danced. Most of the men were watching Paula and wishing they were dancing with her. The others stared because, although the couple was embracing intimately, they were not dancing. Richard and Paula were just standing there, pressing together as if they were trying to merge into one being, engaged in deep, slow kiss that lingered even as music sped up again.

"Damn," Tim said. Major stared with envy.

After a few hours, Tim and Major were ready to call it a night. They sat at a table waiting for Richard.

"He *better* hurry up," Tim warned. "We got class in the morning."

Major looked all around the club. "I wonder where him and ol' girl disappeared to."

"All I know is that fool better *re*appear or his ass is walking to the crib."

"He's probably got her jacked up in a bathroom stall," Major said. "I wish I was him right about now."

"I bet you do," Richard said as he strode to the table from behind them. Paula held his hand, following a step behind him.

"Fellas," Richard continued. "Y'all can go on home without me. Me and Paula are gonna stick around for a while."

"'*Stick*,' huh?" Major asked with a chuckle. "I bet y'all *are* gonna do some stickin'!"

Tim noticed Paula's face remained expressionless despite the crude remark. Other than her eyes being riveted to Richard, her expression was completely blank.

"How are you getting home?" Tim questioned.

"I have a car," Paula answered, her gaze sill fixed on Richard. "I'll take him home."

"You got it goin' on, boy," Major said. "I gotta shake your hand."

Major shook Richard's hand briskly and laughed. Richard smiled triumphantly.

Tim, however, was not laughing. "You sure you wanna do this?" Tim asked. "You know your mom is gonna be worried sick about you."

"I got this," Richard said dismissively. He then gave both of his friends a stern look. "Don't call moms."

"Alright," Tim replied.

He wanted to rail defiantly against the order his friend had the nerve to give. He also registered surprise that Major failed to reply with one of his patented smart-ass comebacks. For some reason, though, neither his defiance nor surprise ever made it to the surface. The two only stared in mute confusion as Richard and Paula walked away and vanished into the crowd.

"Somethin's really wrong with this," Tim said.

"I know," Major responded. "I know... But if hittin' that fine-ass is wrong, I don't wanna be –"

"Shut up, Major."

The moon was full. Its pale light cast a strange glow on Paula's face as she and Richard walked down the street. Richard decided that the glow only added to her beauty.

"I love the way you look at me," Paula breathed.

"I love the way you look," Richard replied.

"I know I've been kind of foul to you," Paula began. "I couldn't help it. It's hard for me to take men seriously. I blossomed early, so when I was fourteen, I looked much older. Ever since then I've had guys my age and older trying to get with me. All they ever want is sex. They're either brutally honest about it or tell transparent lies.

"Even guys I liked wanted nothing more than to show me off to their friends. I got tired of it and just stopped dealing with them. I can understand a physical attraction, but for me, it never went any further than that. I've never met a man that wanted more from me than just my body."

"You have now," Richard assured. "I want *much* more from you than just that."

"I know," Paula confessed. "I don't know how I can tell, but I can see it in your eyes. That's why I don't mind staying with you tonight."

They turned into the lobby of an hourly hotel in a run-down neighborhood. Everything about the neighborhood would normally have paralyzed Paula with fear. Everything about the hotel would normally have made Paula cringe in disgust.

M.J. Stewart

But she felt safe with Richard. She knew no harm would come to her as long as he was by her side.

It was not long before Paula and Richard were in each other's arms, kissing fervently, their hands exploring every part of one another's bodies. There were no traces of awkwardness, shame or hesitation. There was only urgent passion, emphatic foreplay and breathless anticipation. Shortly afterwards, they were undressed, lying atop grimy sheets on a hard mattress and Richard was deep inside of Paula.

Their lovemaking was a dream come true for Richard. In fact, he felt as if he was dreaming at that very moment. His vision swam as he caressed her. He went light-headed when she wrapped her arms and legs tightly around him. Richard could barely believe it was happening.

Paula was everything he hoped she would be. He pulled just away long enough to kiss her from head to toe and back again, tasting every inch of her skin before entering her again. No matter where his lips and tongue roamed, though, they continuously found their way back to her neck. It was flawless and sparkled with a thin sheen of sweat. The salty taste was delectable. He began to nibble on the smooth, soft brown skin of her throat. The nibbling became small bites that drew sharp inhalations and exhalations of pleasure from Paula's perfect lips.

Richard felt a craving building up within him. His mouth began to water and his heart beat faster and faster.

He opened his mouth and felt a sensation of tingling pain in his gums at his upper and lower canine teeth. A strange pull in his stomach compelled him to lower his head to bite.

Something in the back of Richard's mind began to scream at him. He heard his mother's voice imploring him to stop, calling him back from edge of this vile abyss.

Richard finally pulled away.

And then came the pain.

Agony struck him suddenly, causing him to roll away from the surprised Paula. He held his stomach and doubled over in the bed as the dream he had at the hospital came rushing back to him.

Richard remembered the pain he felt in the dream of the misfit slaying Slab. In the nightmare, the pain was a searing emptiness at his very core, but this was even worse. It was an emptiness that consumed him from the inside out. His whole body shuddered as the emptiness threatened to devour him if it was not filled.

"You feel that kid? That's the hunger! Give in to it!"

He recalled the words the misfit uttered to him in his nightmare. The words echoed in his mind again and again. This, however, was no nightmare. The pain was all too real.

Richard realized to his horror that the only way to fill the emptiness was with blood.

"What's wrong?" Paula asked.

It's the hunger, kid!!

"Get out," Richard warned in a low growl.

"No," Paula answered. "I'm calling an ambulance."

She reached for the phone but Richard's hand beat hers to it. In one motion he ripped the phone from the wall and tossed it across the room, where it hit the wall and exploded into countless pieces.

Give in to it!!

"*Get out*," he growled again.

"No," Paula repeated stubbornly. "I wanna help."

It was clear to Richard that the girl was going nowhere. He did not want to hurt her so he gathered all of his strength and forced himself to roll off the bed and onto the floor. Paula watched with worry and confusion as he pulled on his pants. He struggled to his feet and dashed out of the room, slamming the door behind him. Paula would have followed him but she was still naked.

Richard fled down the stairs and raced out of the hotel in crippling pain. He clutched at his stomach as he ran, the burning within him growing with each passing second. As he sprinted into the night, lost in fear and pain, he did not see Paula watching him through the hotel window.

If he had just looked back he would have seen the concern on her pretty face.

If he had only looked over his shoulder he would have seen the man wearing a long black trench coat that emerged from the shadows behind Paula.

He would have seen the man cover the perfect mouth of the startled young woman.

All Richard had to do was look back, and he would have seen Andre sink his long fangs into Paula's smooth, flawless neck.

Chapter 7

The church loomed over the residential neighbor-hood like a protective giant. The belfry reached to the lavender sky of near dawn. A haggard-looking Richard Williams stared at the large Catholic Church as he leaned weakly against the wall of an apartment building across the street.

His face was filthy with dust, dried blood and tears. His clothes and skin were ripped from countless falls as he ran through countless alleys to get to his current location. He did not know why or how long he had been there; he only knew that he could not seem to leave.

Several times he tried to cross the street to go to the church, and each time he did, the pain within him surged to the point that he nearly lost consciousness. Something within him knew that he had to get inside. Whenever he tried, his body rebelled violently.

"No pain," he said to himself as he tried to cross the street once again.

When Richard got to the middle of the street, the pain flared through him. He fell to his knees and clutched his stomach like he had done so many times already. He could feel the bruises that had formed on his midsection from grabbing it so hard.

"No pain," he echoed as he staggered to his feet and continued on his way.

He was just as determined to make it to the other side of the street as his body was determined not to. Even if it killed him, he would make it inside that church. Tears flowed down his face and he thought he would grind his teeth to powder, yet he forced his legs to move.

"To hell with the hunger."

He made it to the curb on the far side of the street. When he licked his desiccated lips, the taste of his blood was strong on his tongue and burned like acid. His nose bled. His head pounded as though it was about to explode.

He mumbled words not even he could understand as he fell to his hands and knees on the church stairs. His knees shook uncontrollably when he struggled to his feet. His brain threatened to burst with every step he took. His blood felt like fire raging through his veins, threatening to burn his heart to ashes. His very eyes burned and his vision became nothing but glaring whiteness.

Richard groped for the handle of the church door and cried out when touched it. The metal felt red hot and it sizzled against his flesh. The door swung open wildly and he collapsed onto the floor of the church. He fell and did not move. His entire being regressed to mind-numbing pain and everything went black.

Camillia was almost out of control. She paced back and forth, wringing her hands until they turned purple. Detective Weller sat by the phone, deep in thought. The sun had come up an hour ago and there was still no sign of Richard. Weller and she had been driving around until daybreak and they had not been able to find a clue.

The telephone rang.

Weller snatched it up while Camillia said a silent prayer. "Hello?" Weller asked urgently.

"Who's this?" asked a voice from the other end of the line.

"Who the hell is this?" demanded Weller.

"This is Tim. Let me speak to Richard or Ms. Williams."

Weller held the phone out to Camillia. "It's Tim."

Camillia took the phone. "Is Richard with you?" she asked frantically.

"I thought he might be home by now," Tim replied.

"He *was* with you!" Camillia was almost in a panic. "What happened last night? Where did you last see him?"

"We went to the movies," Tim explained. "Richard got into it with five gang-bangers." Despite her dark complexion, Camillia turned ghostly pale. Tim continued. "We were split up for a little while but when we found him, we went to a club. He left with a girl from his History class and then me and Major went home."

"What kind of car were the gangbangers in?" Camillia asked.

"I think I saw them getting into a convertible BMW."

"Go to school today," Camillia told him as she tried to calm herself. "Go to his History class and see if the girl shows up. If she doesn't, let detective Weller or me know immediately."

"What's goin' on, Ms. Williams?" Tim pleaded.

"I've gotta go now," she said before hanging up the phone.

Tim hung up his phone as well. This was too much. He had been up worrying about Richard all night. He had to know what was happening. He was startled out of his thoughts by the ringing of his phone, which he picked up before the end of the first ring.

"Hello?" he asked.

"We got trouble," Major said. "I just heard the morning news. Five guys were found dead last night. Two were found in a drop-top Beamer. Tim, those were the guys from the movie theater."

"*That's* what's goin' on," Tim said. "Mage, you were right. Richard's a part of this. I'm on my way over."

Fifteen minutes later Major was ducking into Tim's car. Tim looked over at his friend and shook his head.

"I think Paula's in trouble," Tim told him.

"Me, too," Major returned.

"If she doesn't show up for class, I'm gonna *make* Rich's mom tell us what the hell's goin' on. He's like our brother, man. We have a right to know."

"Yeah," Major agreed.

Tim noted that Major was unusually quiet.

When they reached the campus parking lot, Tim parked in the first parking spot he saw. The parking spot happened to be next to the beat up black Camaro with the tinted windows that he had always avoided. The raggedy car, however, was the last thing on his mind that morning. As Tim and Major got out of the car, the driver side door of the Camaro opened. The tall, pale white man from the movie theater stepped out. Major and Tim froze in their tracks and looked up at Eric.

"What the hell do *you* want?" Tim demanded.

"I wanna help," Eric answered. "And if you're looking for the girl, she's not going to show up today."

Major took a threatening step toward Eric. "How the hell do you know so much? Give us some answers or you push that rusty piece of shit out of here!"

"I know you guys are upset," Eric started. "But you've got to listen to me. I told you Richard was holding things back. I've been following him for a while. I was never able to tie anything directly to him until last night. He killed those five men, and now Paula's missing."

"You sayin' he killed her too?" Tim asked.

"I don't know," Eric lied. "She's exceptionally beautiful. He's probably got her enthralled."

"Enthralled?" Tim asked, starting to lose his temper. "What are you talkin' about?"

"You wanna know what I'm talkin' about, Tim? Major knows what I'm talkin' about. He's suspected it for a long time. You've probably begun to suspect it too, but neither of you want to admit it."

"I'll never admit no shit like that!" Major promised. "I don't know what the hell Rich is, but I know for damn sure he ain't no fucking vampire!"

"Vampire?" Tim echoed.

"I know where he'll be tonight," Eric said. "Meet me in Wolf Lake Park over in Hammond, Indiana at about nine thirty. That's where he'll bring the girl. He brings all the girls there. Do you know the area?"

Tim nodded. "I know it."

"Wolf Lake is a large area so look for my car. I'll be there." Eric got back into his car and drove away.

"So, what's the move?" asked Major when Eric's car exited the parking lot.

"First," Tim began, "we see if Paula shows up. If she doesn't, we go to Richard's house and find out what the hell is goin' on."

Eleven o'clock came very slowly to the two anxious young men. When the awaited time finally came, they were standing outside the classroom door.

They were still standing there at eleven-thirty. The instructor and students had all filed into the classroom before the eleven o'clock hour.

Paula and Richard were no-shows.

Tim turned to Major. "We're goin' to Rich's crib."

Weller held the telephone receiver to his ear impatiently waiting for someone – anyone – to pick up on the other end. He finally came to the conclusion that the phone would not be answered and hung up.

"No luck," he said to Camillia. "No one's answering Father Burns' phone."

Camillia stood by the living room window staring intently out at the sidewalk. She had gained control of herself a few hours ago, which Weller considered an amazing feat under the circumstances. He admired her strength.

"Maybe he's on his way over here," Camillia offered. She tilted her head. "In fact, he's pulling up now."

"You must have ESP," Weller teased.

Camillia managed a weak smile at Weller's attempt to ease the tension. The smile did not last long, however. Weller saw the small smile contort into a look of dread.

"What is it?" he asked.

Camillia said nothing. She ran from the window to the front door with Weller right behind her. He watched her trembling hands fumble with the locks. When she finally got the door open Weller saw the reason for her concern.

Father Burns stood on the porch. He looked very sad as he held the limp, ragged form of Richard Williams in his arms.

Camillia bathed her son and changed his clothes. All the while, he never regained consciousness. He breathed quietly and laid still in his pajamas as Camillia, Father Burns, and detective Weller sat around his bed.

"I found him on the floor of the church," Father Burns explained. "I heard someone cry out and when I came out from the back, there he was."

Tears fell slowly down Camillia's cheeks. Despite the tears, she managed to remain calm as she gently held Richard's hand.

"What's happening?" she asked in a hushed voice.

"I don't know, exactly. I do know that Richard did not kill those people last night."

"How do you know that, padre?" Weller asked quietly and hopefully.

"From what I understand, those killings were extremely ferocious," Father Burns explained. "As you saw when I brought Richard here, he didn't have nearly enough blood on his person to have committed that kind of violence. The relatively small amount of blood on Richard's body appeared to be his own."

Detective Weller sighed. "I'll still need his clothes."

Camillia's head snapped up and around. She pierced Weller with a withering glare that startled the gruff veteran detective.

"He's the only suspect in multiple murders, Camillia. I should arrest him right now. The only reason I won't is because I trust him and the padre. We need to run tests on the clothes to prove the padre right and exclude him as a suspect. We'll still have to ask him some questions, though. You have to understand that."

Camillia's unsettling gaze softened and she took a deep, calming breath. "I understand," she said softly.

The doorbell rang. Camillia reluctantly left her son's side and went downstairs to answer it, fearing that Weller had already contacted more police. When she looked through the peephole and saw Tim and Major, she sighed with relief and opened the door.

"So?" she asked expectantly.

"Paula didn't show up," Tim said.

Camillia's eyebrows scrunched up with anxiety.

"But that tall crazy-looking white boy did," Major added. "He said Richard was responsible for those murders last night. He said Richard has the girl."

"Richard's upstairs," Camillia said. "I don't know who this man is, but he's lying."

"Tell us the truth then, Ms. Williams," Tim demanded. "We need to know what's going on. Maybe we can help. This guy says Rich is a... a vampire. We can't buy that, but somethin' foul *is* goin' down."

"A vampire?" Camillia forced herself to smile. "Don't worry, boys, not about vampires. There are a lot of things goin' on right now, a lot of it we're not even sure about, yet. We'll fill you two in when we know for sure."

"Ms. Williams," Major began. "Can we at least see how he's doin'?"

Camillia shook her head. "He's had a rough night, Major. He doesn't feel well right now. Come back tomorrow. I'm sure he will feel a better by then."

"Alright," said Tim. "I'll see you tomorrow." He and Major walked away as Camillia closed the door.

Camillia went back upstairs to rejoin the others.

"The girl he left with last night never made it to class," Camillia reported.

Weller's chin dropped to his chest. After a few breaths he looked up at Camillia with sadness in his eyes.

"Camillia, I'm going to have to take him in."

Both men saw the anger darkening Camillia's countenance. Her shoulders tensed in defiance.

"Richard did *not* do this," she said. "That strange man the boys talked about has something to do with it. If he doesn't have her, he knows who does."

"How can you know that?" Weller demanded.

"Tim and Major just told me they saw him at Richard's school. They said he told them that Richard has the girl. Obviously, he doesn't."

"That doesn't mean he didn't –"

"He didn't!" Camillia snapped. "If he did, we'd know. *I'd* know! I'd be able to tell just by looking at him."

Weller gazed at the protective mother for a breath before turning to Father Burns. "What do you think, padre?"

"I think what you were afraid of, detective, is coming to pass. Richard is changing. Of that there is no doubt."

"But *how*?" Camillia asked. "How can Richard be...like Andre? We've had blood tests done that proved my fiancé was his father. Andre never even bit me."

Weller glanced at the priest before turning back to Camillia. "The padre believed it was possible that Richard could have been infected in the womb. Maybe that part of him was, I don't know, incubating over the years."

Camillia turned to Father Burns. The desperate look in her eyes beseeched him to say it was not so.

"I fear that's the only explanation for what's happening to your son, Camillia," Father Burns confirmed before quickly adding: "But there is hope. He hasn't changed completely. According to my research I'm positive the change won't be complete unless he makes his first kill. And you were right, Camillia. If *he* had killed the girl, he never would have made it into the church."

"Then Andre is still alive," Camillia declared.

"Yes, he is," Father Burns confirmed. "This 'weird white guy' the boys spoke to is probably Andre's servant. We have to find Andre and destroy him before Richard's change is complete. Perhaps we can use the servant to find the master."

"Look, you two," Weller began. "I agree with everything you're saying, but you have to realize it will eventually come out that Richard was the last person seen with the five murdered thugs as well as Paula. Too many people saw him with them. At some point Richard is going to have to talk to the police, either as a witness or a suspect."

"Can you hold your people off just a little while longer?" Camillia pleaded.

"I'll do what I can," Weller answered. "But if I don't bring him in soon, someone else will. At that point, the best-case scenario is that I'll be pulled off the case. The worst-case scenario is that I'll get tossed off the force. The only reason I'm still on this case is because of the link to the killings nineteen years ago. Well, that, and my boss is giving me more rope to hang myself."

Camillia sat on the bed beside her son and put her hands over her face. She could no longer contain her emotions. Her body shook violently as she sobbed.

Detective Weller left the room. Father Burns pulled up a chair next to the bed and slumped weakly down into it. A tear crept down his cheek.

"This is bullshit," Tim said angrily as he drove away from Camillia's house. "We grew up with them and now they're treating us like strangers. We deserve better."

"What do you suggest we do?" Major asked.

"Since nobody else wants to give us answers, we'll hook up with someone who will."

"You mean the white dude?" Major questioned.

Tim nodded. "Yeah. We're gonna meet 'em, but we're gettin' there early. And we're packin'."

"Packin'?" Major asked. "You mean guns?"

"Hell yeah," Tim answered. "We're gettin' there an hour early just in case that freak tries to set up some kind of surprise. If he tries some foul shit we'll be ready."

"I'm down," Major agreed. "I been itchin' to get some damn answers around here."

Major put all of the bravado and indignation into his tone and posture as he could. And then he turned his head to look out of the passenger side window... and to hide the fear that he knew was all over his face.

The first thing Richard saw upon opening his eyes was his mother looking down at him. Camillia smiled with relief and kissed his cheek. Richard looked around and saw the priest and the detective.

"You alright kid?" Weller asked.

"No," Richard said softly. "I'm far from it." He sat upright. "I'm a freak. I'm a fuckin' monster."

The look on the three adults' faces changed from relief to anxiety.

Camillia looked gravely at her son. "Richard," she implored, "please let me – "

"Let you what?" Richard broke in as he stood up. "You knew all the time, didn't you? All three of you knew!"

Father Burns spoke in his most calming tone, "We suspected, yes, but..."

"Suspected hell!" Richard cut him off. "All these years you kept this from me. What the hell kind of people are you?"

"Look kid," Weller began, "Calm down so we can-"

"Calm my ass!" Richard exploded. "I just found out I'm a motherfuckin' *monster*! How the hell do you expect me to calm down?"

"Listen, dammit!" Camillia commanded in a tone and volume that silenced the three men. "No matter what happens, I'm still your mother!" She grabbed him firmly by the collar of his pajama shirt and pulled him close.

""You don't *ever* talk like this in my presence! Ever! Do you hear me?"

Richard glared at his mother for a beat and then nodded. Camillia forced Richard to a sitting position on the bed.

"Now, you're gonna sit here and listen to what we have to say, right?"

Richard nodded again. "Yes ma'am."

She released him. The anger in her expression gave way to sadness. "I prayed this would never happen." she lowered her head as she spoke. "Every night for nine months I prayed that you weren't *his* son." Richard could see she was trying to hold back tears. "I just knew you were Richard's son, and as you grew older I saw more of Richard in you every day."

"What happened?" Richard questioned. He was saddened by his mother's grief but he was still angry.

"Years ago, my fiancé, Richard, was killed," Camillia began. "I was in a deep depression. I met Andre and I thought he swept me off my feet, but in reality, he entranced me. We spent a lot of time together before I finally found out what he really was. Father Burns and detective Weller saved me before he got a chance to hurt me. To this day I don't know why he didn't do to me what he did to the others."

"Why didn't you tell me, momma? How could you keep this from me?" Richard was almost pleading.

"How can a mother tell her son something like that?" she asked. "How could I tell you that a vampire may have been your father?" She could hold back the tears no more. She sat down heavily next to him on the bed. Even through the tears, she spoke in the same calm, quiet tone.

"I thought about abortion...but when I held you for the first time, I knew I made the right decision. I thought Andre was gone for good. I prayed he was. Even then, in the back of my mind I knew that even if Andre was your father, we could get through whatever happened.

"I could see your strength from the time you were a baby." Camillia's voice began to quiver so she paused to compose herself. After a few seconds she continued. "I'm so sorry, baby. I just couldn't bring myself to tell you, but I know we can get through this if we stick together."

"I'm sorry, too, momma," Richard said with watery eyes. He put his arms around her. They embraced as the priest and the detective looked on. Richard felt his mother's strength flow through him.

"I promise, momma," Richard vowed. "We *will* get through this. We can get through anything together."

"Let's go see what's in the fridge," Weller said to Burns. They left the mother and son alone.

Tim and Major were speeding south down Torrence Avenue thirty minutes before dusk. Torrence would take them directly to Wolf Lake Park south of the city limits.

"Where are we gonna wait?" Major asked. "Dude just told us to look for his car. We don't know where the car's gonna be and we don't know what direction he's gonna come from."

"I just wanna get familiar with the area," Tim explained. "We should see how many roads there are in and out of the park, just to be on the safe side."

Major pointed. "We know the park is right up the street. Why don't you turn down this side street? It may take us past another entrance."

Tim shrugged. "Might as well." He turned the Cavalier left and rolled down the small road.

They traveled the equivalent of three city blocks. Instead of seeing another entrance to the park, all they saw was forest.

"I don't think we're gonna find an entrance to the park on this street," Major observed.

Tim nodded. "Me either, but I wanna drive down a little further, just in case."

After a few more minutes of driving, Tim brought the car to a stop in front of an old boarded-up house. The unkempt front yard was almost as dense as the forest that surrounded the residence. Overgrown grass and weeds covered the walkway.

Neither of them said it aloud, but the house made both of them uneasy. Something about the home and the surrounding wooded area touched something within them, at a primal level, warning them away.

Major frowned. "I wonder when they're gonna tear that fire-trap down."

"I don't see why someone would build a house way back in the woods like this, anyway," Tim said as he performed a three-point turn and drove quickly back toward Torrence Avenue.

Richard had to get out of that damned house. His mother undoubtedly knew by now that he was gone but it did not matter. There was something pulling at him. An irresistible attraction compelled him to leave his home.

It was the night. The infinite depth of the night sky fascinated him more than it ever had. There was a full moon that night and it called to him. Richard had no idea where he was or where he was going, but he was content to follow its mysterious call. He felt at ease as he walked along the moonlit road, like a super-predator surveying his territory.

He knew that his mother would be upset. He also knew that if he did not leave the house he would have probably torn it apart. The craving for blood was starting to consume him. His mother was not safe in the house with him and neither were Weller or Father Burns.

The crucifixes hanging on the walls were starting to give him headaches. He had to leave, to find some way to satisfy the burgeoning hunger within him.

There was nothing but blackness to either side of him. Nothing was visible beyond the road's narrow shoulders. The sounds of crickets and other nocturnal animals were very loud out here but did not bother him in the least. Those were the sounds of the night. Richard was a creature of the night. The sounds gave him comfort.

After a few minutes more of walking, the moonlight revealed to him a rather large, decrepit house a few yards off the road. Every opening to the house was boarded except the door. The house looked as if it would fall at any time, but somehow, Richard knew it would not. The house appeared to have been empty for some time. Richard instinctively knew that was not the case. There was something inside that house, something he had to find; something that had to find him. He located the walkway under a blanket of thick weeds as if it was in plain view, made his way to the front porch, and opened the door.

Richard had never been in this house before but it was as familiar to him as his own home. He made one turn and was standing in the living room. The room was rich with African tapestries, paintings, carvings, and sculptures. Other than the artwork, the entire room was black and gray. He also saw five unusually large German shepherds lounging around the room. The dogs looked up at him with a lack of interest and lowered their heads. This time Richard felt no fear of the animals.

"It's about time you got here."

The familiar voice came from behind him. Richard turned to see the misfit sitting on a black leather couch sharpening a machete with a whetstone. Standing behind the misfit was a man with his back to Richard. The man stood there with his hands in his pockets admiring the art on the mantle and wall. He was about Richard's height and build. He wore a long black leather trench coat.

"Eric is right," said the man without turning around. "I've been waiting for you to come home."

The man turned around slowly. His skin was medium brown. His hair was cut short, his jaw and chin were clean shaven. His voice was smooth and calming, ideal for lulling the unwary into a false sense of safety.

His face, on the other hand, was the exact opposite. It was disgustingly contorted, wrinkled and cracked beyond belief, with a long, beak-like nose and cheekbones that were unnaturally high and severely angled. His eyebrows were thick, jagged black lines that stretched in a sinister arch from the bridge of his nose almost to his hairline. There were no human eyes in his eye sockets, only obsidian orbs that seemed to absorb what little light there was in the dimly lit room.

The man pulled his hands from his pockets, revealing fingers that were long, ugly things with bony knuckles and curved claws for fingernails. He held his arms wide as if he expected Richard to run over and give him a loving embrace. He smiled an evil smile that displayed a mouth full of twisted, yellow, pointed teeth.

"Come give your old man a hug."

"NO!" Richard screamed, waking from his nightmare. He sat bolt upright in his bed.

Camillia was in the kitchen cooking when she heard her son's cry. She dropped her spoon and sprinted up the stairs. When she burst into the room she found it empty. The window was wide open and there was a large hole ripped in the screen.

A cool evening breeze blew into the room and brought a chill to Camillia that made her shiver. Weller joined her a moment later.

"What happened?" the detective asked breathlessly.

It took a while for Camillia answer. She was staring at the window and fighting back the panic that so desperately attempted to overwhelm her. The rush of emotions ultimately swept her strength and breath away. All she could manage was a whisper.

"Richard's gone."

Chapter 8

Richard was no longer wearing pajamas. He wore a leather jacket, t-shirt and blue jeans that he grabbed before going out the window. The hospital where he once worked was unusually quiet. He walked the silent halls in a daze. His former coworkers greeted him as they passed and were somewhat surprised at Richard's blank stare and the distant "hello" he gave them in return. They had no idea that his distance was the result of him restraining himself from attacking them.

He got on the elevator and pushed the button marked "B" for the basement, only vaguely aware of where he was going. A faint smell led him; a scent that reached his sensitive nostrils even through all of the strong sanitizing agents that permeated the hospital.

The voice of the misfit replayed in Richard's mind...

The hunger, kid! Give in to it!

Richard knew he had to do just that. The hunger left him no choice. The elevator door opened to a dim hallway. He walked out slowly and kept walking until he reached an unmarked door. He tried to open the door but it was locked. With the slightest exertion of effort, he forced it open and stepped into the room.

He did not bother to turn on the light. The weak light from the hallway was more than enough for Richard to make his way through the room. Even if the room was pitch black, he knew he would have had no trouble finding his way. He could see in the darkness as well as he could in light, and maybe better. Light irritated his eyes.

There was an industrial-sized refrigerator on the other side of the room. Richard walked over to it and pulled it open. The refrigerator door was padlocked, but the stainless steel lock surrendered to Richard's augmented strength as if it was made of paper. An assortment of small, labeled bottles lined the shelves of the large refrigerator. Each bottle was filled with a dark red – almost purple – fluid. Richard lifted one of the bottles from the refrigerator. When he took the top off of the small bottle, the fluid lightened to a deep crimson.

The liquid smelled...off, somehow. Nonetheless, his hunger, his *thirst*, bade him to ignore the irregularity. He put the small vial to his lips.

"What the hell's goin' on here!?" boomed a deep voice.

The lights came on and Richard noticed that written on the label of the vial were the words "HIV POSITIVE." Richard snapped back to his senses and dropped the bottle on the floor. The small vial broke and the cold, dark blood spread slowly into a small puddle. Richard turned to see Slab filling the doorway.

"You sick motherfucker," Slab accused. "I knew your little skinny ass wasn't right in the head. You weren't really about to do what it looked like you were about to do, were you?"

"Get out of here, Slab," Richard snarled in warning. "You don't know what you're dealing with right now."

"I think *you're* the one who'll be leavin'," Slab replied. "And I know just what the fuck I'm dealing with: a light-in-the-ass nigga who's about to get rolled on!"

The hulking orderly approached Richard and grabbed him by the collar. Slab tried to move the smaller man but Richard would not budge. Richard looked down at the two massive hands and looked up into the orderly's eyes.

Slab saw two black globes where Richard's eyes had once been. Richard smiled an evil, fanged smile.

"Alright..." Richard said with a wolfish grin. "You can stay if you want to."

As terrified as Slab was, he could not seem to tear his eyes away from the awful sight. He released Richard and backed away slowly until he was out in the hallway. When Slab reached the hall he turned and ran.

Richard turned back to the open refrigerator. This time he read the labels on the vials. He picked up a bottle marked "A" and took its lid off. He lifted the bottle to his lips and this time he was undisturbed. The contents of the bottle were quickly drained and Richard sighed in relief.

Pain unlike any of his former aches ripped through him. It was so acute that he could not find the breath to scream. He clutched at his stomach and fell heavily to the floor. His mind cried even though his lungs, larynx and mouth could not, deafening him to any other sound.

He writhed around on the floor crying and slavering, and then, as quickly as it had come, the pain went away. A residual soreness lingered so Richard remained on the cold floor, expecting the pain to return. He welcomed the return of breath into his lungs with deep gulps.

"Ain't nothing like the real thing," someone said.

Richard looked up, shivering uncontrollably as his eyes met the eyes of a man in a long black leather trench coat. Even though the face was normal, handsome, even, and the digits on his hands were well-manicured fingers, Richard knew that this was the man from his dream.

"That's one of your mother's favorite songs, you know. She was huge fan of Marvin Gaye and Tammi Terrell."

"Who are you?" Richard asked, his voice a near-inaudible whisper.

"You know, who I am. Come with me."

Slab and three security officers burst into the room.

"Here he is –" Slab began, but the room was empty.

Nine-thirty came and went. Tim and Major were sitting in Tim's car in a fast food restaurant parking lot on Torrence Avenue, just a few minutes north of Wolf Lake.

"It's about that time, huh?" asked Major.

"Yeah," Tim said as he started the car.

Tim drove at a moderate pace as he and Major looked for the old Camaro. It took a while but eventually they pulled to a stop a few yards away from the beat up car.

"I didn't see the car come by when we were at the restaurant," Major said.

"Neither did I," Tim replied. "It must've come from the south end of the park." Tim looked seriously at his friend. "You ready, Mage?"

Major snapped a clip into his Glock 19 nine-millimeter pistol and smiled at Tim. "Always." He reached into his shirt and pulled his necklace with the small golden crucifix from beneath his jacket. "Just in case," he said.

Tim checked his handgun, a .44 Magnum Colt Anaconda revolver, and tucked it into his pants.

Major whistled. "That's a big ass gun."

"Yep," Tim concurred. "It puts big-ass holes in things."

"I'll make up for the size with quantity," Major said as he slipped his nine into the inside of his jacket and made sure his Saturday-night special was tucked in his pants.

They got out of the Cavalier and walked up to the Camaro. The back and side windows of the old car were deeply tinted so Tim walked around to the front of the car to see if the misfit was there.

"You lookin' for me?" came the misfit's voice.

Major and Tim peered into the trees but saw nothing. Seconds later, the tall, pale man seemed to materialize from the shadows.

"C'mon," Eric the misfit whispered, "We don't have much time, and we've got to be quiet."

The two lifelong friends looked at each other for what seemed like an eternity. They both took deep breaths and followed Eric into the darkness of the forest.

"Where are you?" Richard called into the night.

No answer came as he walked slowly through the woods. He looked in every direction but failed to see the mysterious man in black. The pale moon glow gave the forest a chilling illumination. The cool night breeze blew through branches and made the shadows dance. Richard thought he saw movement behind every tree.

The sound of twigs snapping underfoot carried to him on the breeze. He turned quickly in the direction of the sound to see Paula stepping from behind a large tree. Her exquisite body was covered by a long, sheer, white nightgown that clung enticingly to every curve.

Even though she looked at Richard, there was a haunted quality to her gaze that made it seem as if she looked through and beyond him. She took two slow, mesmerizing steps in his direction and then went still.

"Paula?" Richard whispered.

"Take me," she answered.

Something was wrong. Richard sensed it from her vacant expression and stiff posture to the utter lack of passion in her voice. At the same time, he felt her body heat wash over him, awakening his manhood. Her scent, a heady blend of her natural musk, the remnant of a fragrant perfume, and, most importantly, the metallic sweetness of the blood coursing through her veins, pushed all thoughts of her strangeness from his mind.

Richard took a few tentative steps toward the enthralled young woman. He felt the hunger building up inside of him as if it was a living thing. It started slowly, as a strange heat in the pit of his stomach. With every step he took in Paula's direction the heat spread within him.

His thoughts drifted back to the missed chance back at the hotel. He would not miss his chance this time. When he finally reached her, he put his hands on her soft shoulders. He looked deeply into her eyes and placed a gentle kiss on her full lips. With one hand, he tilted her head to the side to expose her neck.

Richard opened his mouth and bared his elongating fangs. He hesitated when he saw that there were already two small puncture wounds on the side of her neck.

His attention was abruptly diverted by moonlight reflecting off of something small and metallic in the darkness of the surrounding woods. For some reason, the reflection seared his eyes as if he were staring directly into the sun. He shaded his eyes with his hand and glared in the direction of the flash.

"He sees us!" Major whispered frantically as the moonlight twinkled on the surface of the golden cross he wore around his neck.

"Let's get the hell out of here!" Tim said.

Their weapons forgotten, Tim and Major sprinted to the road. Eric followed with a dark smile on his face.

Richard heard the sound of more than one person fleeing through the brush. He took a few hurried steps in the direction of the sound but was stopped short by an all-too familiar voice.

"Don't concern yourself with them," the voice said.

Richard turned to see the man in black standing next to Paula. He did not look much older than Richard but Richard knew that his looks were most definitely deceiving. He was the oldest man Richard had ever met.

This was the moment Richard had been dreading; the moment he knew would come when his mother finally confirmed what he was. All of the pain, all of the nightmares and all of the sleepless nights were merely a prelude to this moment.

Every muscle in Richard's body screamed for him to run away yet he could not force his feet to move. His heart beat faster as he was seized by a storm of emotions. The fear and loathing in Richard's face were impossible to hide. He stood and stared at the man in black for a long time before he spoke.

"You're Andre," Richard said. "You're the...the *thing* my mother told me about."

"Yes," Andre admitted. "I'm the side of the family that your mother tried to hide from you."

"What do you want from me?" Richard demanded.

"I want you to give in to the hunger. I want my son."

"I'm not your son. Richard was my father."

Andre scoffed. "Richard was a sperm donor. He fertilized Camillia's egg, but it was my seed that nourished you. You're more my son than you would have been his...even if I had let him live."

"What if I don't want to join you?"

Andre chuckled. "That's not even a consideration. We both know you want it. The hunger in you is too strong for you to deny. The power you have now is not even a hint of the power you *can* possess. You know it's true."

"I know that I'm a fuckin' monster," Richard argued.

"I understand your fear," Andre sympathized. "I, too, was afraid when I was first turned. I know this is all new to you but that cold blood at the hospital is *not* the answer. This is the answer." He lifted his hand to indicate the young lady standing next to him.

"I don't want that," Richard lied.

Andre ignored the denial and continued. "Only the sweet, warm, living blood of a human will sate you. I'm sorry to say that she won't completely satisfy you because, as you've seen, I've already sampled her. But don't worry, son. She'll do for the moment. You'll need to make your own fresh kill to truly extinguish the burning you're feeling inside and come into your full power."

"You're a sick son of a bitch," Richard said.

Andre shrugged lightly. "Perhaps. And if immortality is indeed a sickness, I hope I'm never cured."

"But at what price?" Richard challenged. "You don't have a soul. You have to kill every night to survive."

"I don't have a soul?" Andre burst into insane laughter. "I have a different soul every night!"

The laughing stopped as suddenly as it started. Andre looked deeply into Richard's eyes.

"The soul is life, and life is in the blood, so that is the means through which I acquire a soul. I have to take lives to continue my own. That's a miniscule price, I would argue, for eternal life."

"That's a price I won't pay," Richard promised.

"You're strong, Richard, I'll give you that. You're strong like Camillia."

"Don't you say her name," Richard warned. "You're not worthy of saying her name."

"Her strength is the most significant trait that attracts me to her. I can use that kind of strength. Once a strong person is broken, they stay broken. They become just as strong *for* you as they were against you. I never wanted to kill Camillia, Richard. I wanted her to be my bride."

"Leave my mother out of this," Richard growled.

"I want us to be a family. I want us to spread our seed throughout this crumbling world. You are the key, my son. You have no idea how special you are. But you will come to know. I have come to show you."

"You're insane," Richard said.

"No," Andre disagreed. "It's only logical. This earth is well on its way to hell as it is. What better god than me could there be for a world already bloated with disease and wickedness? All I need are you and your mother. I would've broken her years ago if not for that meddling priest and his cop friend. But I'll break you first, boy. And then I'll have Camillia."

"LEAVE HER OUT OF THIS!" Richard exploded into motion, moving so fast that he would have been a blur to the human eye. He crashed into Andre and the two men hurled toward the trunk of a large tree.

Richard felt Andre's body lose substance and dissipate. Andre evaporated into mist and Richard was clutching nothing but air. He slammed into the tree alone, bounced off of it and hit the forest floor.

Richard got up slowly and shakily and looked around. Andre was gone. He turned his back to the tree and the only person he saw was Paula. She stood in the same spot gazing blankly into the night. Richard turned back to the tree and saw Andre standing right behind him.

Before Richard could move, Andre grabbed his arm.

"You'll find me much harder to handle than a few young punks," Andre told him.

Andre heaved and Richard went flying head over heels through the brush. Instead of hitting the forest floor again, Richard came to a complete stop, still airborne, and hovered five feet above the ground.

"I see you're familiar with a few of your abilities," Andre acknowledged. "I know you enjoy them. Inhuman strength and speed, all of your senses heightened, flight...immortality; these are mere droplets in an ocean of power that will be yours to command. All you have to do is say yes to the hunger. Start with Paula."

Andre dissolved into a cloud of mist that drifted off in every direction until it was out of sight.

Once again Richard and Paula were alone. She looked at him with dreamy eyes and repeated the only words she had spoken that evening.

"Take me."

Richard's legs moved involuntarily. Before he knew it, he was a step away from the lovely young woman. He forced himself to stop. The denial ignited his hunger and the pain that accompanied it. Breathtaking agony raged through him again, dropping him his knees.

No one would know he told himself. *If I just got one little taste, it would only be between me and the night.*

Richard would do anything to stop the pain, anything to quell the hunger. Undreamed of powers could be his. He could have anything he wanted, any woman he wanted. All he had to do was the one thing he already wanted to do more than anything he had ever wanted in his young life. All he had to do was sate his hunger.

The pain eased in response to his acceptance. The hunger diminished just enough for him to stand and take another step toward Paula.

What would he tell his mother? How would he stop the anguish his mother would feel when she found out that he had given in? Richard knew he would rather die than hurt his mother, just as she would die for him. This pain was nothing compared to how he would suffer if he broke his mother's heart by succumbing to the hunger.

Andre said himself that Richard had his mother's strength. Richard knew that Camillia would never give in to Andre, so neither would he.

Richard left Paula and raced into the night.

Paula stood alone in the shadows, oblivious to all of the nocturnal sounds. The crickets sang their haunting tune and small animals scurried across her bare feet. For long minutes she continued to stare into space. The moon had risen higher in the sky and the shadows on the forest floor had shifted yet Paula did not move.

A small rustling of leaves came from just beyond her eyesight. She looked to her left as a dark figure stepped from the darkness. The shadows slid away to reveal Andre. He strode over to the entranced young woman.

"I'm sorry, Paula," Andre began. "The boy's will is stronger than I anticipated. He's almost too much like his mother. I didn't think he'd be able to resist you. Oh, well," Andre sighed. "I can't let you go to waste.

Andre put his arms around her and bit into her jugular vein. He drank deeply, gorging himself on her lifeblood. When he was done, he stepped back and let Paula crumple to the ground. Her complexion had turned from a hazel brown to a sickly gray. The puncture wounds in her neck were larger now, but no blood flowed from them, for there was no blood left in her lifeless body.

The Cavalier and the Camaro were parked in a vacant lot. Eric, Major, and Tim stood outside their automobiles having a heated conversation.

"Believe me now?" asked Eric. "You saw those fangs *grow* out of his mouth. You saw the control he had over the girl. You saw the glare from that cross burn his eyes."

"I don't wanna believe it," Major said quietly. "But I guess I have to."

Tim remained silent.

"Now you know why you were kept in the dark," Eric continued. "Richard's mother and the others are trying to keep this quiet. They're looking for a cure, but I got news for you: there *is no cure*. While they're spinning their wheels looking for something that doesn't exist, Richard is killing a different woman every night."

"If he's a vampire," Major started, "why was he able to go to school every day? Vampires can't stand daylight."

"I've studied vampires for years," Eric told them, one of the few truths he had spoken. "Some of them can move about in the day but they choose not to. It's painful for them and their powers are much weaker."

"How did this happen?" Tim asked.

"Nineteen years ago a vampire knocked Camillia up. He was killed before he could kill or turn her. Instead of getting an abortion, Camillia had the baby. She hoped her dead fiancé had impregnated her before his murder.

"When Richard was younger he seemed normal. Just recently, though, the dark side of him started to show itself. It happened so gradually that no one really noticed until it was too late. Now, the change is complete."

"I can't believe this is happening," Major said.

Tim remained silent.

"There are a lot of things in this world people don't think are possible, that they refuse to believe because they don't want to believe. Almost everyone thinks vampires are a myth, but if you do enough research, you'll find that many myths and folktales are based on facts. Sometimes the particulars get distorted and sometimes they don't. After a while people just stop believing."

"So you're tryin' to say that werewolves, fairies and all that other shit is real?" Major questioned.

"I've never come across any of those other things," Eric said. "I hope I never do. When the general public hears 'fairy' they think tiny, cute people flying around granting wishes and shit. But if you read the original stories, you'll find that fairies can be some scary fuckers straight out of your worst nightmares. No thanks. Vampires are more than enough for me. I can't say those other things don't exist, though. Hell, for years I didn't think vampires existed, but as you saw tonight, they most definitely do."

"So what are we supposed to do?" Major asked.

"There's only one thing *to* do," Eric answered. "We have to do what his mother couldn't when she was pregnant with Richard."

"You mean kill him," Tim finally chimed in. "You're sayin' we should kill him."

"I'm saying we *have* to kill him," Eric corrected. "There's no cure for his sickness. The only thing we can do is stop him before he kills again and spreads this disease all over Chicago and beyond."

"How can we just kill him?" Major asked. "We grew up with him. He's like our brother."

"Not anymore," Eric said. "He's changed. He's not the man you two used to know. Richard's a monster now."

Major shook his head. "There's another way," he argued. "There's gotta be another way."

"Is there?" Tim asked hopefully. "Is there another way we can do this?"

"I'm sorry, fellas. I wish there were, but there isn't."

"Maybe you're right," Tim said. He spoke softly, his voice tired and defeated. Major looked at him with surprise. Tim's shoulders slumped as he continued. "I can't stand to see him like this." Tim's eyes grew moist. "I know deep down inside Richard can't stand to see himself like this. He was a good man. He was the best brother I've ever met."

Major asked the obvious question: "You're not serious, are you?"

"I think his soul's already with the Lord, Major. I think his body is just being used by that...that thing." Tim lowered his head. "We have to stop him."

Major turned to Eric. "No offense, man, but that's some white people shit. Black people don't fight monsters. We run from them motherfuckers."

"Major!" Tim admonished. "This ain't the time for silly-ass jokes, man."

"Who the hell's joking?" Major shot back.

"C'mon, Major," Eric said with mock sadness. "No one else who's willing to do it will be able to get close enough to do it. Richard won't let them. Are you in or not?"

Major looked at Tim for a long time before he hung his head and answered. "We don't have much choice, do we? God forgive me... I guess I'm in."

Eric fought to hold back a smile. It took a great effort but he was able to keep a serious expression on his face. "Ok," he began, "This is how we'll do it..."

Chapter 9

At six A.M. the next morning, Father Burns, Camillia, and detective Weller sat in a back room of St Anselm's Church. Each one had a cup of coffee and they all wore a grave expression.

"Have we lost him?" Weller asked.

"I pray we haven't," Burns answered.

"I don't think we have," Camillia added. "Not yet."

"What makes you think that?" Weller asked.

"It's just a feeling..."

"A good feeling," came a voice from the door.

All three turned to see Richard standing in the doorway. He looked exhausted and beaten. His clothes were soiled. His jacket was torn. Even though he looked as if he should have been covered with cuts and bruises, he did not have so much as a scratch. That realization made all of them uneasy, but the morning sun beaming down on him without him displaying any discomfort went a long way toward tempering their concern.

Camillia jumped up and ran to her son. She hugged him firmly and kissed him on the cheek. Weller and Burns both smiled and breathed deep sighs of relief. Camillia and Richard went to the table and sat down with the other two.

"Where were you?" Camillia asked.

"Hell, momma," he answered. "I met the old man last night."

"Andre," Father Burns said.

"He's not your father," Camillia stated. There was a feral timbre in her voice that gave them all pause.

Richard nodded. "He's not. But he wants us to be a family, anyway. He thinks we're supposed to build a nation of vampires."

This is the night I make you my queen.

Camillia remembered Andre's words as if he had spoken them to her the night before. The fear that seized her every time she recalled that phrase was a keen as it was nineteen years ago.

This is the night I make you immortal.

"Why us?" Camillia asked.

"It started with you, momma. You were special to him, somehow. He thought you'd make the perfect partner."

"What else happened?" Weller questioned. "I know he didn't exactly sit down with you and tell you this over a couple of beers."

"He tempted me with a girl from school. Paula. She didn't deserve this. The poor girl was already half-dead." Richard inhaled deeply, as if he was taking in her scent again. Hunger flashed in his eyes. "I won't lie, though. It was hard to turn her away."

"But you did," Camillia said.

"I did," Richard confirmed. "I told Andre that he'd never turn me. I attacked him and he handled me like I was a weak puppy. I'm no match for him but we gotta find a way to stop him. I got a feelin' that if he can't make you and me give in, he'll try to kill us."

A calm but fierce expression spread across Camillia's face. "That means we have to get to him first."

"But where do we start?" Weller asked. "I've been working with Keith Milton as well as the padre, here. We aren't any closer to finding him than we were when this began. Andre's not making the same mistakes he made the first time we dealt with him."

Father Burns turned to Richard as he answered Weller. "We start with you, Richard. You can find him."

"I don't know where he is," Richard said.

"You don't *think* you know," Burns corrected. "You may be surprised by what you actually do know. Like it or not, you two are connected.

"Your nightmares are the key. Every one you have is a clue. Each dream is likely something your subconscious knows about Andre. If you can recall anything from your nightmares you may discover that you already know where he can be found."

Richard thought for a moment, then his face lit up with recognition.

"A house!" he began. "I saw an old boarded-up house in my last nightmare. It looked like crap on the outside but the inside was, what's the word? It was immaculate, all kinds of expensive African art. The walls and furniture were all black and gray."

Father Burns stiffened. Weller's head snapped up. Camillia's eyes went wide.

Richard noticed the change. "Sounds familiar, huh? I went into the house and saw that freaky-lookin' white guy and a whole bunch of huge German Shepherds in the living room. Then I saw Andre."

Burns leaned forward. "Think hard, Richard. Do you know where the house was?"

"It was a few yards off a small road somewhere in the boonies. The house was surrounded by darkness. It might've been near where we squared off last night, but I was so zoned out I can't remember exactly where I was. From the time I went out the window last night until I got to the front door here a minute ago, everything except Paula and the fight is a blur. This is just a guess, but it might have been somewhere south of here."

Weller's eyes lit up. "Southeast."

Father Burns turned to him. "Why do you say that?"

"A hunch, something Milton made me think about."

Camillia's expression changed. She looked as if she was doing a math calculation in her head. Her eyes lit up.

"From the northwest side of the city to the southeast side *outside* the city!" she said. "You think he's doing something like the opposite of what he did back then."

"It's not iron clad, but it does make sense," Father Burns allowed.

"Either way, we have a little more to go on than we had," Weller said. "You guys wanna start searching now?"

"I think that would be best," Burns replied. "The earlier we start, the more daylight we'll have."

"Let's go," Camillia said resolutely.

Weller held up a finger. "Gimme a second. I need to make a phone call. I have a reporter to thank."

He went to the phone resting on a table in the corner of the room and dialed Milton's number.

The phone was picked up on the other end on the third ring. "Hello?" came an unfamiliar voice.

Weller frowned. "This doesn't sound like Keith."

"It's not," replied the uniformed officer standing in Milton's apartment. "This is the CPD. Who is this?"

"Oh no," Weller breathed. "This is Detective Weller, special investigations. Where's Milton?"

"We answered a disturbance call at this address from a downstairs neighbor," the police officer explained. He looked across the room at the dead body sprawled in the middle of the floor in a pool of blood.

Milton's body was a mess of deep cuts and violent bruises. His neck was twisted at a sickening angle.

"Keith Milton's dead. You may want to talk to the homicide detective over here, sir. Looks like someone took him out last night. It's pretty messy."

That afternoon, Eric sat on the front porch of the Williams home tapping his foot impatiently and checking his watch over and over.

"Damn, those guys are slow," he said to himself. He walked out to the sidewalk and looked up and down the street. When he returned to the porch, Tim and Major came out of the house. "Everything ready?" he asked. "Did you set everything up to my specs?"

"Yeah, everything's set up," Tim grunted. "I still don't like the idea of breakin' into Rich's crib like this."

Eric frowned. "What, then? Would you rather take him on man to man? He'd tear us apart."

"You sure this is gonna work?" Major asked.

"I've done it before," Eric lied. "It's never failed. All we have to do is stick around and watch the house."

"Damn," Tim said, "I hate this. I'm gonna hate myself for a long time."

"It had to be done," Eric insisted.

Major rubbed his face with both hands nervously. "That doesn't make it hurt any less."

"You're right," Eric said with fake sympathy. "But think about all of the lives we're saving. It's like you said, Tim, Richard's soul died a long time ago."

Major and Tim remained silent.

"Let's get out of here," Eric suggested.

Just then two police cars pulled up to the front of the house. The three men turned to run through the back yard but stopped short. Through the chain-link fencing on the perimeter of yard, they saw two more police cars pull up in the alley.

"Oh shit!" Tim said.

The policemen got out of their cars with pistols and shotguns cocked and ready. One officer pulled shouted: "On your knees! Hands on your head!"

More police cars, sirens screaming, came on the scene.

The three men did as they were told. It seemed as if all of Camillia's neighbors either came out of their homes or looked out of their windows.

"This is embarrassin'," Major said.

"Chance we had to take," Eric explained. "We had to do this in the daytime. There was no other way."

He looked around and silently wondered which nosey-ass neighbor called the police.

The three men went through the whole process. The police forced them to the ground and put a knee on the back of their necks. All three were handcuffed and tossed inside three different police cars.

Later that afternoon, after a fruitless search of several areas in the southeastern outskirts of the city, detective Weller's and Father Burns' cars came to a stop in front of the Williams home. Richard and his mother got out of Weller's car and headed to the front door.

"I have some church business to attend to," Father Burns said through his window. "I'll be back well before sundown."

"I have to look talk to homicide about Keith," Weller added. "If you need me, you've got my pager number."

"Alright," Camillia called.

She and her son went to the house. When they got to the porch the next-door neighbor spoke to them through the window.

"Camillia," called the elderly woman.

"Yes Gladys?" Camillia answered.

"Some men broke into your house early this morning."

Camillia and Richard grew very concerned. "Who were they?" asked Richard.

"Two of them were friends of yours," Gladys said to Richard. "It was Tim and Major. I don't know who the third man was. He looked scary, though. He was tall, skinny, white as a sheet. I knew you two weren't home so I called the police."

"Thanks, Gladys," Camillia said. "We'll find out what's going on." Camillia and Richard went into the house and locked the door. Camillia turned to her son. "Sometimes it's good to have nosey neighbors."

"Why would they break in here?" Richard asked.

"They're worried about you, Richard. They know something is going on but they don't know what. They've been asking me questions but I haven't given them any answers. I guess they tried to get answers on their own. But what were they doing with that weird guy?"

Richard shrugged. "I'll call the cops and find out where they've been taken. We can get them out and ask."

"We can find out where they are," Camillia agreed. "But we should leave them there. Let their parents get them out. I'll take out a restraining order on them, too.

Richard raised his eyebrows. "A restraining order, momma? That's a little drastic, isn't it?"

"Not at all," Camillia countered. "If they get too involved they might get hurt. And they're working that man. Who knows what lies he's telling them? We need to keep them away from us until this is over."

"You're right," Richard said, "If they're Andre's radar..." he could not bring himself to finish the sentence.

Camillia and Richard called the police station and found out where Tim and Major were being held. They told the officers that the young men were playing a practical joke.

They informed the police that they were not going to press charges on Tim and Major, but they would appreciate it if they kept the young men in custody for a day to teach them a lesson. They knew Camillia through detective Weller and decided to go along with her.

"Now that all that's taken care of," Richard said to his mother, "I'm gonna go take a nap. Wake me up when Father Burns gets here."

"You know I will," Camillia assured him.

Richard went up the stairs and into his room. He took off his jacket but was too tired to bother with the rest of his clothes. He sat down on the bed and reflected on the last few days, trying to process all that had happened. The effort only served to exhaust him further so he lay back across the bed.

A loud click sounded from beneath the bed and a sharp pain tore through Richard's upper abdomen. The blow took his breath away, but his mind flooded with a scream of agony and rage. He looked down at his torso to see a large wooden spike protruding from his stomach.

A deafening roar exploded from him when he tore himself away from the bed. He was roaring like a crazed animal when his mother burst into the room.

"RICHARD!" Camillia cried

Her son was raging around the room. He punched several holes in the wall. A wild kick reduced his nightstand to splinters. Camillia knew better than to approach him in this wild state.

Richard held the gaping wound in his stomach with one hand and with the other he flipped the bed over to reveal a small spring-loaded device beneath his bed. He stormed over to his chest-of-drawers and sent it flying across the room.

"Richard, *please!*" Camillia begged as she took a cautious step toward her son.

He looked up at her and she saw the pain and fury in his eyes. Her heart began to beat faster and she suddenly became very afraid of him. But he was still her son. She went to him when he calmed down a bit and leaned against the wall, growling softly like an injured animal.

"C'mon, baby," she said in her most comforting voice, "I'll get you to a hospital." She reached out and gently touched his shoulder.

Richard shoved her away, baring his fangs in a warning snarl. Camillia stumbled back and fell heavily to the floor. She looked up at her son with pleading eyes.

"God, no..." Camillia swore. "Fight it, baby. Fight it!"

Richard gave one final growl and then leapt through the closed window, tearing a large portion of the wall away as well. Camillia ran to the ruined wall and peered through the hole.

Her son was gone.

Detective Weller was motoring north on the Dan Ryan expressway when his pager buzzed. He checked the number and saw it was Camillia's. He pulled over to the shoulder, and called her back on his car phone.

"Hello?" Camillia's voice was wild and breathless.

"Camillia?" Weller asked. "What's wrong?"

"Our time's up!" Camillia cried. "Richard's lost control."

"What the hell happened?"

"His bed was rigged with some kind of contraption. A spike was set to shoot through the bottom of his mattress and through him. The pain set him off."

"Who the hell –"

"Major and Tim!" Camillia answered the question before Weller could finish asking it. "They were arrested while we were out searching for Andre. One of our neighbors saw them breaking into our house. She said a scary looking man was with them. She described him as tall, skinny and as white a sheet."

Weller rubbed his face with his free hand in exasperation. "That son of a bitch," he sighed. "The spike, was it wooden?"

"No," Camillia answered. "It looked like it was made of wood, but I checked it out. It's some kind of synthetic material, Formica or something."

Weller thought for a moment. "With a setup like that, there's no guarantee the spike would find the heart. A trap with that much risk of failure would've been loaded with a silver spike, not a wooden one, to poison him for maximum damage in case it missed the heart."

Camillia grew uneasy listening to Weller talk about the best way to kill her son, but she had to face the reality of their situation, as grim as it was.

"So...what are you saying?"

"Even if it went through his heart," Weller realized, "it would've hurt like hell but that's it. That trap wasn't rigged to kill him. It was only supposed to piss him off."

"Well it damn sure worked," Camillia said. "He left the house and I don't know where he went. He's going to hurt someone. I could see it in his eyes."

"Does he know Major and Tim did it?" Weller asked.

"He has to. He knows they broke into the house."

"Does he know where they're being held?"

"Yes. We called the police station and found out."

"I'm pretty sure he'll try to find his home boys and find out why they tried to kill him."

"You're right," Camillia agreed. "Richard's on a rampage. We've go to get to that station before he does."

"No chance of that, Camillia. But we can warn them. Where are they being held?"

"They're at the hundred-and-eleventh street station."

"That's my next call, then. I'm on my way there. See if you can get in touch with Father Burns and tell him to come get you. If you can't reach him, go to the nearest church and stay there. It'll be dark before long. If Andre tries to come after you, you'll be safe in a church."

"Good luck, detective," Camillia said.

"Thanks, Camillia. I'm gonna need it!"

Weller hung up the phone, put his light on the roof of the car and sped off down the expressway.

Camillia hung up the phone and dialed Father Burns' number. She let the phone ring seven times before she hung it up. She went through a drawer under one of the kitchen counters and brought out a pencil and a piece of paper. She wrote a note for Father Burns just in case he was on his way over to let him know that she was going to catch the bus to St. Anselm's church. The note also told him that he should go to the police station on one hundred and eleventh street.

It did not matter to her if Andre found the note. He would find her no matter where she went, and she would be safely inside a church before sundown.

Major, Tim and Eric sat quietly in a holding cell at the police station.

"You sure you guys don't want to call home?" an officer asked them through the bars.

"Positive," Major and Tim said at the same time.

"No home to call," Eric added.

The officer shrugged and walked away.

Eric looked at Tim and Major. "Call home? How the hell are you two supposed to tell your folks that you got arrested for breakin' into your best friend's house and riggin' his bed to kill 'em because he's a vampire?"

"Yeah," Tim agreed, shaking his head.

"So what do you fellas think?" Major asked. "You think it worked? Do you think Richard is...?"

Tin nodded. "Major's right. We have to pierce the heart right? We don't know if we missed or not."

"It didn't have to pierce the heart," Eric said with that false sadness once again. "That bullshit is just that: novel and movie bullshit. Wood and silver are like poison to those things. The heart would be quicker, but a wooden bolt that size anywhere in his torso will be fatal. " The lies came so easy it was almost laughable. "I'm sure the trap did its job."

The trap did indeed do its job. At that very moment, Richard was entering the police station. He walked to the front desk and the female officer seated there. She looked up at him with a look of concern and a little fear. He looked terrible. The front of his shirt was crusted over with drying blood. Every part of his body was haggard except his eyes, which were bright with hatred.

The officer stood and approached him cautiously. "You're hurt. Do you need an ambulance?"

"Oh, you mean for this?" Richard asked with a mirthless smile, indicating the bloody mess of his T-shirt. "No, I'm alright. It's just a scratch. If it's not too much trouble, ma'am, may I talk to the three gentlemen that were brought in earlier this afternoon. The ones who broke into a house over in the South Shore area."

His tone was so incongruent with his appearance that the officer did a double take.

"Maybe we should get somebody to look at that wound first," she suggested.

Richard's smile disappeared. He gazed deeply into the woman's eyes. "Maybe you should do as I ask."

A faraway look shrouded her face. "Maybe I should do as you ask," she agreed.

One of the many phones in the station rang. A male police officer answered. "Hundred and eleventh street station," he greeted.

The voice on the other end of the phone was urgent:

"Look, this is detective Weller, special investigations. A kid might come through there. You won't have any trouble spotting him. He'll look like he's hurt real bad. If he wants to go in the back, don't let him. Stall him if you have to, but whatever you do, don't piss him off."

"Is he dangerous?" the officer asked.

"No," Weller lied. He knew that if the police thought Richard was dangerous they would respond aggressively. If it came to that, he did not know whether Richard or the police would be in the most trouble.

"He's valuable to us. He has some information that we need for a big-time bust. He's a little excitable, though. If you piss him off he'll walk and we'll be up a creek. Just humor him until I get there."

"You got it, detective." The officer hung up the phone and scoffed. "Humor, my ass," he mumbled to himself. "If he gets out of line we'll straighten him out the way we do everyone else..."

Chapter 10

The police officer led Richard to the hallway that would take them to the holding cells. When they stepped into the hall a male officer jogged up from behind and stopped them.

"Hey kid," the officer called. "Come with me."

"For what?" Richard asked.

"I've been told that you should wait for detective Weller to get here. If you'll just come back to the front with me..."

"I don't think so," Richard said.

If there was one thing the officer could not stand, it was non-compliance. He remembered Weller telling him to be nice, however, so he checked his temper and tried to reason with the younger man.

"C'mon, fella," he said. "It's not that long a wait."

He put his hand on Richard's shoulder. That was a mistake. Weller told him not to piss the young man off but the officer did not know the young man would be pissed off so easily. He saw Richard's hand flashing in his direction and the next thing he felt was flight.

Richard propelled him across the room head over heels like a ragdoll. The unfortunate man crashed into a wall, rebounded to the floor, and lay still. Two policemen rushed Richard with their nightsticks drawn.

"Protect me," Richard commanded the entranced policewoman beside him.

She pulled out her gun and took aim. A look of shocked surprise registered on the approaching officers' faces. They had just enough time to throw up their hands when she fired two shots into each man. Other officers in the station drew their guns and ordered the woman to drop hers. She answered by firing two more shots before a hail of bullets from the other officers cut her down.

Richard caught several bullets as he continued down the hallway. The blasts sent him reeling and stumbling to the floor.

"What the hell's goin' on out there?" Major asked.

"Sounds like all hell's broken loose," Tim added.

Eric smiled. "It has," he said. "If everything's going as planned, your buddy will be back here in a few seconds."

"What are talkin' about?" Tim asked suspiciously.

"What plan?" Major questioned.

That maniacal smile spread wider across Eric's insipid face. "The master's plan. Our trap wasn't set to kill Richard. The spike I gave you wasn't even real wood. But you better believe he's mad as hell, and he knows by now that you two did it. He's coming for you now!"

Tim grabbed the frail, pale man by the collar and shouted, "What's goin' on here? Answer me!"

The gaunt misfit showed surprising strength. He was only a couple of inches taller than Tim and at least sixty pounds lighter yet he snatched Tim's hands away with ease and tossed him to the other side of the cell. Tim hit the wall and fell to the floor, stunned.

Eric turned to Major. "What about you, shorty?" he challenged. "You want some?" Major backed quietly away from the grinning lunatic.

Seven officers slowly walked toward the still bodies of Richard and the fallen policewoman. The rest of the police stood well back. They all had their guns drawn and ready. One of them checked the woman for a pulse and felt nothing. He indicated to the others that she was dead. He then reached over to Richard.

Richard's eyes opened to reveal two glowing red spheres. The officer stopped in his tracks. Richard did not even give the man a chance to cry out. His right hand knifed up to the officer's neck and his left went for the officer's gun. Richard flung the policeman into the six men directly behind him.

Three of the men went down and the remaining three opened fire. Richard twitched and shuddered as the bullets struck him but he rose to his feet anyway. The police could believe not believe it was happening. Richard lifted his appropriated gun and fired at the officers until all three men lay still on the floor.

The other officers in the station opened fire on Richard. He dropped his gun, let out an evil roar and became a whirlwind of violence. He was a blur of claws and teeth as he hurled himself into the crowd of shocked police officers. His inhuman speed did not allow the officers to get a clear look at their target. A few lucky shots found various parts of Richard's body but the vast majority of them missed. In their panicked shooting spree, several stray bullets struck fellow officers.

The sound of gunshots mingled with agonized screams and unholy roars. Blood and bodies flew in every direction. Snapping bones added to the cacophony and created a nightmarish melody of destruction.

The officers left standing watched in horror as their comrades were cut down. It finally registered that their bullets were doing them no good. Someone yelled over the hellish din: "Fall Back! Fall Back!"

Those who were able turned and fled the station through the nearest exit. Soon, most of the officers were gone, either having fled or died. Richard stood in the middle of the station to survey his handiwork. The station floor was littered with ammunition shells, shattered glass, destroyed furniture and ruined bodies.

Some of the people on the floor crawled slowly to the exit. The few surviving injured that still could walk were dragging or carrying out the survivors that could not. Richard let them leave.

Gore dripped from his hands and was splattered all over his clothes. The heady scent of blood filled his nostrils and stoked his appetite yet he had not tasted one drop of his victims' blood. Even in his frenzy his desire was not to feed but to destroy. Besides, no one there was worthy of being his first. As much as his hunger throbbed in the core of his being, he wanted his first taste of living blood to be special. He knew he would have to give in to the bloodlust sooner rather than later, but he was determined to hold out just a bit longer.

After a few moments the entire station was empty except for the prisoners in the back and the corpses left in the wake of Richard's onslaught. The outside of the station was alive with the sound of sirens and voices but the inside was deathly silent save for ringing telephones.

"It stopped," Eric noted with a disturbing chuckle. He was pressed against the bars as if trying to squeeze through them. "It's quiet out there, now. You know what that means?"

Tim and Major glared at him.

Eric's grin turned into a bone-chilling laugh. "That means he's on his way."

Major and Tim sat on a bench on the opposite side of the cell. Major leaned forward. "We know what Richard is. What kind of monster are *you*?"

Eric turned toward Major. His disturbingly idiotic grin was replaced by a serious, almost wistful expression. "I'm not a monster. Not yet, anyway. But I struck a deal with Rich's old man. I help him push Rich over the edge and the old man makes me like them."

Tim straightened up. "You told us the vampire that got Ms. Williams pregnant was killed."

Eric waved a long, bony hand in dismissal. "Ha...I told you two a lot of shit to get you to help me pull off this scheme. It was easy, all we had to do was piss Rich off."

Tim and Major looked at each other in confusion. Eric caught the shared look and the grin returned.

"That's right, boys" he explained. "I was never trying to kill the kid. The plan was always to get him good and mad, and we did it. Now I'll get to become a vampire. You guys wouldn't believe the powers these sons of bitches have. Just think, the power to fly, to have any woman you want. These guys can even turn into smoke. Fuckin' *smoke*, man! You ever hear of anything like that?"

"Damn," Major said. "You're one sick motherfucker."

"Yeah," Tim agreed. "You need serious help."

"Oh, you two already gave me all the help I needed. When all this is over I'll kill you quickly if Rich doesn't beat me to it."

Eric laughed then, with that madman's laugh of his.

"They gave you too much help."

Eric looked around to see Richard standing just outside the cell. Tim and Major looked stunned when they saw their friend. His clothes were riddled with bullet-holes and his face had a number of holes in it as well. The big bloody spot on his shirt was frightening proof that their trap had been sprung.

The look in Richard's shimmering red eyes as he glared at his two best friends caused a chill to run through both of them. The fury in his visage was tinged with contempt, betrayal, and hunger in equal parts.

"Rich!" Eric exclaimed delightedly. "I thought you'd never make it!"

"Oh, I was gonna make it," Richard assured. "I have a few debts that need to be paid."

Eric stepped closer to the bars, a gleeful rictus stretching from ear to ear. "Before you start tearing heads off, Rich, why don't you get me outta here?"

"Good idea," Richard said with a toothy grin. He reached into the cell with one arm and grabbed the misfit's collar. Richard gave a quick, strong yank that brought Eric face first into the bars with a loud clang.

"Hey!" Eric yelled, spitting blood and several teeth as he struggled in vain to free himself from Richard's grasp. "What the fuck are you doing?"

"I'm doing what you suggested," Richard explained. The evil grin morphed into a bestial snarl. "I'm tearing heads off." He put his other hand through the bars in order to grip Eric's face with both hands. "And I'm starting with yours."

"You can't!" the misfit screamed. "Me and your old man made a deal!" Eric pushed against the bars with all of his might in a fruitless attempt to escape Richard's vice-like grip.

Richard's face darkened. The red gleam in his eyes sharpened. "Your deal is with Andre. He is *not* my Father."

Richard twisted Eric's head around to an impossible degree. The sickly sound of crunching bones and snapping cartilage echoed in the cell.

Eric's head was turned around so far that, even though his back was to the other two men in the cell, his face pointed in their direction. When Richard stopped twisting, Eric stared at Major and Tim with sightless eyes and a pained expression frozen onto his face. Richard released him and let the body drop to the floor.

The prisoners in the adjacent cells cried out in frightened amazement. Tim and Major looked at Richard with abject terror in their eyes. Richard looked at his two best friends and smiled.

"Whatup fellas?" he asked.

"You tell us," Tim said quietly.

"What the hell's happened to you, Rich?" Major asked.

"What happened?" Richard replied. "This happened."

He lifted his bloody T-shirt to reveal the large puncture wound in his stomach. It was crusted over with dark dried blood. There were countless small bullet holes in his body from the scuffle with the police a few minutes earlier. A few of the wounds were still bleeding. Most of them had already started to heal.

"Why?" Richard asked with sincere disappointment. "We were homies. We grew up together. You see all this death tonight? It's because of you two."

"Look at you, man," Tim began. "What are you?"

"You've killed people before tonight," Major accused. "Those gangsters you fought the other night were all found dead. We saw you with Paula last night. Now, she's missing. We saw you when you were about to, about to –"

"Bite her?" Richard finished. "That was you hiding in the bushes out at Wolf Lake." He pointed at Eric's corpse. "That lousy son of a bitch deserved to die. Those cops out there: self-defense. The urge to kill is still in me, though. I've been fighting it but it's harder than you can imagine.

"What hurts more than anything else is you two turning on me. I thought I could always count on you two brothers. Now I know I can't." The look of sadness gave way to one of rage. "You tried to kill me."

Richard grabbed the bars and pulled. Tim and Major cringed at the screech of the metal bars against the stone floor. The floor and ceiling at the ends of the bars began to crack and shudder. The bars gave way and were pulled from the entrance of the cell. Richard dropped the bars to the floor and stepped slowly into the cell.

"C'mon," Major pleaded. "Think about what you're doing."

"I've been thinking about this since your trap punched a hole me," Richard growled. He turned his attention to Tim. "I expect something like this from Major. He's been full of shit his whole life. It wouldn't take much for him to turn on a brother. But you..." he approached Tim slowly as his two friends backed away. "I never thought you'd let anything come between us."

"This ain't just anything," Tim shot back.

Richard nodded in agreement. "You're right, Tim. This is the end."

Major and Tim made a break for it. They tried to dart around Richard to get out of the cell. He reached out with blinding speed and grabbed Tim by the neck, snatched the larger man off his feet, and slammed him against the cell wall. Tim's feet dangled two feet above the floor.

Major ran a few more steps, resigned to leave his two best friends, but he could not. It took all of his courage to come back. He ran to Richard and wrapped one arm around his friend's neck, squeezing with all of his strength. With his other hand, he clutched at the arm that holding Tim in the air.

"Let 'em go," Major grunted as he struggled uselessly.

"I'll get to you in a second, Mage." Richard reached behind him with his free arm and, with a flick of his wrist, sent Major flying out of the cell. Major crashed into the cell bars across the corridor and slid to a sitting position on the floor. The prisoners in that cell backed away from the bars and called for help.

"God help you," Tim said to his oldest friend.

"It's too late for Him to help me," Richard said. He bared his fangs and Tim watched as Richard's canine teeth, already inhumanly long, curved and sharp, extended another half inch. "And it's too late for Him to help you."

"No, it's not!" someone shouted from outside the cell.

Richard turned to see detective Weller and Father Burns standing side by side. Weller held a small crossbow in his hand that was loaded with a sharpened wooden stake. Father Burns held his silver staff with the golden-wreathed crucifix. Richard quickly shaded his eyes with his free hand and turned away from the blessed talisman to face Tim.

"It's not too late for either of you," Father Burns said.

"Just put Tim down," Weller bade. "I promise we'll work this out."

"I'm surprised your buddies let you two old bastards through, Weller. Don't you know it's dangerous in here?"

Weller shrugged one shoulder. "I've been working here for twenty five years. I know a couple of secret ways in and out."

"Use them, then, and get back out of here, both of you," Richard warned without looking at them. "I'm not about to give you a chance to use that wooden stake. If you shoot it Tim's catching it."

"We won't use it," Weller promised. "Not if you put the kid down. But if you kill him, I swear to God I will use it."

"Don't surrender to the anger," Burns implored. "Anger fuels the hunger. It'll push you over the edge."

"Too late, padre," Richard returned. He refrained from looking in the direction of the crucifix. "These three motherfuckers tried to kill me. One's already dealt with and I'm not leaving here until the other two are done."

Weller reached slowly into his pocket and pulled out a small crucifix. He handed the cross to Major and motioned in Richard's direction. Major rose to his feet eased toward Richard and Tim as quietly as he could.

"If you kill Tim, you won't leave here alive, Richard," Burns vowed. "We know it's not too late for you, but you have to be strong. Think of your mother, Richard. You have her strength within you. Use it. Be strong for her."

"Leave my mother out of this!" Richard growled. He was still looking down and away from the rest of them. His voice dropped to a calm tone. "Major, if you take one more step I'll snap Tim's neck like a pencil."

Major froze. His eyes met Tim's. Major looked at the cross in his hand, looked back at Tim and nodded. Major tossed the cross across the cell. Tim plucked it out of the air and pressed it against Richard's cheek.

A sizzling sound echoed through the corridor. Smoke rose from Richard's face and the cross. Richard unleashed a high-pitched, feral howl and dropped Tim in order to clutch at his burned cheek. Tim hit the floor running. Richard moved his hand for an instant and the men caught a glimpse of a brand on the side of his face in the shape of the crucifix.

Richard gave them all one final glare. His eyes had turned into pits of shadow. His lips pulled back to reveal a mouth full of pointed teeth jutting from black gums. His horrific image wavered in the others' vision just before he evaporated into mist. A second later the mist itself faded from view. The four men left in the cell looked at each other in stunned surprise.

Father Burns was the first to speak. "We don't have much time. His rage is feeding his power and hunger. The bloodlust will become too strong to resist. We have to destroy Andre before Richard turns completely."

"You mean he hasn't already?" Major asked.

"No," Father Burns answered. "If he had, it would've been evident in his face."

"It looked pretty evident to me," Tim noted.

"When you burned him with the cross," Burns explained, "the true beast showed itself. If Richard had crossed over he would've looked a lot worse."

"One whole helluva lot worse," Weller added. He remembered Andre's face when they confronted him all those years ago. The thought made him shudder.

"Who is Andre?" Tim asked, having a pretty good idea of the answer.

"Richard's maker," Burns confirmed. "He seduced Camillia while she was pregnant...and managed to infect Richard while he was still in the womb. We hoped and prayed we destroyed him years ago. Andre is the key to Richard's sickness. If we can destroy Andre before Richard crosses over, Richard will revert to human form."

"What do we do?" Tim asked the two older men.

"Yeah," Major said. "How do we find Andre?"

"All we have to go on," Weller said, "is a dream Richard had about an old boarded up house surrounded by darkness. That could be anywhere in this blasted city."

Recognition sparked in Major and Tim's eyes. "That sounds like the house me and Major saw the other day!"

"What else did he say about the house?" Major asked. "Did he say anything about the lawn being overgrown? Was the walkway hidden by all the grass and weeds?"

"I'll be damned," Weller said. "That's exactly how Richard described it."

"Take us there!" Father Burns commanded.

"It's night-time," Tim reminded them. "By the time we get there, Andre will probably be out hunting."

"Then we'll wait for him to return," Father Burns said.

Weller shook his head. "We can't wait until morning, not if we want to save Richard. I don't think he'll go another night without giving in to the hunger."

"You two don't have to come," Burns offered. "I don't have to tell how dangerous it will be."

"Richard is like our brother," Tim said in a near whisper. "I'll help any way I can."

"Yeah," Major agreed. "Rich said I was full of shit, that he wasn't surprised I turned on him. It'll shock the shit out him when he finds out that I helped save him. Excuse my French, Father."

"You two are good friends," Burns commended. "I would insist that you stay away, but honestly, we all the help we can get. The detective and I can try to warn you of the danger but words can't describe what we will likely face tonight. "

Tim and Major glanced at one another as the priest went on.

"You have to be strong. You must have faith in yourself. Most importantly, you must have faith in the Lord. Be honest with yourselves, gentlemen. If you doubt your faith, you will be effectively powerless against Andre. If you don't believe, it will be much safer for all of us if you did not come."

"I'm comin'," Tim pledged.

Major looked at his friend for a moment and then looked at the priest. "I'm a Baptist. I may not act like all the time, and I don't go to church like I should, but I believe in God. I believe Jesus Christ died for our sins," he touched the crucifix hanging at his chest. "But I'm worried about Tim. He's Muslim, and not real devout either. "

Tim glared defiantly at each of the men in turn, but he did not deny Major's statement.

"Do you believe in Allah?" Father Burns challenged. "If you can look into your heart and know that you believe, you will have His protection."

Tim nodded. "I do," he assured. "And I'm comin'."

"Like I said, then," Major repeated, "Rich thinks I'm full of...it. I gonna prove him a liar."

"Let's go, then," Weller said. "SWAT is gearing up to crash the joint. If the CPD catches us in here, they're not letting us go until we answer a million questions."

Chapter 11

It was early evening when Camillia knelt at a pew in the front row of St. Anselm's Catholic Church and prayed as hard as she had in her life. The church was almost empty except for her and two other people who were also kneeling and praying in the rear pews.

The sound of the outside double-doors of the vestibule opening echoed in the large space. Camillia felt a cool breeze blow through the nave. She looked over her shoulder to see a female police officer entering the church and making her way toward the altar. Camillia went back to her praying. The policewoman walked up behind Camillia and tapped her on the shoulder.

Camillia looked up quickly, startled. "Yes?" she asked.

"Are you Camillia Williams?" the officer questioned.

"Why?"

"Detective Weller sent me here to pick you up. He told me to tell you that your problem has been solved. He wouldn't tell me what the problem was, just that it was none of my darned business." The officer grinned. "He used another d-word, but I won't say that in a church.

Camillia smiled. "Sounds like Weller."

"He told me to bring you home. Him, Father Burns, your son and your son's friends are waiting."

Camillia could not have removed the smile from her face if she tried. She breathed a sigh of relief and quietly thanked God. The officer led her outside to the patrol car. Fifteen minutes later, they came to a stop outside of Camillia's house.

Camillia jumped out of the car and hurried to the front door. When she made it to the sidewalk, however, she pulled to a stop. She looked around and realized what it was. None of the cars she expected to see were there. Weller's Cutlass Ciera, Tim's Cavalier and Father Burns' station wagon were all missing.

"Where are all the cars?" she asked the officer.

Camillia turned, but not in time. She caught a flash of the officer's nightstick just before she heard a sharp crack and felt a bright burst of pain on the side of the head.

Everything was going dark, but Camillia acted on pure adrenaline. She stumbled in her fight to keep her balance against the spinning landscape. In her dizziness, she saw her attacker produce a set of handcuffs and step forward.

Camillia's survival instincts kicked in. She swung a closed fist wildly in the general direction of the officer's head. The officer thought Camillia was about to topple over, so she was taken completely by surprise and reacted too slowly. The desperate punch caught her right at the base of the chin and dropped her to one knee.

Still struggling to stay on her feet, Camillia snatched the handcuffs away from the policewoman. She thought briefly about trying to take the gun or the nightstick, but cuffs were closer. In her unsteady condition, she knew she could not handle the stick and would be just as likely to shoot herself with gun.

Camillia ran to her door on unsteady legs as the pain and dizziness grew in intensity. She managed to unlock the door stumble into the house, and kick the door closed again. She was able to crawl up the foyer stairs while darkness closed in around her vision.

The first thing she saw upon awakening was the woman officer standing near an open window. Either there was no screen or it had been removed. A moment later Camillia realized that she was in her darkened bedroom lying on her bed, handcuffed to her headboard. A safety pin had been jammed into the cuffs' keyhole and broken off. Camillia did not eve remember doing it.

Careful not to move too fast with her head still throbbing, she rose tiredly to her feet and looked around the room. The only light came from the faint green glow of her digital alarm clock, but it was enough for her to see.

"Where is Andre?" Camillia asked calmly.

Andre slipped into view on the other side of her bedroom window. The home's basement extended about four feet above ground level, which elevated the sill of the first floor windows to roughly seven feet above the ground. Andre was about two inches shy of six feet tall. For her to see his head and shoulders above the sill of her first floor bedroom window, he had to be standing on a ladder or floating in the air.

Camillia knew he was not on a ladder.

Her bedroom window faced the home next door, and at night, when the backyard lights and lights within the home were turned off, the area between her and her neighbor's homes was immersed in deep shadow. If her nosey neighbor had been watching through a slit in the blinds, as she was wont to do from time to time, she was either too afraid to scream or had fainted.

Camillia noticed that Andre looked exactly as he had nineteen years ago. There was no sign of aging anywhere on his face. He still had the short-cut hair, the calm expression on his handsome face, and those deep, dark brown eyes.

He wore a black trench coat buttoned to the top with the collar turned up. Camillia guessed what else he was wearing. If his fashion sense was the same, he was wearing black slacks and well-shined black Stacy Adams dress shoes.

Andre smiled that beguiling smile of his. "The years have been very kind to you, Camillia. Those mahogany eyes still captivate me. You're as beautiful as ever."

Camillia looked at him with cold contempt. "You look the same. The years haven't done a damn thing to you."

"That was very clever," he noted, looking down at the cuffs. "You made sure my attendant couldn't get you out of your home. You've been educating yourself about my kind. That's good. It'll shorten your learning curve when you become my queen."

Camillia's baleful glare did not waiver.

"I didn't expect you to be happy to see me," Andre admitted. "I know what you've been through recently."

"I'm sure you do. You're the cause of everything I've been through recently."

"Let me make it up to you," Andre offered. "Join us."

"Who the hell is 'us'?"

"Your son and me."

"Richard won't join you. He's got too much of me in him. You want to do something for me, Andre? All you can do for me is die."

Andre laughed. "That's the one thing I *can't* do, sweetheart. Besides, I know you don't mean that. You feel the same way you felt all those years ago."

"I do mean that. What I felt for you was never real and you know it. You had me under a spell."

"That's not true," Andre insisted, sounding wounded by the accusation. "I was everything you wanted and then some. You were young. I'll give you that. You hadn't learned to tell the difference between what you wanted and what you needed. Deep inside you knew you didn't need me...but you *wanted* me. I presented you with a choice and you chose me."

"You're a murderer and a liar. The only natural feeling I could ever have for you is disgust."

Andre sneered. "What feeling did you have for Richard senior?" Surprise registered on Camillia's face. "Yes, my love. I knew about your fiancé. What feeling did you have for him?"

"What do you know about him?" Camillia demanded.

"I know that he was the only thing standing between me and your devotion. I know that he died with your name on his lips."

"You monster!" Camillia snapped.

"Did you think we met by mere chance, you and I? I leave nothing to chance. I knew everything about you long before I made my presence known to you at that movie theater. That man was not your destiny. I am your destiny. Look at me and tell me I'm wrong."

Andre looked at her with those familiar, haunting and mesmeric eyes. A far-away expression came over Camillia's face. Andre smiled.

"You *are* my destiny," Camillia breathed.

"Yes," Andre said. "With you and Richard by my side, I can fulfill my own destiny. We can bring about the culling. Invite me into your home, my love, so that I can consummate our union properly."

"What difference does it make if I invite you in or not?" Camillia asked. "You have the power to make me do whatever you want."

"It doesn't work like that," Andre replied. "You must invite me into your home, just as you must invite me into your life. If I compel you to accept my gift, you'll only be a thrall...a slave. I don't want that for you. I don't want that for us. Join me freely and you can rule by my side as the mother of evolution."

Camillia smiled. "That has a nice ring to it."

She stepped seductively to the window, one arm trailing behind her where it was cuffed to the headboard, and leaned out of the open window invitingly. Andre drifted higher and then closer to Camillia. He put his arms around her and kissed her cheek. He bared those animal-like fangs and began to lower his head to her neck.

And then his eyes all but bulged out of their sockets.

Intense pain flared through his entire body and smoke rose from his stomach. He looked down with painful surprise to see Camillia's free hand pressing a small silver crucifix into his midsection.

Andre cried out like an injured animal and shot backward. He somersaulted and landed on his knees in the grass between houses. When he looked up at Camillia, he looked nothing like he had before.

His deep, dark brown eyes were now gleaming orbs that glowed red in the shadows. His eyebrows had sprouted into a thick mess of black, wiry bristles that joined at the bridge of his nose to form one long streak across his forehead. The smooth brown skin that once covered his face became hideously wrinkled with a sickly gray pallor.

Andre's mouth and nose were fused into a stunted canine snout. His ears had grown larger and changed into shape vaguely human and vaguely bat-like. Every tooth in his mouth was long and pointed. There seemed to be far too many yellowish fangs for the twisted mouth.

Camillia looked down at him with contempt and loathing. "You did it once but you'll never entrance me again you fucking beast. I know what you are and I know how to resist you. You'll never have me or Richard."

"WHORE!" Andre roared, turning his glare to the ground to avoid seeing the hated cross. His voice was unnaturally loud and deep. It was little more than a bass rumble that was barely understandable. "I already own Richard! As of this night, he belongs to me!"

"We'll fight you, Andre." Camillia was amazingly calm. "But if you insist on having us, c'mon. Start with me." Camillia still held the cross out toward Andre and took a step further back into her bedroom.

"If you won't join me, bitch, you'll die!" Andre looked over at the female officer.

Until that moment policewoman had just stood there in a daze. She suddenly pulled her gun from its holster and aimed it at Camillia.

"Do it, Andre," Camillia dared, a triumphant smile on her face. "But always know that I was the one 'bitch' you couldn't have."

The officer fired four times.

Camillia was thrown back violently against the wall. She slumped to the floor with a painful grin on her face. She still held on to the cross.

"You can kill this body, *sweetheart*," she taunted in a pained whisper, knowing full well that her voice was reaching Andre's supernaturally acute ears. "But my soul belongs to the Lord." Her voice grew weaker and her breathing grew labored yet she gathered the strength to continue. "And you're wrong about Richard. He's too much like me to give in to you."

Her voice faded to silence. Still she held on to the small silver crucifix.

Gladys, the nosey next-door neighbor, was at home watching television when she heard Andre's agonized wail. She immediately ran to the phone and called the police. When she heard the gunshots, she hunkered down on the floor and called the police again to urge them to hurry. The gunshots were more than enough incentive to keep her from going near the window, no matter how badly she wanted to peek at the house next door.

Andre was still enraged. This was the first woman to ever resist him and he did not quite know how to react. He could not take his fury out on Camillia the way he wanted to. She had never invited him into her home, and even if the policewoman tossed Camillia out of the window, she was already dying from the gunshot wounds. He would feel no pleasure tearing apart a woman who was already dead.

Andre had to destroy something. He paced back and forth in the shadows before coming to a decision. He looked up at the female police officer. She stood at the window quietly with the smoking gun in her hand. He beckoned her to him and she dropped her gun and dove through the open window. Andre caught her, threw her easily over his shoulder and leapt into the air, quickly disappearing into the night sky.

The policewoman was found later on the other side of town, broken and mutilated.

Richard was losing it. He was walked on one of a series of north side streets that held nothing but adult bookstores, topless clubs with live stage shows, and small establishments that provided peep shows for small amounts of money.

The whole strip was alive with flashing neon lights every color of the rainbow. They displayed "XXX", "ADULTS ONLY", and "LIVE GIRLS". Different kinds of music blared from erotic-themed establishments and combined to form a haunting melody rife with the promise of sinful pleasures.

Richard walked around in a daze. He had appropriated a black leather jacket from God knows where to hide his tattered and bloody T-shirt. The only things he was aware of were the flashing lights, the painted women on every street, and the hunger.

His vision blurred and swam as different men and women floated in and out of his vision, approaching and propositioning him. His wounds had healed but he still looked sinister. Every would-be solicitor turned and walked away when they got close enough to see the look in his eyes.

The pain was as strong as it had always been but Richard was learning to keep his composure. He was almost shivering with hunger and was still choosey about who would sate it.

Just any woman would not do. He had to find one that met his lofty standards.

He was about to pass an establishment that looked so small from the outside that he would have missed it had he not noticed the small handwritten sign that read "PEEP SHOWS" taped to the shadowy doorway. There were no windows and no flashing neon signs. There was only the sign, the lock and an eye slot on the door.

Something about the place stopped Richard in his tracks. For some reason that he could not explain, he knew that what he was looking for was somewhere within this establishment.

He walked into the small place. The lobby was dim and had a damp, musty odor. There was a counter that stood about five feet high. On the far side of the counter were a few steps that led to an elevated floor.

There were three doors in the lobby. There was the door through which Richard entered. There was another door behind the counter. The third door was on the far side of the lobby. Richard saw a dark-haired Italian man seated behind the counter.

"You wanna check out a show or what?" the proprietor asked.

Richard nodded.

"Great," the man said sarcastically. "You know how this works?"

Richard shook his head.

"Ok," the man said, "Five dollar cover, another three and I give you back three in quarters. Go through that door, choose a booth, and put a quarter in the coin slot. Boom! You see a beautiful dancer. You get thirty seconds for each quarter."

Richard's first inclination was to punch a hole in the man's chest and go into the back for free. He decided against it and paid the eight dollars. After collecting his quarters he went through the door that led to the booths. A long, narrow corridor led to a row of doors. Each door led to a different booth. Instinct led Richard to the far end of the corridor and to the last booth.

The inside of the tiny room was even more damp and musty than the lobby. The very air was sticky and beads of perspiration popped up on Richard's forehead. A small light shining on the ceiling revealed a wide window set in the wall opposite the door.

There was a metal panel on the other side of the window that concealed what lay behind it. Richard dropped a quarter into the slot and the metal panel rose. A hazy red light came on behind the glass to reveal a small, nearly empty room. There was only a solitary chair set in the middle of the room and a door on the far wall.

The door on the far wall opened and a dancer stepped into the room. The woman was dressed in a gold, tiger-striped teddy and black garters that held up a pair of fishnet stockings. She wore a pair of black, lacy six-inch stiletto heels.

She appeared to be in her mid to late twenties. Her skin was tanned golden and her face boasted exquisitely delicate East Asian features. Her long black hair draped past her shoulders and down to her full breasts. She had a tiny waist that curved out to a flawless pair of round hips.

Richard's ravenous eyes followed those hips down to her beautiful legs. Her fishnet stockings impeccably accented the curve of shapely thighs and calves.

She was, in a word, perfect.

The dancer gave Richard a bold smile. Music began to play at a low volume. She did a few sensual movements of her hips as she wiggled down into the chair. She sat with her legs spread wide and slid down the shoulder straps of her teddy.

The top half of her lingerie fell softly into her lap to reveal taut, pink little nipples on full breasts. Richard stared, utterly entranced by the exotic dancer on the other side of the glass. She smiled again and a second later the red light went out. Richard's newly enhanced vision allowed him see her clearly even after the room was plunged into darkness. The dancer remained seated as the metal panel slid down to conceal her.

It was all planned out. She made sure that it took all thirty seconds for the first part of her show. She would sit there, like always, until the excited man on the other side of the window put his next quarter in the slot. Whenever the red light came back on and the cover rose, she would dance with her breasts exposed for thirty seconds.

When the light came on the third time, she would make a thirty-second show of stripping completely out of the teddy. For the next thirty seconds, she would dance seductively wearing nothing but her panties, garters, stockings and shoes. She would take off the shoes and the garter just before the light went out.

This would go on until she was stripped down to her panties and high heels. She made it take the whole three dollars in quarters for her to get nude. The only exception would be if the watcher incentivized her to undress faster by placing paper money in the dollar slot.

This time, however, it took an unusually long time for the light to come back on. The dancer was surprised. She saw the lust in the young man's eyes and was sure this would be one of her more lucrative shows. When the cover finally lifted and the light came on, she was even more surprised to see that the room was empty. All she saw in the glass window was her own reflection.

She stood there expectantly for a moment expecting the young man to come back. When he did not, she shrugged, rose from the chair, and turned to leave.

Richard was standing right behind her. The dancer jumped and gasped, inhaling deeply to release a terrified scream. That impulse faded when she looked into his eyes. She stood there in a daze, mesmerized, as Richard reached out to her. He put a hand behind her head, pulled her face to his and kissed her deeply.

Her soft, yielding lips excited him, causing the pain within him to slightly ease. Richard peeled away the teddy and everything else the woman wore. She stood naked before him for a moment and then she began to undress him. The red light went out and the metal panel came down once again.

In the lobby, behind the counter, a little beep sounded and a small light flashed to alert him that someone's time was up. Usually when this happened, the light would stop flashing in a few seconds due to yet another coin being placed in the quarter slot. If it took too long for the flashing light to go out the man would call a few of his bouncers from another room to go into the booth and remove the deadbeat.

The proprietor waited thirty seconds. The light did not stop flashing so he did what he was supposed to do.

"Yo! Bruno, Vince!" the proprietor called. "We got another one!"

Two huge Italian men stepped through the door behind the counter.

"Which one, Tony?" one of the men asked.

"Number seven," the proprietor answered. "It ain't gonna be lucky for that little bastard. He's a kid, kinda skinny, so be careful. Don't rough 'em up too bad, ya know? Just break a few teeth, maybe."

The two big men went into the corridor and walked down to the booth.

"O.K. kid," Vince called, "It's time to go!"

They walked into the room to find that it was empty. They looked at each other and shrugged.

"You sure it was seven?" Bruno yelled in the direction of the lobby.

"Yeah! Seven!" Tony called back.

"There's nobody back here!" Bruno said.

"He didn't come out this way," Tony yelled. "Find 'em!"

"Well," Vince began, motioning toward the window. "You think he's back there?"

Vince took a quarter from his pocket and dropped it into the coin slot.

"No," Bruno said. "There's no way to get back there from this room. But hell, we may as well get a peep while we're back here. Who's workin' right now?"

"I think it's that Chinese chick."

Vince grinned. "She's hot. Best one we got by far."

The metal panel lifted. The soft red light switched on. Bruno and Vince gasped when they saw what was on the other side of the window. The Asian dancer sat entirely naked and spread-eagle in the chair. Her tan skin was ashen. She stared at the two men with dead eyes. Two puncture wounds in her neck wept thin streams of blood.

"I think you better get back here, Tony!"

The two bouncers stared at the shapely, lifeless body as they waited for their employer. They heard Tony's footsteps grow louder as he approached. He barged inside with an irritated frown.

"What the hell's goin' on in –" Tony stopped short when he saw the dancer. "Oh...shit."

Detective Weller's car came to a stop in front of the old boarded up house. The men sat in the car for a few seconds and just looked at the big ragged construction. It was an intimidating sight. The dark forest, an extension of Wolf Lake Park threatened to swallow the house whole. A terribly overgrown yard and old boards covering the windows gave the house a forbidding look.

Father Burns' station wagon pulled up behind Weller's car. The tall priest got out of the car with his crossbow and his six-foot, gilded-wreathed crucifix. He made sure the crossbow was securely loaded with a small silver stake and adjusted the customized bandoleers that crisscrossed his torso over his long gray trench coat.

One of the bandoleers was loaded with more sliver spikes and the other with wooden spikes of the same size. The silver was to neutralize vampires. While their bodies were pierced with silver, their powers would be weakened and they would be overwhelmed by pain. Ideally, the silver would immobilize them by pinning them to a surface so that Father Burns could get close enough to finish them with a wooden spike through the heart. Every spike in his bandoleer had been consecrated at the altar of St. Anselm's Church.

When he was satisfied everything was in place, he walked over to Weller's car. The detective stepped out of the car wearing his long tan trench. A twelve-gauge

Mossberg shotgun was slung over his shoulder, sling strap fitted with custom silver slugs.

"That's his place?" Weller asked. "That doesn't look like Andre's style."

"Yes," Father Burns agreed. "Compared to the apartment he used when we last encountered him, this would not appear to be to his taste."

"Well, this is definitely the house Tim and I drove past," Major said.

"And this house fit's Richard's description exactly," Burns added. "According to Richard's dream, the interior of the home is more Andre's style."

Tim took a deep, nervous breath. "There's only one way to find out for sure."

"Everyone ready?" Weller asked.

Tim and Major climbed out of the back seat of the Ciera and all four of them checked their gear. Each man was armed with crucifixes dangling from chains around their necks. Weller, Major and Tim all made sure their guns were loaded. Tim had his Colt Anaconda. Major had his Glock 19 and his Saturday night special.

Weller eyed the two youngsters and their weapons. "Where did you two come by those guns, fellas?"

They both shrugged.

"Found it in a garbage can in the alley," Tim lied.

"Here, and there," Major said.

Weller grunted. "If we're alive at sunrise, we'll have a nice, long talk about this. Major, grab that bag on the back seat for me."

Major reached into the car and pulled out a large, heavy duffle bag.

"What's in this thing?" Major asked.

"Extra ammo and other stuff you'll see when we get inside."

They approached the house slowly with watchful, wary eyes. The structure was not particularly large but it exuded a cold and oppressive presence they could all feel. The home resembled some resting beast, a latent force that not even the nocturnal animals dare awaken. There were absolutely no natural nighttime sounds, not even the song of crickets or toads. They were more than slightly unnerved by the unusual silence surrounding the house. All they could hear was their own footfalls.

"I know I don't have to tell any of you to be careful," Burns whispered as the men were halfway to the porch, "But I would feel better if I did. There's no telling what kind of traps may be set up to protect Andre."

"If this guy is tougher than Rich," Major began, "I wouldn't think he needed protection."

"He needs it in the daytime," Weller explained, "when he's sleeping."

Father Burns stopped in his tracks. The other men turned to see what the problem was.

"What's wrong?" asked Tim.

"His protection," Burns answered. "In Richard's last dream, he mentioned Andre's living room being filled with–" Father Burns' sentence was finished by a deafening bark from behind that sounded more like a small explosion.

All of the men jumped. A chorus of thunderous barks followed the first one. The men turned to see at least a half dozen incredibly large German shepherds. The smallest dog was no shorter than three feet tall on all fours. All of the canines foamed at the mouth and each mouth was evilly contorted with black lips, black gums, and dripping snarls.

The dogs crouched at the street end of the near-invisible walkway and advanced slowly on the men.

"BREAK!" exclaimed Tim.

The four men broke into full sprints toward the house. The monstrous canines took off after them. The dogs gained on them as if the four men moved in slow motion. Major was the first to reach the front door. He fully expected the door to be locked but he tried it anyway. The door miraculously opened. He pushed it open and rushed into the foyer. Tim came in behind him. The older men, however, were not as fleet of foot.

Father Burns was a few feet in front of detective Weller. Major and Tim watched in horror as the distance between Weller and the dogs grew shorter at a frightening pace. Just before Weller reached the porch stairway, the fastest dog was almost upon him.

"Weller, look out!!" Tim screamed as the lead dog pounced.

Weller showed incredibly quick reflexes and agility. He spun, fired his 12-gage, and spun back toward the house in one motion, never breaking stride. The airborne dog let out a high-pitched scream and changed direction in mid flight as the silver slugs hammered into it.

The loud discharge of the weapon caused the other dogs to hesitate, but only momentarily. The shot bought Weller a second but that was all the time it took for Weller and Burns to make it safely into the house. Major slammed the heavy wooden door just as the berserk dogs crashed into it. They snarled, barked and scratched violently but the door held.

The closed door plunged the house into darkness that was quickly countered by a small flashlight that Father Burns produced from the deep pockets of his trench coat. Major hastened to engage the deadbolt lock, hook the chain, and slide the latch on the door.

"Thanks for the warning, Tim," Weller panted. "I knew the dogs were back there but I was afraid to look." He extended an open hand to the younger man.

"Don't mention it," Tim said. He took Weller's proffered hand and shook it firmly.

"Someone needs to find a light switch," Major suggested, "with a quickness."

Father Burns played his flashlight around the room again. He paused at lamps on end tables and a ceiling mounted light fixture. None of them had bulbs.

Major frowned. "What the hell? I know there's electricity. I can hear the little hum, like a generator somewhere around here."

"I suppose vampires don't need light," Father Burns pointed out.

"Why would he need electricity, then?" Tim wondered.

"Good question," Weller said. No one had an answer.

"In Rich's dream," Major began, "you said the dogs were in the living room." Major looked around fearfully. "You think..."

"I think if any dogs were in here they'd be on us by now," Weller responded.

Father Burns clicked a switch to increase the brightness of his flashlight and used it to survey the living room. "This is definitely is Andre's place. It's just as Richard described. It's exactly the same as Andre's old apartment."

"Yeah," Weller added. "His tastes haven't changed in nineteen years."

"He lets the outside look bad to keep people out," Tim concluded.

"So what now?" Major asked.

"We search this house until we find his resting place," Father Burns answered.

Major looked around nervously. "So… uh… no one is going to suggest anything stupid like splitting up to cover more ground… are they?"

"Not a chance," Weller assured.

"Ok," Major said with relief. "Just checking."

The dogs stopped barking.

Major tensed and turned to the door. He was as startled by the sudden silence as he had been by the dogs' appearance. "Are we *sure* Andre's not here?"

Weller nodded once. "I'm pretty sure we would know it by now if he was."

"Yeah," Tim said despondently. "He's out there feeding. Like Richard."

"What about those damned dogs?" Major went on. "Maybe they have another way in."

"True," Weller allowed. "If they do, we just have to be ready to use up a lot of ammo."

"What do we do when we find where he sleeps?" Tim wondered.

"Ultimately we have to take his head and his heart to make sure he can never return," Father Burns said with a grim expression.

"That's right," Weller concurred. "But first, we'll immobilize him by rigging his resting place the way you two rigged Richard's bed."

The statement stung Tim and Major equally. They both understood that they had pushed him over the edge. The weight of their guilt – both for what they did to their friend and what they unleashed upon the world – drew their gazes down to the floor.

"Richard," Tim said softly. "I'm sorry man."

Richard was walking home. He was a half-block away from his house with a satisfied smile on his face.

He had finally eased the pain. The moment the dancer's hot blood touched his tongue he started to understand what Andre had been trying to tell him. From the time the salty, coppery fluid hit the back of his throat and slid sensuously down his esophagus, Richard felt better than he ever had in his life.

Incredible energy pulsed through his veins like comforting liquid flame. It infused every part of being, fortifying his body and bringing razor-sharp clarity to his mind. He was stronger, faster... he simply felt... *powerful*. The only thing he could not figure out was why he waited. It seemed crazy to have denied himself for so long.

The night no longer seemed to call to him the way had during the last several days. There was no longer a need. Richard had *become* the night. The blackness of the night sky invigorated him. Though he could not remember ever consciously noticing his heartbeat when he was human, he became acutely aware of its absence after he changed.

Richard was also keenly aware that he no longer needed to breathe. Nonetheless, he drank the cool night air deeply into his lungs with a passion he had never experienced. While he did not need it, it was part of the night, like him, and he wanted to indulge in every aspect of his new self.

He would have to convince his mother to join him. She had no idea what she was missing. He was not sure if words would be able to accurately describe the exaltation he felt. At last, he was able to realize that his mother was being entirely too stubborn. If she could just get a taste of the power that she could have...

Camillia's problem was that she could not imagine the scope of what was happening. Richard would convince her, though. Andre would never be able to talk her into it but maybe, just maybe, her only son could. He had to. No matter what happened, his mother was still the most important part of his life and he wanted to share this power with her. And on an instinctive, primal level, he knew that the only way she could fully embrace this elevated existence was to do so voluntarily.

Richard turned into his walkway and almost skipped merrily to his porch. He unlocked the door and walked in, expecting his mother to be waiting at the front door as she always had, but this time she was not.

"She must be out," Richard said to himself as he closed and locked the door.

A strange mix of smells stopped him abruptly when he entered the house.

Gunpowder and blood.

For some reason he could not fathom, the scent of blood did not tweak his hunger in the least. There was something about the scent, something unsettling and familiar that filled him with dread.

He followed the scent to his mother's bedroom. The closer he got to the room the stronger the smells grew. He entered the bedroom and looked around, and then his eyes went wide and his jaw dropped. Camillia sat on the floor beside her bed, under the window, propped up against the wall, in a pool of blood.

One arm was raised above her head, suspended by handcuffs fastened to the headboard. There was blood smeared on the wall behind her. In her right hand she clutched her small silver crucifix. She had been bleeding profusely from multiple gunshot wounds but the flow of blood had slowed to a frightening trickle. Her heartbeat was so weak and so slow that even Richard's super-naturally augmented hearing could barely detect it.

Fear and anger and confusion, and quite possibly the crucifix hanging from the wall and the one held in his mother's cold hand, smothered any trace of the hunger.

"Momma..." Richard whispered.

His mind started screaming. It felt as if a massive fist had punched him in his gut. His heart grew hot and felt as if it was swelling to the point that it would explode. A storm raged within him yet he could not find the strength to cry out. He hurried to his mother and dropped to his knees. He cradled her head in his arms.

"Momma..." he whispered again.

He experienced a whole new type of pain. The pain inflicted on him by his bloodlust was pleasurable compared to the agony he felt upon seeing his mother lying helplessly near death. Tears began to stream uncontrollably from his eyes and he started to shake.

"Momma... please, don't..." his voice cracked.

Camillia opened her eyes. She looked up at him slowly and tiredly. She forced a weak smile to her lips. Richard tried to smile back at her but he could not. The hurt was too great.

"You gave in tonight, didn't you?" she asked, her voice barely audible.

"How did you know?" Richard asked.

"The eyes," Camillia began. "They look so much like *his*, now."

"I'm sorry, momma," Richard gasped. "I couldn't... I just..." Richard could not continue. Instead, he changed the subject. "Who did this?"

"You know damn well who did this," Camillia answered, managing a stern tone even in her debilitated state. "*He* did this. He did it because I wouldn't give in."

A thought occurred to Richard, and with it, a surge of hope. "I could turn you, momma," he offered. "I could make you like us. I could save you."

"That wouldn't save me, son. I don't want to be like Andre. I'd rather meet God and Jesus. Now that you see what he's capable of, son, do *you* want to be like him?"

"No, but it's too late." He wiped tears from his cheeks.

"It's not too late, baby," Camillia confided. "As long as you have *some* of me in you, you can beat him. We gotta stick together, Li'l Rich. Me and you..." she inhaled deeply, released a shuddering exhalation, and stopped breathing.

"Momma...?"

Richard rocked his mother gently back and forth in an attempt to rouse her. She did not move. He looked up at the distant sound of sirens approaching.

"Momma?"

The sound of the sirens grew louder.

When Camillia did not respond, he placed her gently on the floor.

The dam holding back the full force of his agony, despair and rage finally burst.

"MOMMA!!" Richard screamed.

The cry extended into an unintelligible, inhuman wail that shook the walls of the home.

Gladys cowered on her knees and peeked through the curtains of her living room window. Several minutes had passed with no more gunshots so she was comfortable parting the curtains an inch to spy on the Williams home.

She saw the lights and heard the sirens of approaching police cars and ambulances. She then heard a sound louder than all of the sirens put together. The sound was similar to the roar she heard earlier, right before the gun shots. The roar she heard earlier, however, was filled with rage. This one was filled with agony and sadness. Gladys felt the despair wash over her.

She jumped and shrieked when the picture window at the front of Camillia's home exploded outward in a spray of shrapnel-like wood and glass. A dark figure darted from the window much too fast for Gladys to identify. All she saw was a blur.

When the police and paramedics arrive, Gladys was tempted to go outside to tell them what she witnessed but she could not force herself to move. Not only was she paralyzed by disbelief and fear of what she saw, she was sure the police would never believe her.

She was watching when Richard went into the home. She was fairly certain that the inhuman scream and the blurred figure that flew out of the living room window minutes later could be nothing else but him. The last thing she wanted was to be called a crazy old lady. She enjoyed living alone and had no desire to give her children a reason to move her in with them. She certainly did not want to give the authorities a reason to lock away in some sanitarium.

Inside the Williams home, paramedics worked feverishly on the bullet-riddled woman. She had lost a dangerous amount of blood and it looked as if she would not survive. The police watched with sadness as the medical people did all they could. One of the police officers knew Camillia.

"I met her through detective Weller," the uniformed officer said to his partner. "She survived that 'vampire' serial killer back in the seventies. She was a good woman, a strong woman."

One the paramedics looked up. "Was? She's stronger than you realize, man. We just got a pulse!"

Chapter 12

Father Burns, detective Weller, and the two younger men started their search in the basement. Weller added the light of his flashlight to Father Burns' light to illuminate the entire basement. The subterranean level of the home was a broad unfinished space as broad as the house. Plumbing pipes and electrical wiring snaked to and fro overhead. The floors and wall were slate gray poured concrete that radiated and magnified the autumn chill. The basement was dank and musty and confining despite the absence of interior walls.

The only furnishing in the stifling space was a wide, floor-to-ceiling freezer unit on one of the walls. It was connected to a gas-powered generator.

"And there's the answer to why he needs electricity," Tim said.

Major eased over to the freezer. "That's weird," he noted. "He feeds on blood. Why does he need a fridge?"

Weller trained his light on the refrigerator while Major slowly opened it and peeked in.

"SHIT! SHIT! *SHEEIT!*" Major screamed. He slammed the door shut and did a panicked dance as he leapt away from the freezer.

Weller looked curiously at Major and then at the freezer. He handed his flashlight to Tim. "Hold this, kid, and open that door." He hefted his Mossberg. "Padre," he called to Father Burns, "keep your light on that door and get ready to back me up with the crossbow... just don't shoot *me* with that thing."

The detective stood a foot clear of the freezer door with his shotgun at the ready. Tim stood to the side, grasped the door handle firmly and snatched it open.

"Oh, for Christ's sake," Weller moaned.

Father Burns gasped, took a step back and made the sign of the cross.

Several frozen bodies had been stuffed inside the freezer unit. There was no blood, only twisted and broken and naked bodies. There were men and women of varying ethnicities. Weller kicked the door closed before he or Father Burns could get an accurate count of the frozen corpses. Neither man wanted to count them.

"What was it?" Tim asked. Fortunately he stood behind the door at an angle that did not allow him to see the horror inside the unit.

"Bodies!" Major snapped. "Dead fucking bodies!"

Father Burns shivered with disgust and confusion. "Vampires prefer living blood. Why would he store dead bodies in a freezer?"

"My guess," Weller offered, "dog food."

"What?" Major asked.

Father Burns understood. "His dogs need to eat."

"But there're deer and shit out here," Major said, "not to mention rabbits, raccoons, possums."

Weller turned to Major. "How much would you bet none of those things come near this damned house?"

"Exactly," Father Burns said. "Animals can sense the presence of the undead. Predators and scavengers may be bold enough to come near, but prey animals would give this entire area a wide berth. The dogs would have to venture far and wide to hunt. My guess is Andre would want to keep them relatively close. What good are guardians that are never around?"

Tim stepped away from the freezer unit."Let's get the hell out of this basement."

They did. It took a little longer to search the main floor. The home was not big, but the main floor boasted many small rooms. By the time they made their way to the master bedroom on the second floor, they had searched everywhere for a coffin with no luck.

The master bedroom was as strikingly decorated as the rest of the home but they could find nothing out of the ordinary. Weller went to the last space they had not searched: the bedroom closet. He opened the closet door and found nothing but clothes.

"I thought this guy had to be encased in something dark when he slept," Weller said in a frustrated tone. "The windows are boarded but not blackened. Sunlight would filter in during the day. We haven't found anything even remotely resembling a coffin."

"I don't know," Tim said. He recalled what Eric said about some vampires being somewhat tolerant of sunlight. Was that a lie like almost everything else he told them? "Maybe that coffin stuff is just a popular myth about vampires."

Weller shook his head in disagreement. "It's been said that the rare vampire comes along that can survive daylight. Andre's not one of them. We found something like a coffin in his apartment back then. It was an upright job hidden in a storage cabinet."

"In my studies," Burns added, "I've learned that vampires intolerant to the sun do indeed need to have a reliable way of allowing absolutely no sunlight to touch them when they sleep. These boarded windows would not be adequate protection. There has to be some kind of light-proof encasement here."

"I guess that rules out king-sized beds," Major said as he plopped down tiredly onto Andre's bed. He attempted to bounce a little but the bed gave very little resistance. "This thing is pretty stiff."

He reached down and pulled the cover off the mattress. They saw that the mattress did not rest on a box spring. It was placed atop of an oak box formed in the same dimensions as a king-sized box spring.

"What have we here?" Weller asked.

He rummaged through his duffle bag and pulled out a small battery-powered lantern, which he placed on the floor and switched on. With the brighter and more stable light, he and Weller clicked off their flashlights and Father Burns gave the box a closer inspection.

They found a small handle on the side of the oak box. Father Burns set his crucifix-staff on top of the bed and lowered himself to a kneeling position on the floor. Weller gave the handle a tug and the whole side of the box swung down on a hinge to reveal a dark hiding place underneath the bed.

"Bingo!" Weller exclaimed.

"Damn!" Tim said. "He sleeps *under* the bed."

"Nice piece of detective work," came a deep, smooth voice from the door. The four men turned to the voice.

"Andre," Weller announced.

Andre's gaze went from Weller to Father Burns. "You gentlemen have aged very badly."

Weller scoffed. "Wish we could say the same for you."

Andre looked at the detective. "Your friend Keith Milton sends his regards."

Weller's eyes narrowed, his anger and desire for vengeance momentarily overshadowing his fear. "You're a sick bastard."

Andre ignored the insult. "I noticed that he took a particular interest in my exploits in the seventies, so I took a particular interest in him last night."

Father Burns snatched up his crucifix with one hand and lifted his crossbow into firing position with the other. Andre spun out of the doorway and out of sight.

"Using the same old tricks, old man?" Andre called back from the hall. "Well, I have a few new ones."

He darted back into the doorway brandishing a .22 caliber pistol and fired two shots at Father Burns before ducking back into the hall. All of the men started moving when they saw the gun. They dived to the floor on the other side of the bed, but one of the shots struck the priest in the arm and the crossbow went flying.

"I don't believe this shit," Major said breathlessly to himself. "A vampire with a Saturday night special."

"Father," Weller began, "Your arm..."

"It's alright," Burns assured, "The bullet passed right through. It hurts like the devil, though."

"Do we go after him?" Tim asked.

"This is his house," Major said. "He could be hiding anywhere."

"We can't just sit back here and wait for him to come to us," Tim argued.

"Why the hell not?" Major shot back.

"We have to go after him," Father Burns grunted through his pain. "Keep your weapons ready and your crucifixes in plain site. His shots weren't fatal only because he couldn't look in the direction of my staff."

The four men rose from behind the bed with their crosses and weapons held high. When they did so, they saw the huge German shepherds that greeted them in the front yard stood there blocking the door.

The dogs attacked.

The sounds of gunfire and screams and the pained yelps of animals resounded throughout the home. Andre waited patiently outside the room, amusing himself by watching the shadows dancing madly in the room and the hall in the lantern light.

Minutes later, three surviving dogs came trotting out. All of them had something in its mouth. One of the dogs emerged with two crucifixes dangling from chains clamped in its bloody muzzle. The second dog carried only one crucifix. The third dragged out Father Burn's crucifix-staff.

Andre averted his eyes until the dogs went down the stairs. He smiled and stepped back into the room.

The four men were still alive. They all bled from various bites and scratches, but they were alive.

"My dogs are obedient, as you can see," Andre boasted. "I wanted them to get your religious trinkets out of the way and they risked their lives to do it. Now I have the pleasure of killing you with my own teeth and claws."

Father Burns grimaced as he lifted his crossbow with his damaged arm and reloaded it with his other hand. "We still have our weapons."

"I'm not concerned about your silver and wooden ammunition," Andre assured. "They have to actually strike me to do any damage."

Weller leveled his shotgun. "We did it before, we'll do it again."

Andre nodded. "As *young* men, yes. I allowed my rage at your intrusion to distract me. That bolt nicked my heart and it took nearly twenty agonizing years to heal. By the time the sun touches the horizon, I promise, you will know my pain."

He advanced on them. All four men opened fire. They knew their chances for survival were slim but they were not going out without a fight.

Andre danced in and out of view quicker than their eyes could follow, never giving them a clear shot. Between the four of them they kept him moving. Every time he got too close Father Burns let fly a silver bolt before gnashing his teeth and fighting through the pain of reloading his crossbow with an injured, painful arm.

"Backs to the wall!" Weller commanded.

He followed his own advice, reloading his Mossberg while the others continued to fire at their inhumanly elusive target. Tim and Major scored the most hits, which were not many. Their shots were not silver and so did minimal damage, but they were powerful and painful enough to cause Andre at least a moment's pause.

Father Burns tried not to think of that terrible night nineteen years earlier but the scene was too similar. Just like that ill-fated night, they fought the vampire in the vampire's own residence, in his own bedroom. Father Burns prayed even as he loaded, aimed and fired, that Tim and Major would not meet the same fate as the officers who died alongside him and detective Weller.

In one impossibly swift lunge, Andre closed the distance between himself and Major. A loud cracking sound reverberated just before Major's scream. His gun went flying across the room. Major went to his knees with Andre clutching his wrist.

Major had not said anything to the others when the dogs took everyone's religious paraphernalia but his. He reached into his shirt with his free hand, pulled out the small golden cross hanging from the thin chain around his neck and pressed it against Andre's hand.

Andre laughed and squeezed Major's wrist, shattering bones with an audible crunch. Major could only gasp in breathless agony.

Weller, standing next to Major, opened up with his shotgun. Andre spun out of the path of the silver slug. Weller blasted again and again, his Mossberg causing a storm of thunder and lightening in the enclosed space. Andre paused for a fraction of a second on the other side of the room, produced the .22 again, and shot Weller in the stomach. Weller fell back against the wall grimacing with agony.

Andre pounced. He ducked Burns' next bolt and shrugged off Tim's shots as he closed on Weller. He grabbed the Mossberg by its superheated barrel and snatched it away, nearly taking the detective's fingers with it. He used the shotgun to bat away yet another silver crossbow bolt and then flung the rifle at the priest.

Father Burns dodged as quickly as he could but he was not fast enough. He barely managed to keep his head as the flying shotgun tore the crossbow out of his one-handed grip.

Tim continued to pull the trigger of his .44 even though it only clicked. Before he could reload, Andre lifted Weller from the floor and with an easy flick of his arm he sent him sailing into Tim too fast for the younger man to dodge. Tim and Weller went down in a heap.

Andre stood before the beaten men. The vampire was riddled with bullet holes. His trench coat bore much larger holes from a few near misses of Weller's silver bolts, but he was alarmingly unhurt.

"You were the biggest fool of all, Major. You came here wearing that cross with absolutely no faith to power it. Why do you think my pets left it with you?" He growled, glaring at the others with glowing eyes and a feral smirk,

"Now, it's my turn."

He took a step forward but hesitated, cocking his head as if he could hear something the others could not. A slow, ugly, fanged smile spread slowly across his face.

And then the others heard it. It started out as a distant rumbling that, after two seconds, began to make the room tremor lightly. In a few more seconds, the small rumble grew to an extended roar.

Andre's smile spread impossible wider.

The four men had just enough time to hit the floor as the window behind them crashed in. A dark, howling figured hurled through the boarded window as a spray of flying glass and splintered wood rifled through the room. The dark figure slammed into Andre, the force of the blow sending them both flying out the room and into the hallway. A rush of air caused the door to slam shut.

Andre was swept from the room by something he could not see clearly but he knew full well what it was. When he slammed into the wall across the hallway he

quickly gained his footing, grasped the dark figure firmly with one powerful hand and lifted it into the air. He found himself staring into Richard's face. Andre took in the younger man's maniacal eyes and grinned.

"You've crossed over," Andre said. "I can see it." He breathed deeply. "I can smell it."

"Was that Rich?" Major asked.

"If it was," Weller said, "I hope he's on our side."

The door crashed in. Richard and Andre came stumbling into the room and fell to the floor.

"I guess he is on our side," Tim noted as he watched Richard and Andre struggling.

Father Burns ran out of the room and the other three followed close behind. The priest stopped when they were halfway down the hallway and turned to the others.

"We have to find our crucifixes," Father Burns told them. "That's the only way we'll be able to help Richard."

"We have to find the dogs," Weller reminded.

"I don't think that'll be a problem," Tim said quietly. All four men looked down to the end of the hall to see the German shepherds guarding the top of the stairway, crouched and ready, teeth bared.

"I don't see crucifixes," Major said. "All I see are teeth."

There was nowhere to run. The only opening was a boarded window at the opposite end of the long hallway.

"That's the only way out fellas," Weller pointed out. "If we go out that way and come back in through the front, maybe we'll find our gear. So... who's first?"

"Pardon me, Father," Tim began, "but fuck it! I'm out!"

Tim turned and ran. The other three men sprinted behind him. The dogs immediately gave chase. The four men knew the dogs were not after religious symbols this time. They were after blood.

In a move fueled by adrenaline and fear, Major snatched his Saturday night special from his belt with his left hand and pivoted to shoot at the dogs while he ran. He was an inexperienced shooter to begin with and the broken wrist ruined his shooting hand. Shooting with his off hand while running was a valiant but useless effort.

Tim said two silent prayers as he raced to the boarded window. The second prayer was that they all survived the fall. The first prayer was that the boards covering the window were as brittle as they appeared.

He shielded his face and leapt as hard as he could. The glass and wooden boards gave way with a loud crash. An instant later Tim was rolling down the steep roof. He felt himself tumbling uncontrollably and was certain he would soon be plummeting head first to the ground.

Tim reached out blindly for something to grasp. His tumble stopped abruptly and he hung from the edge of the roof by a rusty gutter.

The other three men made their way down the roof a little more carefully than Tim had. Soon Weller, Burns, and Major were sitting on the edge. Tim was still dangling.

The most adventurous of the three dogs came soaring through the smashed window in pursuit. It was moving too fast, though. When its four paws lighted on the glass and wood strewn roof they slipped out from under it. The dog went tumbling down the slope, snapping at the men as it passed, and went over the edge only a few inches away from Tim.

The fall did not kill it. The big dog scrambled back to all fours and barked savagely as it waited for the four men to inevitably join it.

Weller turned to Major. "Hand me that pea shooter." Major did so with so hesitation. Weller took aim and pulled the trigger, expertly placing one bullet in the big dog's shoulder. When the dog faltered Weller pulled the trigger again and put the dog down with a headshot.

The other two dogs remained at the window barking wildly. After a few seconds of that, they went silent and padded away from the window.

"Good shooting," Father Burns complimented. "But how are you still functional after getting shot?"

Weller patted his torso, immediately winced and then smiled with embarrassment. "Vest, of course."

"What do we do now?" Major asked.

"We jump," Tim said nervously as the gutter creaked and bent. "If those mutts are as smart as Andre said, they're on their way to meet us on the ground floor."

"He's right," Father Burns agreed. "We can forget about getting to our crucifixes. We have to get to the cars before the dogs do. I have more gear in mine."

"Here goes nothing!" Tim released the edge of the roof and dropped to the ground. He landed on his feet and fell to his backside.

"That wasn't so bad!" he called up to the other three. "C'mon!"

The house was not very tall. The worst damage that could occur from jumping from the roof was probably jarred knees. Burns and Weller, however, had a lot more wear-and-tear on their knees than the younger men. They had to be careful.

Weller took a deep breath and jumped. He fell heavily to the ground and rolled a couple of times before he rose to his feet. Father Burns slid to a sitting position on the edge, made the sign of the cross, and followed. He landed much the same as Weller did but he did not get up.

He clutched his leg and grimaced in pain. Major jumped without a second thought. He landed on his feet, took a few running steps to keep from falling and then gained his balance.

Tim and Weller helped Father Burns to his feet and the four of them rushed back to the cars. When they were almost to the curb, the mad dogs burst from the house. The station wagon was the closest so all four men piled inside. The dogs, however, did not give up their pursuit.

One of the huge German shepherds jumped on the hood of the car. It barked and scratched and snapped at the windshield while another dog trotted patiently around the vehicle. Father Burns honked the car's horn and revved the engines in an attempt to frighten the dogs away. The animals would not be scared off.

"Stop this, Richard!" Andre yelled as he tossed the teen across the bedroom. Richard crashed into the wall and fell to his knees. He stood up and glared at Andre.

"Come with me, son," Andre cajoled. "The two of us have a lot of hell to raise... quite literally."

It took some effort for Richard to calm himself. "You were right," he confirmed. "I have crossed over. I've never felt so powerful in my life. I was ready to join you."

"Good," Andre said quietly with a malevolent smile. "Why all of this foolishness, then?"

"I decided to talk mom into joining us..."

The smile dropped away from Andre's face. He knew where this was going.

Richard continued. "But then I went home. Why did you kill her, Andre?"

"She would never have joined us," the older vampire explained. "Her ability to resist me was stronger than I realized. You must understand what I'm trying to accomplish. I want to build a new order, Richard, with you and I as the monarchs.

"I'm sorry about your mother, son, but she's unimportant, now. What matters is the *culling*."

"She's important to me, more important than you and your lunatic culling."

"You don't know what you're saying, boy." Andre's gaze darkened with his mood.

"I know what I'm saying. I'm not your son, and I won't live like you."

"You have no choice," Andre reminded. "You've tasted blood. You can't deny that you loved it. I understand your sorrow about your mother, but it will pass. You have an eternity to get over it. Join me."

"I won't live as a monster," Richard said with icy calm. "I'd rather die."

"Then so be it." Andre said, and then he exploded into motion. In the fraction of a second it took Andre to cross the room, Richard's form melted away into mist.

Andre shot through it and crashed through the wall into the adjoining room. He turned, fangs bared and eyes glowing red. Snarling, he went back into the room and looked around for Richard.

Andre turned just in time to see Richard rushing at him with blazing eyes and flashing teeth. The younger vampire held the silver bolt from Burns' crossbow. The spike was two feet long and was sharp on both ends. The silver sizzled against Richard's flesh but he used the pain to fuel his vengeance.

Andre reached out and caught Richard's wrist with a clawed hand before the silver could touch his flesh. The two vampires struggled all through the room. They smashed Andre's chest-of-drawers and a glass nightstand as they wrestled with the silver bolt. Richard slammed Andre into the wall next to the smashed door.

"I'm a little tougher than last time, eh pops?" Richard taunted. "It's from givin' in to the hunger. I've got youth on my side, though. You're old, Andre, your time on this world is just about finished."

"Not yet, boy," Andre whispered.

With a burst of strength, he forced the two of them across the room and through the broken window. They landed hard on the ground and rolled away from each other. Richard shot to his feet, the bolt still burning his hand. As Andre righted himself Richard threw the weapon at his chest. Andre sidestepped and the bolt sailed through empty air. It struck a tree like a giant dart, a third of its length embedded in the trunk.

The vampires rushed each other with inhuman speed and clashed violently. Richard took the worst of it, unable to match his maker's speed and strength. Andre got his hands around Richard's neck and slammed him into the wall of the house several times and then to the ground. Andre straddled Richard and began to strangle him.

"For centuries," the vampire growled, "I've searched for the perfect womb for my seed. For almost two decades I've healed and planned and waited for the moment the three of us could bring this world to ruin. I may have to start over, and I have an eternity to do just that, but for making me waste my time, I'll rip your fucking throat out."

To Richard's misfortune, his father was doing just that. Richard struggled uselessly against Andre's hands. Pain seared though his neck as Andre's talon-like fingers plunged into his skin. Richard wanted to transform into mist again but the pain would not allow him to concentrate or summon the strength to do it.

His vision began to blur. He became light-headed. Andre's image began to waver before his eyes. And then, out of the corner of his eye, he caught sight of something painfully reflecting the light of the full moon. It was the same gleam that he saw in Wolf Lake Park; that burned his eyes and gave away his friends' hiding place. Richard focused on the light and saw the small golden cross that Major sometimes wore. It was lying on the ground, apparently dropped when or after Major went through the window.

Merely looking at the cross hurt Richard's eyes but he dared not tear his gaze away. Something inside urged him to reach out to it. It was the same feeling that forced him into the church a few days ago. The difference was that then he was only a hybrid, still in the midst of his terrible transformation. Now it was too late.

The feeling, however, did not subside. Before tonight the cross and his faith would have been the only things that could have saved him, but a vampire could not touch a consecrated religious symbol. The mere thought of him picking up the cross was ridiculous, yet that was all he could think to do as Andre throttled him.

Richard recalled his mother's words:

As long as you have some of me in you, you'll be able to beat him. We gotta stick together...

But how? How could they stick together? His mother was gone, thanks to Andre, whose hooked, razor-sharp nails Richard could feel scraping his trachea.

Almost on its own, Richard's hand reached for the cross...

...you have some of me in you...

He did have her in him. Camillia's face, beautiful and angry and determined, filled his mind. She was the strongest person he had ever known. Richard wished he had his mother's strength. He needed it at that moment.

Richard felt feel his own blood ooze down his neck beneath his father's deadly grasp. Richard's hand inched closer...

Pain tore through his fingers, palm and arm as it came closer to the crucifix pendant. His watery eyes seared at the sight of it.

We gotta stick together Li'l Rich, me and you...

"Fuck the pain," Richard mumbled to himself.

He snatched up the pendant and pain erupted in his hand. His whole body began to spasm uncontrollably but he forced himself to hold on. Smoke billowed from his closed fist and the smell of his hand burning filled his nostrils. Richard wanted to cry out, but he could not. Andre's death grip kept any sound from escaping.

Andre did not take note of the smell. All of his senses were trained on clawing out Richard's throat. When he saw the tears and felt Richard's body quaking beneath him, Andre believed himself to be the cause. He squeezed even harder and smiled.

Richard's face contorted hideously. His eyes turned as black and dull as coal. The skin on his face turned from a light brown to a dull gray. His lips twisted and pulled away from his gums in a horrific rictus. Every tooth in his mouth grew impossibly long and razor sharp. His gums blackened and distended while his nose and his lips began to fuse into a bestial muzzle.

Andre was almost laughing with satisfaction. The true beast within Richard emerged in a last-ditch effort to save its host. Andre knew it would not work. He was centuries old, with the strength borne of countless blood feasts. Richard was less than a mewling newborn in comparison. It was a shame such potential had to go to waste, but Richard chose his own fate, and now, his death was only seconds away.

Richard grabbed the back of Andre's head with his free hand. He then brought the cross around and up and thrust it onto Andre's forehead.

Andre let loose an ear-piercing screech. It was a terrible sound, full of fear and shock and suffering. He tried to remove Richard's hands but the boy's grip was unyielding. Andre's face distorted worse than his son's. His clawed fingers tore at Richard's hands and wrists but Richard would not let go. The smell of burning flesh in intensified as the monsters fought to destroy each other.

The younger vampire rose to his feet, still holding Andre's head as he lifted him above the ground. Andre's screech dropped to a bass, guttural growl. He swung his arms and legs in the air wildly, still trying to break free of Richard's grasp. The crucifix continued to steam and burn between Richard's hand and Andre's forehead.

Richard looked behind Andre and saw the silver bolt he threw minutes earlier. About three quarters of it protruded from the tree. One sharp end of the bolt was imbedded in the tree trunk. The other deadly point stuck straight out toward them.

Richard took flight. He rocketed through the air in a straight line to the protruding stake. While airborne, Andre glanced over his shoulder. His unholy eyes widened in surprise and horror as the sharp point of the bolt rushed closer. He tried to morph into mist but cross and the pain it caused sapped his strength.

Andre struggled against Richard with a renewed vigor that was fueled by his fear. Richard, however, mustered the strength to hold on. His strength was bolstered by his determination as well as the power he drew from the memory of his mother.

Richard stopped abruptly in mid flight. He came to a halt a foot away from the stake. Andre however, had neither the strength nor focus to stop himself as quickly. His impetus kept him going and Richard gave him a powerful shove for good measure. Andre's momentum impaled him on the silver bolt. His body did not stop moving until his back struck the tree trunk. The bolt, coated in black, sizzling, and smoking blood, emerged from the center of Andre's chest.

Andre opened his mouth to scream but he could not make a sound. He reached back and pushed against the tree but he did not have the strength to move himself even an inch. Andre looked at Richard with black depthless pits that once contained his eyes. He opened his frothing mouth and forced out a rasping whisper:

"You've crossed over, boy. I still have you. I'll *always* have you." He went into violent convulsions that lasted for a few seconds. And then he was still.

The dogs tearing and barking at Father Burns' car went silent. The animals had confused looks on their faces and looked around at their surroundings. The massive beasts lost interest in the men inside the car and trotted off in different directions. The station wagon was left with cracked windows, deep scratches, and a number of dents. Luckily for the four men, however, the big old station wagon held.

"What's going on?" Tim asked with relief and disbelief.

"Andre's hold over the dogs must be broken," Father Burns answered. "Andre's spell can only be broken if he if he intentionally releases them or if he dies."

"How do we know the dogs didn't go off and hide somewhere?" Weller asked.

"Yeah," Major agreed, gingerly holding his forearm just below his broken wrist. "They might be tryin' to fake us out so we can get out of the car."

"Let's find out," Father Burns said. He stepped out of the car and immediately stumbled to the ground.

"Is the leg broken?" Detective Weller asked.

"I don't think so." The priest climbed carefully to his feet and tested his balance. "It hurts but it's not broken." He took a few seconds to gather himself and then took a few tentative limping steps away from the station wagon. The predawn woods remained silent.

"I've got a better idea, padre," Weller called to him. "Get back in."

Burns did as Weller said. He started up the station wagon and drove it across the overgrown lawn and stopped right at the stairway to the porch. The priest reached into the glove compartment and came out with another crucifix. This one was made completely of silver and was small enough to fit in the palm of his hand.

Father Burns turned to the others. "Are you coming with me?" he asked.

"Might as well," Weller responded. "I sure don't wanna be a sitting duck in this car."

"Let's go," said Tim.

"Oh...what the hell," Major added.

They got out of the car and made their way back into the house. They searched the house carefully from the living room to the back rooms. They went back upstairs and looked through the bedrooms. They entered the ruined bedroom and went to the smashed window.

They looked out the window into the backyard and saw Richard standing before Andre's corpse. The four men rushed downstairs and out the back door. Richard was still standing there. He kept his back to the men. Father Burns looked at Andre.

"He's dead," the priest told the others, uttering the words he had been longing to say for the better part of two decades. "That bolt is piercing right through his heart. You did well, Richard."

Richard did not turn to look at his longtime friends. He stood there with his back to them and his hands in his pockets.

"So... it's really over?" Weller asked.

Father Burns remained silent and stared at Richard. Weller looked at the priest and then at Richard. Something was clearly bothering both men. Tim saw the uneasy looks Burns and Weller gave one another. Weller's unanswered question spawned alarming questions in Tim's mind.

Major broke the uneasy silence. "What's everybody so damn quiet for? We should be dancing a freaking jig! Andre's dead! It's over..."

"No," Richard said. "It's over for Andre but not for me."

"What are you talking about?" Major asked.

Richard turned so all four men could see him under the frosted moonlight. His eyes were glowing red. The points of his long canine teeth were hanging from his mouth. He took his hands from his pockets to display long bony fingers and sharp, twisted, claw-like fingernails.

"But Andre is..." Major began.

"He's dead," Richard confirmed. "I killed him."

"Rich, no..." Weller pleaded.

Richard nodded. "Right after I left the police station..."

Major's expression of confusion turned to dread. "You drank someone's blood," he accused.

"Why?" Tim asked.

"I can't describe it," Richard said. "The pain I felt...the only thing that would stop it was blood. And now, the power I feel, the strength... it's like nothing in this world. You could never understand."

"So it begins again," Father Burns announced sadly. "You won't be able to resist the bloodlust, Richard. You know what must be done."

"Yeah," Richard conceded, "I know what must be done. I also know that you won't be the ones to do it."

"We have to," Weller assured. "You were like the son I never had, kid, but I can't let you live like this."

"You don't understand, detective," Richard explained. "I can't let *you* destroy me." Richard turned and looked at Andre's still form dangling from the bolt and sighed. "He wanted a hug," Richard said with a sad smile, "I'll give him one. I'll give him a hug from me and momma."

The four men watched in astonishment as Richard moved with incredible speed. He launched himself through the air and impaled himself on the part of the stake that protruded from Andre's chest. The sharp point of the stake emerged from the middle of Richard's back. He wrapped his arms around Andre's shoulders and hugged him tight.

A hellish roar exploded from deep within the young vampire. The four men put their hands to their ears to keep their eardrums from bursting.

The sound caused the very air around them to vibrate harshly. The boarded windows exploded and tiny shards of glass and wood flew through the air like shrapnel. At the front of the house the windows and headlights of both Weller's and Burns' cars burst.

The four men writhed around on the ground in pain as the sound threatened to rupture their eardrums. And then, suddenly, the earsplitting noise ceased.

The men remained on the ground for several more seconds. Their ears continued to ring. They all were dizzy with headaches. After struggling to their feet, they looked skyward. The heavens were laced with a red-orange tint as the dawn's first light kissed the eastern skies. The light banished the night's chill and chased the shadows away. The new day promised warmer weather more fitting to summer than the chill of the previous weeks.

They looked at the two bodies impaled on the stake. The shadows retreated and sunlight bathed Richard and Andre, causing both bodies to burst into flames. The four men watched the burning bodies with equal parts sadness and morbid fascination.

After a few minutes, the only remaining evidence that the bodies ever existed was the acrid stench of burnt flesh and a pile of ashes at the foot of the tree. Soon, not even that remained. A morning breeze swept through to carry away the ashes and the smell.

No one spoke. No words were necessary. Nothing they could say would accurately describe the emotions threatening to overwhelm them.

Father Burns made the sign of the cross. The other three men said silent prayers to themselves.

Epilogue

A few days later, Father Burns, detective Weller, Tim and Major paid Camillia a visit. She was lying in a hospital bed watching television. When the men came into her room she favored them with a weak but sincere smile. All four men were covered with bruises, scratches, and bandages. Major's right arm was in a sling. Father Burns walked with a crutch.

"You guys look pretty bad," she said quietly.

"I guess that makes five of us," Weller teased.

"Yeah, I guess so," Camillia agreed.

"We wanted to come see you earlier," Father Burns started as he braced himself on his cane. "But you've been unconscious for a few days."

"The doctors told me," Camillia answered. "I guess it could've been worse." She turned her attention to Weller. "Did you finally close the case, detective? It's been open for almost twenty years."

Weller nodded. "You bet your ass I closed it."

Camillia grinned. "How did you explain it to your colleagues?"

"Like I wrote in the report," Weller began, "I followed a lead that took me out near Wolf Lake. The killer ambushed me with a gun but I fatally wounded him. In the firefight, a gas-powered generator was damaged. It exploded and the house went up in flames."

Father Burns added: "The fire investigators will find the remains of the 'killer' and a few of his victims." They all knew the priest was referring to the poor souls in Andre's basement freezer but knew better than to say it aloud in the hospital room.

"The bodies are burned beyond identification but I'm sure they'll accept my account of what happened," Weller concluded.

"Sounds exciting," Camillia noted.

"You don't know the half of it," Father Burns assured.

Tim was growing restless with obvious unspoken concern that no one seemed willing to address.

"Ms. Williams," Tim began, no longer able to remain silent. "Richard..."

"I know," Camillia cut him off. "Richard's gone. If he survived he'd be here right now. I guess he did the right thing after all."

"He did," Major assured. "He did the right thing."

"Richard sacrificed himself to save countless others," Tim said quietly. "And for you."

"That's just like my boy. He'd do anything for his momma."

"I'm so sorry Camillia," Burns offered.

"I am too," Camillia sighed.

"I brought you this," Weller said as he pulled something from his torn trench coat. He placed it on the stand next to Camillia's hospital bed.

Camillia turned to see a framed picture of her and Richard. In the photograph, Richard was holding her high in the air with both hands. They both had big happy smiles on their faces.

"He always was strong," Camillia said as tears began to stream from her eyes. "That's how I'll remember him...strong."

Major smiled with forlorn eyes. "Yeah, he is. He's strong like his momma."

END

Keep reading for a preview of the next book in the Heralds of the Culling saga:

Blood of the Third

Heralds of the Culling

Book 2

MJ Stewart

CHAPTER ONE

Major's Story

I have a story for you...a doozy of a story. You probably won't believe it, but your belief or lack thereof doesn't change *my* reality. If you don't believe it, maybe you'll at least find it an interesting tale.

And cautionary.

I've already forgotten more about my life than I can remember. As the years pass – and believe me, many more years will pass while I walk this earth – I know I will forget much more. There are three moments in my life, however, that I will never forget. They're memories that not even an eternity can diminish.

The first is what I call my dark baptism. To be more accurate I'll call it the loss of my virginity. I'm not talking about the loss of sexual innocence. That was great. It happened in the mid-eighties. It was awkward and terrifying, in a good way, but that's not what I'm talking about. What I'm talking about is the loss of my spiritual innocence. I lost that in the early nineties, in a way no one should.

Richard, Camillia, and Andre; son, mother, and... something else, revealed to me a side of this world that I never thought existed. Richard was one of my two best friends. The other one was Tim. He was right there with me through it all. There were a couple of older guys there, too, named Detective Weller and Father Burns.

I can't remember their first names. Hell, I don't think I ever knew their first names. Before all hell broke loose I didn't know them well enough to care. Afterwards, well, their first names didn't seem to matter much anymore. They were who they were, a cop and priest.

I can't speak for Weller and Burns, but what Richard, Camillia and Andre showed all of us would change Tim and me forever. When we made the idiotic choice to play a part in it, we ended up seeing things that neither of us would ever forget, no matter how bad we might want to.

The worst of it was the end...at least what I *thought* was the end. I can still see Richard and Andre in their death-embrace, both of them impaled on the same wooden stake driven deeply into that tree. Their cold flesh ignited like tinder when the first rays of the morning sun touched their lifeless bodies. Tim, Father Burns, Detective Weller and I watched them burn until there was nothing left of them but ashes at the base of the tree.

The second memory is my wedding day. Six years had passed since Tim and I left Chicago. We couldn't stay home after Richard and Andre. We stuck it out until the end of the fall semester so our grades would transfer from the South Chicago community college to an HBCU (Historically Black College and University) about forty miles northwest of Houston. I'd never been to Texas. Tim had been in the past when visiting family up in Sealy. It felt right to both of us.

We could have moved to the moon, though, and it wouldn't have made a damn bit of difference. No amount of distance or time was ever going to erase the memories of Chicago during that time. Fighting Andre, Richard's horrific change, and his subsequent honorable suicide were the types of things that gave people lifelong recurring nightmares.

Having already spent one year at a community college, Tim and I finished our bachelor's degrees at the Texas university in three years. I chose to stick around and earn a master's degree. Tim went right to work in computer networking, and it wasn't long before he was making good money. He lived a single man's dream.

Tim leased a plush loft in Midtown, drove a classic Mustang that he restored and tricked out until it was worth five times as much as a new one, and enjoyed the company of a parade of women that would make a voluptuous video vixen green with envy.

I, on the other hand, met a beautiful woman during my last year of undergraduate work. Her name was Denise but I called her "Kitty." Her sexy phone voice reminded me of Eartha Kitt's Catwoman character from the 1960's era Batman reruns. We fell in love almost instantly and moved in together after only a few months of dating. A few friends and a bunch of family members thought we were moving too fast. They did not believe we would last. We got married two years later.

The contrast between Tim's life and mine were stark and – if you had known us before the crisis with Richard and Andre – ironic. Tim had always been the one looking for a serious relationship. I was always the insensitive skirt chaser. Tim really hadn't changed very much. He was still looking for a serious relationship but was never able to find the right woman. Until then, he decided he would have as much fun as he could while he searched.

I was the one who had changed. While I watched Richard and Andre burn on that brilliant sunlit morning, something burned away within me. I realized that my flippant attitude and my whole "I don't give a damn" outlook on life had been a shield. It was a barrier I put up to keep from dealing with the seriousness of adulthood. That shield crumbled to ash as surely as Richard and Andre had. From that moment on I took the world and myself much more seriously. And it's a good thing I did. Had I not, I never would have been able to appreciate a woman as special as Denise.

On the morning of my wedding day a tap on my shoulder awakened me. I thought it was Denise but then I remembered she had spent the night at her parents' house. My eyes snapped open, and I jumped up. The face that greeted me caused my blood to go cold and my heart to beat like a drum solo from hell.

"Richard!" I yelped.

He sat on the edge of my bed grinning from ear to ear.

"Calm down, Mage," he said in a soothing voice. "I can't hurt you."

"Of course not," I realized. "This is dream."

I knew it was dream, and not just because Richard had been dead for years. For as long as I can remember I've always known when I was dreaming. That knowledge always took a little of the sting out of nightmares no matter how intense they were. I could always force myself to wake up if the nightmare got too bad. This wasn't a nightmare, and even though it was a dream, I was happy to see my old friend.

What made it even better was that it was the Richard I grew up with. His grin contained normal teeth instead of bestial fangs. His skin was medium brown without the ashen undertones of lifeless flesh. His fingers were human fingers with unremarkable fingernails, not long twisted digits tipped with black claws. This was the Rich I knew before Andre entered our lives.

I smiled back. "It's been a while since I've dreamed about you, Rich."

"So are you ready to jump the broom?"

"Hell yeah," I told him.

"Out of the three of us I figured you'd be the *last* one to get married."

I nodded. "Me, too."

"That makes twice you've surprised me, Mage."

"What do you mean?"

"Tim tried to give you a blow-out, 'no ho's barred' bachelor party last night. Emphasis on the ho's. He was gonna rent out a whole strip club for you but all you wanted to do was go bowling."

"I've matured, Rich, but I'm still me. If I'd let Tim have his way I would've got some drink in me, probably a little weed, and had a gang of butt-naked freaks shakin' ass in my face on the last single day of my life. I would've been so deep in trim I'd be too weak to walk down the aisle this morning. Better to start our marriage off on the right foot."

"Glad to see you've grown up a little," Rich said. "Is momma coming down for the wedding?"

"Definitely," I answered. "She said she wouldn't miss this for the world. She can't believe I'm getting married, either. You know what she told me when I brought Denise to the crib one summer and introduced them?"

Richard executed a perfect imitation of his mother. "She said: 'Boy, that girl's too good for you. You better not screw this up!'"

I frowned. "How the hell did you know...? Oh, yeah, this is my dream."

Rich shrugged and smiled. "Something like that. But anyway, congrats, man. I'm really happy for you. Now wake your ass up."

My alarm clock was blaring. I sat up slowly and slapped to top of the clock three times before finally hitting the button to turn it off. Even though I knew I'd been dreaming, it seemed so real that I looked for Richard at the foot of the bed. It depressed me a little when he wasn't there.

The rest of the morning and early afternoon were spent running last-minute errands with Tim, who was my best man, and the other four groomsmen. The day flew by, and before I knew it, I stood at the church altar watching in awe as my beautiful bride and her father made their way down the aisle.

My wife's bright, perfect smile shone like the sun. She looked like a brown angel. Her white dress drifted around her like soft clouds. Her veil was a radiant halo that framed her lovely oval face as she glided to the altar. Before a church full of family and friends we held each other's hands tightly and promised that we would be together for the rest of our lives and, God willing, in the afterlife as well.

My mother-in-law went all-out for the reception. The food was excellent and the decorations were exquisite. Denise led the crowd in a spirited bout of the electric slide, the Harlem Shuffle, and every other line dance she knew (and she knew pretty much all of them). Tim and I, both thoroughly tired of line dancing, decided to watch from the wedding party's table.

Tim raised his glass for an informal toast. "So, how are you enjoying your first few hours of marriage?"

I laughed. "I'm loving it."

"You got a good girl, there, Mage," Tim noted. "The two of you make a great couple. Don't screw it up."

"Don't even sweat that, brother," I assured. "I ain't letting her get away for nothing."

"You know," Tim began, "out of the three of us, I figured you'd be the last one to get married."

"Damn, that's what Rich told me."

Tim looked surprised. "When did he tell you that?"

"This morning."

Tim looked even more surprised. "Say what, now?"

I laughed. "Calm down, man. It was a dream."

"Whew," Tim breathed. "I thought you were losing it." He was silent for a second, no doubt wishing like I was that Rich was sitting there with us. "I still dream about him every now and then, too."

I sighed. "As great as today's been it just doesn't seem right without him."

Tim put his hand on my shoulder. "I'm with you, man. I'm with you. But I think he *is* here." He placed a finger on my chest. "I think he's in your heart and mine, and especially in his mom's heart."

We looked out at Richard's mother and smiled. Except for a few gray hairs she didn't bother to color and a little darkness under her mahogany brown eyes, Camillia Williams looked exactly the same as she did six years earlier.

She was out on the dance floor out-electric sliding most of the people our age. How she had been able to go on after all that happened was beyond my understanding. Andre killed her husband and went on to put her and her son through hell. I was thankful she hadn't been there with us me at the very end. I don't think even she would've been strong enough to endure the sight of her son killing Andre and then himself, to watch them burn in the sunlight.

"So let me ask you something," Tim said.

"Shoot," I replied, glad that he had distracted me from that unwanted memory.

"Does this marriage mean our 'day of memorial' is officially over?"

"Not a chance," I promised, raising my glass. "To Rich!"

"To Li'l Richard," Tim replied. We tapped glasses again.

There's one more memory that will never fade. It's the memory of the circumstances that brought me to this place, to this time, to tell you this story.

---

https://majorstewart.com/blood-of-the-third

www.ingramcontent.com/pod-product-compliance
Lightning Source LLC
Chambersburg PA
CBHW062009170626
46813CB00001B/87